CITY GIRL VS COUNTRY BOY

FOREVER LOVE #1

JORDAN FORD

NOTE FROM THE AUTHOR

Dear Reader,

I'm so excited to be able to share this new series with you. I came up with the initial idea years ago. You can learn more about the inspiration in the **Behind the Scenes booklet** (https://dl.bookfunnel.com/6ynsy69pnx). The series has changed and developed a lot since first conception, but the fact that it runs like a TV show in my mind has always stayed the same.

The characters in this book have been thrust together unexpectedly, and we're going to follow their lives as they try to make it work. Be warned: it's going to be an emotional ride. I've cried several times while writing this book, but I think that's a good thing. I already love these characters...this makeshift family. They've touched my heart, and I hope they find a home in yours too.

Being able to set this series in New Zealand and share a part of myself like this is really special. I know there will be words and phrases you may not understand, so I've put together a Kiwi Dictionary for ya. If you come across something that doesn't make sense, you'll no doubt find it here. You can download your copy by **following** **this** **link** (https://dl.bookfunnel.com/gtguyptohn).

Thank you for taking a chance on this book. I can't wait for you to dive into this new world with me.

I'd also like to thank my amazing team: Rachael, Lenore, Beth, Kristin and Emily. Plus, my amazing review team and my awesome reader group. You guys are so instrumental in helping these books be worthy of publishing. I value your input and feedback so much.

I'd also like to thank my dad for his abundant knowledge of rugby and helping me with these first few important chapters as well. And thank you to Greg and Rose for letting me visit your farm and learn all I can about how one operates. You guys have given me so much of your time and I'm so, SO grateful.

I am blessed enough to come from a very supportive family. May I never take their love for granted. Being family isn't always easy, you have to work at it, but I don't know what I'd do without them, and I am so very grateful to live life right alongside them.

And to the constant, unchangeable being in my life. The

one who will never leave me nor forsake me. The one who loves me, who fuels my imagination and who walks this journey with me every step of the way. Thank you, Lord. I love you so much.

xx

Jordan

1

HARPER

"All right, fine. We can pick things up when I get back."

I smile up at my boyfriend. Well, ex-boyfriend. That's what we've decided. It's for the best. He's leaving for his big OE adventure. A full year in Europe, traveling, working a little, sightseeing. That's been his plan since he was fifteen, and even I can't change it.

Not that I would.

I want him to have this experience. It's his dream, and I won't go crushing it.

Sliding my hand from his shoulder to his chest, I stare at the small white buttons of his polo shirt. They seem safer than his brilliant blue eyes. There's something so disarming about them, and if I gaze into them while I say goodbye, it'll only make it hurt more.

I've already decided that I'm not going to cry.

We're making the right decision, no matter how awful it feels.

"It's not too late to change your mind, you know." Dylan bumps my forehead with the tip of his nose.

I snort and giggle against his chest. "Um, you're about to walk through security. I think it's *way* too late for me to change my mind." I glance up, studying the shape of his pointed chin and long, narrow face. It seems to epitomize Dylan—long, lean, sure of himself. There's no bulk to him, just this confidence that exudes strength. "And as for picking up where we left off, let's just hold that idea lightly. I don't want to spoil your adventure. I don't want to stop you from falling for some European model or something."

My smile seems forced, but also genuine, if that's even possible.

I'm being honest. I seriously don't want to hold him back. He's been saving and planning for this for three years. He deserves every ounce of fun and joy he can get.

"I guess I don't want to stop you from falling for your economics professor either," he quips.

I snort again, and he captures my smile with his lips. Gliding my arms around his neck, I press my body against his, clinging to this final goodbye.

We're doing the right thing.

I have to keep reminding myself of that.

"Flight NZ301 to Auckland is now ready for boarding. Please make your way to the gate."

Pulling out of the kiss with a gasp, I check the departure board. "You better go. You can't miss your first flight. It'll screw up your entire plan."

Dylan chuckles and brushes his lips across mine one last time. "Never mess with the plan, right?"

I let out an abashed laugh and bob my head.

"See you when I get back." He winks and walks away, hitching his meticulously packed bag onto his shoulder.

I stand where I am, the bustle of Wellington Airport turning into a blur as I'm rooted to the spot, watching my boyfriend of nine months leave me.

He turns one last time to wave goodbye, and as soon as he's gone, I wrap my arms around my waist and shuffle out to my car. The huge suspended statue of Gollum gives me a creepy look as I head for the exit, and the smell of cheap, overpriced airport coffee burns my nostrils when I walk past the cafe by the sliding doors. I could use a good coffee, but I can make one at home. I left my brother and sister sleeping, but they'll be waking up soon, and although they're old enough to look after themselves, they're my responsibility at the moment. I want Mum and Dad to come back to a pristine house. That's what they expect, and I'm going to deliver.

Jumping around an overloaded luggage trolley, I ignore the excited jabbering of a family heading off on holiday and instead focus on the things I can control, like paying for the parking ticket and pulling the keys from my pocket, spinning them around my index finger while I try not to feel sad.

We're doing the right thing. We discussed this before we even got together. Dylan had his plan, and I had mine. He wants to travel the world. I want to go to university with my two best friends. This coming year is going to be amazing, a whole new chapter. I just kind of wish that Dylan could be part of it. He invited me to travel with him so many times, but I want to get my degree first. I'm only eighteen, and I don't feel old enough to flit off around the world just yet. Besides, my parents aren't loaded like Dylan's. We're not poor or anything, but they definitely don't have the funds to send me off for a one-year trip on the other side of the world.

Pulling my phone from the front pocket of my handbag, I text Dylan's mum like I promised I would. She wasn't too happy that her eldest son insisted she didn't come to the airport. The only person he wanted there was me. It was our last goodbye, and he didn't want anyone getting in the way of that. His family had to say goodbye at home while I jittered by their front door, avoiding a few resentful glares from his mother.

As the text swooshes away, a plane rises into the sky above me. I squint into the early morning sun and watch it go. It won't be Dylan's plane yet. Thankfully, I'll be well on my way home by the time he takes off. I don't want to see him flying away from me.

"Stick to the plan, Harper," I mutter to myself, trying to bolster my spirits.

I know what I'm doing. I'm excited for the new year. It's only two days away, and it's going to be great. A whole new chapter. January is fully booked with summer fun. Zoey, Alaina and I have it all mapped out—beaches, parties, shopping, prepping for our first year out of high school. We're like full-fledged grown-ups now!

My phone starts ringing just as I reach my car. I frown, hoping it's not Dylan or his mother. I've said my good-byes. I can't talk to them again or I might—

"Mum," I whisper with a smile. "Hey."

"Hey, sweetness. I just had to call and see how you're doing. Did you do it? Make the final break?"

"Yep."

"How hard was it?"

Wrenching the car door open, I plunk into the driver's seat and stare out the window. "It pretty much sucked, but I comfort myself with the fact that I stuck to my plan. That's what Dad always says, right? Make it and stick to it. Don't deviate and you'll eventually get all the things you want and need."

Mum does her closed-mouth chuckle. I can picture it so clearly in my head. It's the laugh she makes when she doesn't fully agree with you. "Yeah, although sometimes life tries to get in the way."

"Not for me." I shake my head. "I'm starting Victoria University in February as a single woman. I'm going to focus on my studies, on hanging out with my besties and just enjoying this new phase of my life. It's gunna be awesome." My voice cracks and I suck in a quick breath.

It *is* going to be awesome, I remind myself, and I'm not going to let some gorgeous guy with blue eyes and a sweet smile ruin it for me.

"Harper?"

"Yeah?"

"I'll be home tomorrow, and I've got a monster hug all ready for you."

Her soft promise makes me warm, and I lean my head back with a smile. "Thanks, Mum."

"How's it going at home? Willow and Oz being well-behaved?" I laugh as I think about my siblings. This is the first time my parents have left me in sole charge for this long. It's only been four nights, but Mum's still called every day.

"Just as good as they were yesterday," I tease her.

She laughs. "I'm sorry. I can't help it. It's not that I don't trust you. I just miss my babies."

"Mum! They're twelve and fifteen. Hardly babies."

"You know what I mean. You're all my babies."

"You and Dad are supposed to be having fun with your friends, not thinking about your kids."

"Oh, I am. We're having a great time. I forgot how beautiful the South Island is. I can't believe we haven't holidayed here more. It's ridiculous, considering how close we are to it. Anyway, we're heading out to Milford Sounds today. I've always wanted to go there, and it's going to be a stunning drive."

I smile at the excitement in Mum's voice. She's away with Dad and their best friends, who they haven't caught up with in years. It's kind of like a reunion holiday, and it's making Mum sound like an effervescent tween, until she lets out a disgusted, sad sigh.

"What's wrong?" I ask.

"Beck would have loved this. I can't believe he's not with us."

I go quiet, sticking the key into the ignition so I'm ready to leave as soon as this call wraps up.

"We should have insisted he come. Being here without him just makes us realize that we haven't stepped up enough. We've been pushed away too easily, and it's got to stop. It's time we start butting in. Even if he is still with that woman, that's no excuse. When we get home, your dad's heading up to see him, uninvited. It's time to rebuild bridges."

I nod, not sure what to say.

I haven't seen Uncle Beck in years. He's not even my real uncle; we just call him that because he grew up with my dad. There were three of them—Lance, Richie and Beck. Best friends who grew up together and became like family. Until they all got married and life pulled them to different parts of the country and then the world. Even with modern technology, it's hard to keep up relationships when you live so far away.

That's why this trip was so important to my parents. It was the first time the three guys were going to be together again. Until Beck pulled out six weeks ago with no explanation. My parents nearly canceled the trip, but Richie and Leanne were specially coming home from China for it. Too many plans had been set in place to pull the plug, so they went without him.

"You should call the twins to say hi before they head back to Suzhou," Mum murmurs.

I roll my eyes. "Mum, I haven't spoken to them in a couple of years."

"All the more reason to call them."

"It'll be awkward."

"They are the closest thing you have to cousins, and it'd mean a lot to Uncle Richie and Aunty Leanne, especially because we couldn't coordinate all of us getting together this year. They're staying with friends in Auckland. I'll get Leanne to text you Stacey's number."

I groan.

"Come on, please? Do this for us. Aunty Leanne is batting her eyelashes at me right now. You have to say yes, or she might cry."

"Hello, Manipulation, my name's Harper."

Mum giggles and I give in with a sigh, putting the phone on speaker so I can program a reminder in. "Fine, I'll give them a quick call this afternoon."

"You're an angel!" Aunty Leanne calls out to me.

My lips quirk with a smile. "Whatever."

"Hey, sweetie." Mum's voice goes low with a serious edge. "I know you're a smart woman who always makes the right choices, and sometimes those decisions don't make you feel fantastic. I just want you to know that I'm proud of you. It's hard right now, but take heart, okay? If it's meant to be, Dylan will come back next year, and you'll pick up where you left off. Or you might meet someone who's even better for you."

I snicker. "Dylan and I were kind of perfect for each other. I mean, we're really similar. We study well together."

Mum laughs. "There's more to a relationship than studying well together. And haven't you ever heard that opposites attract?"

"You know what I mean. And stop acting like you don't like Dylan."

"I do like Dylan. I've always liked him. I'm just trying to make you feel better about your decision."

Another plane flies over my car, and I lean against the steering wheel to watch it go. A deep sadness pierces me, so I lurch back in my seat, closing my eyes and gritting out, "I know we're making the right choice by letting each other go. I just have to keep reminding myself of that."

"You're always so thoughtful about everything you do. Trust yourself." I know Mum is trying to ease my pain. "And I know it's tough, but sometimes the things you think are perfect turn out to be something else entirely. You have to let go in order for your hand to be open to receive something new." I smile. She's used the open palm analogy before. A closed fist can't take anything; you have to unfurl your fingers first. "I know this is impossibly hard for you to do, sweetie, but try to go with the flow on this one. Not everything has to be set within a rigid plan. Life sometimes has other ideas."

I shake my head. "Life without direction will get you nowhere. Plans are good. They keep you focused."

Mum laughs. "You sound just like your father."

That makes me grin. I'm more than happy to be compared to my brilliant dad.

"That's my girl!" Dad yells in the background.

Mum and I laugh together, but the sound soon peters out.

"I better let you go and get ready for your big day," I murmur, tracing my finger over the top of the steering wheel.

"Your heart wants its perfect match." Mum finishes her point with her usual eloquence. "My heart beat for your father long before I met him. And your heart is beating for someone too. Maybe it's Dylan, or maybe it's the last person you ever thought you'd be with."

2

TANE

I shunt a cow into position and whistle for the next one to keep moving down the line. They pretty much know what they're doing, and there's a little meal to munch on while they're waiting to get milked.

"Good girl." I pat one on the butt, and she lifts her tail.

Jumping out of the way, I avoid the splatter of cow poo and head down into the milking pit to join Beck. He's already got the hose out and is washing down the concrete before we start putting the suction cups onto the last row of cows.

This morning's milking session has actually run pretty smoothly.

Getting up at five every morning would suck for most people, but not me. Especially over summer break. I don't mind the crisp morning air. Sure, the winter is harder. It can be frickin' cold. But summer. That's where it's at. The sky is already pale blue. It's gunna be a cracker of a day. I don't think Beck has too many jobs planned, so I'm hoping to skip out and play some touch with the boys later. Cam's leaving on holiday soon, and I want to hang out with him as much as I can.

I haven't asked Beck if I can borrow the car yet, but it shouldn't be a problem. He never minds me hanging out with my rugby boys. He knows they're good guys. Trusts me with them.

"Cruel Summer" starts playing through the radio, and I snicker as I press the suction cup to get it whirring before slipping each metal tube onto the cow's teats.

It's only taken me five years, but finally Beck has graduated from the Beach Boys and the Beatles to solid gold hits from the 80s. I'm hoping if I keep nudging him, in the next five years, we might actually make it to music from the twenty-first century. It's kind of painful, but thankfully I'm an eclectic guy. It doesn't take much to please me in the music department, so I start humming along to whoever sings this song as I work my way down the line.

I'd rather be here dodging cow poo and listening to music from the wrong decade than with my mum in Upper Hutt right now.

I still can't believe what she did to Beck.

I still can't believe she wants me to hear her explanation.

She's been texting me nonstop since I refused to go with her. What does she expect me to say?

Oh yeah, of course you cheating on Beck is totally acceptable, Mum. I get it. He's only the nicest guy on the whole planet; why wouldn't you screw his worker?

I'm livid.

You know, it's lucky Beck was the one who caught them at it and not me. If I'd walked in on them bumping uglies, I would have done more than just thrown a few obscenities at them. Beck was way too controlled, if you ask me.

I have no idea how long they've been having this affair, but Grant was fired on the spot, and rightly so. They've moved down to Upper Hutt together. Grant's sister lives down there or something. I don't really give a shit. All I know is that I'm not going, and if I never see my cheating mother again, I won't be sorry.

My guts pinch with that sore, ugly feeling that keeps nailing me every time I think about her. I haven't told Beck about any of her texts yet. I don't want to burden him with it. He let me stay when he could have so easily told me I had to go with my mother.

But Beck's not like that.

He's the closest thing I'll ever get to a dad, and he wouldn't kick me off the farm, not when I basically fell to my knees and begged him to let me stay.

"It's all right, mate." He waved his hand at me. "Of course you can stay. You're old enough to make your own choices."

I'd choose him every time. Yeah, it's not exactly loyal, but Mum attacked my loyalty with an axe blade the second she chose to start cheating on the guy who saved our lives.

"As soon as we're done with this lot, I'll get them secure in Paddock 26. You start washing down the shed, and I'll come back to help sterilize everything," Beck yells at me above the whirr of the pumps.

"Yeah, sweet as." I raise my eyebrows at him.

His lips twitch but don't break into a smile. It's like he's forgotten how. Not that he's Mr. Smiles or anything. When I first met him, I was kind of terrified. He was like a hulking bear with his bushy beard and assessing gaze. I was this scrawny little kid and figured he could knock me out with one swift blow, but he never did. The guy is the quiet type—solid and unwavering as a pine tree. He keeps the feels on lockdown unless absolutely necessary. But he knows how to have a laugh, and since catching Mum six weeks ago, he hasn't laughed once.

I wish I could make it better for him, but he's hurting, and hurts take time to heal. I get it. My stomach aches when I think about it too. I've been let down by people I trusted before. Those wounds cut deep.

Beck never talks about it, but he used to have a wife. She died, so it's kind of different to what he's facing now, but I wonder if old feelings of loss are resurfacing or something.

Shit, Mum. How could you do it to him?

My anger simmers, acting like a corrosive as it eats through my system. I want to lash out at her, but every time I grab my phone to call and give her a piece of my mind, I stop myself. It's better to just ignore her. She can text me a hundred times a day if she has to. I'm not responding. My silence will do the talking for me.

She knows I'm pissed.

And there's nothing she can say to me that will ever make me understand how she could hurt the best thing that ever happened to us.

Love is not supposed to be like that.

Love is loyal, no matter how you might be feeling at the time.

You don't cheat on your mates.

You don't cheat on your partner.

Beck has my complete loyalty, and if I can have my way, after I finish high school next year, I'll be working this farm right alongside him.

3

HARPER

I glance over my shoulder to check on Willow. She's still on her phone. I need to get her off that thing. We've always had screen restrictions in this house, but Mum and Dad aren't here right now, and I know Willow's locked in some epic conversation with her ballet girls on Hangouts. They're probably talking dance moves or swooning over that new teacher who's just joined the school. Apparently, he's twenty-six and has a *tour en l'air* that rivals any dancer in New Zealand.

I don't even know what that move is.

Anyway, I think Willow said he's Russian or something. Whatever he is, the girls love him, and I can just imagine their flushing giggles when he glides into a room.

"Your turn." Oscar taps the table, pulling me back to a painful game of Monopoly. I hate this game with a passion, but when he asked if I wanted to play, I knew saying yes was the right thing to do, so I did.

Mum and Dad gave him a laptop for Christmas, and before they left, they made sure I understood the rules. He wasn't allowed on it 24-7. Mum and Dad are expecting me to look after my siblings, and telling my little brother that I'd rather ignore him and read a book is not what they'd want to hear, especially if it means he's not on the screen for a couple of hours.

So, I'm getting demolished by a kid at a game that was designed by Satan himself.

"Um…" I roll the dice while Oscar grabs another chip from the bowl, scooping out a huge mound of dip. My nose wrinkles as he shoves it into his mouth, a little dip squirting onto his lip as he crunches down. He really knows how to pack it away, and I'm so tempted to tell him to slow down a little. He's a solid kid, some would say chubby, but he's also twelve and will no doubt go through some growth spurt, and all his soft edges will inevitably turn into hard muscle. That's what Mum said anyway.

I'm not going to say anything, but chips aren't that good for him, so after I've moved eight spaces, I subtly shift the bowl out of his reach while he picks up a Chance card and reads it out for me.

"Advance to the nearest station." Oscar looks at the board and grins. "Yes! I own that, so you have to pay me—" He double-checks the card. "—twice the rent of which I am otherwise entitled." His posh put-on accent is overrun with an evil cackle.

I roll my eyes and collect up my meager stack of money. "You're taking it all." I force my voice to be upbeat as I hand over the last of my cash. "Congratulations. You won!"

"No, you can still mortgage your properties and stuff."

It's an effort to hide how I truly feel.

"Great." Forcing a tight grin, I bob my head and remind myself that at least he's not on a screen, and my parents will be proud of me when they find out I've been the ultimate sister by letting my brother completely pants me at this stupid game.

Willow laughs, and I glance at her but don't bother asking what's so funny because her earbuds are in. That girl doesn't know how to live without music constantly playing around her. She won't be able to hear me, so I don't say anything and nearly whoop with delight when the doorbell rings.

"I'll get it." I jump up, straightening my loose button-down shirt as I head for the front door.

I still haven't gotten changed since the airport this morning. I was tempted to throw my pjs back on and crawl into bed when I got home. Oscar was watching a movie and Willow was still asleep, but I played the good girl and stayed dressed in case my siblings wanted to go out later.

Running my fingers through my hair, I neaten it up at the back and pull the door open with a smile. Even if it's a salesman with the latest phone plan I don't want, that's no excuse not to be friendly.

But it's not a salesman.

And it only takes me ten seconds to desperately wish that it was.

"Miss Hughes?" The police officer pulls the hat off his head, tucking it under his arm and looking at me with an expression that sets off warning bells in my chest.

They scream so loudly and thump so hard, I miss his name.

"…and this is Officer Patten." He indicates the woman beside him. She gives me a kind, sad smile, and my confusion runs into overdrive.

Logic is telling me to calm the hell down. I have no idea why they're here. They've probably come to the wrong house or something.

But they said your name.

I check the driveway to make sure my little hatchback is still there. The family wagon is in the garage, and I can't think of anything else that might be stolen.

The thought I'm trying to avoid squeezes its way into

my brain, radiating through my head and warning me that there's only one reason why they would be here.

Something's happened to Mum and Dad.

I cross my arms, willing my voice to come out strong. "Is everything okay?"

"We're really sorry to have to tell you this, but there was an accident. A head-on collision at high speed. Your parents were involved."

My ears start buzzing. Between the sirens in my chest and the hum in my brain, it's kind of hard to hear.

I tip my head, straining to understand. "Are they okay?"

The female officer looks to the ground while her partner delivers the final blow. "There were no survivors."

I grip the doorframe, swaying on my feet and having to ask again, "I'm sorry, what?"

"What's going on?" Oscar appears behind me, rising on his tiptoes so he can look over my shoulder. "What are they doing here?"

I stare at their blue uniforms, so pristine and crisp. I've always admired the police. Respected them. Right now, I'm fighting the urge to accuse them of outright lies.

No survivors.

What does that even mean?

What does…?

I rub my forehead, my fingers trembling.

"Harp?" Oscar tugs on my shirt, his hazel eyes swirling with fear. "What's the matter?"

Swallowing is impossible. There's no fluid in my mouth right now. I can barely breathe.

"Do you have a family friend or a neighbor we could call? Someone to come over and support you?" the female officer asks.

"Why do we need support?" Oscar snaps. "Harper! What is going on!"

"Mum and Dad," I manage to choke out. "Car accident."

Oscar gasps. "Are they okay?"

I blink at my burning eyes. All I can manage is a stiff shake of my head. I can't say it. I can't form the word *dead* or *died*. I can't even say *passed away*. How do I tell my little brother that news?

"I'm sorry to inform you, but your parents have died." The police officer's voice is soft, yet brutal.

"What?" Oscar whispers. "What did you just say?"

"I'm sorry, son." The officer takes a small step toward the door. "They were in a head-on collision. No one survived."

"They're dead?" Oscar's voice cracks, and then he starts hyperventilating.

I grip his shoulder, desperate for my senses to kick back in. I need to help my brother. I need to—

He lets out an anguished wail. It's so loud and dramatic, just like they do in the movies, and all I can do is stare at him, useless and inept as I lean against the doorframe. My head is spinning when Willow walks into view. She looks as though she's ready to smile, to tease Oscar for once again being the showman, but he launches into her arms, nearly knocking her off her feet and sobbing against her chest. She pats the back of his thick hair, the color draining from her face.

She stares at me, her eyes wary as she starts rubbing Oscar's back. She looks like a delicate reed against his shaking bulk. Her long, slender fingers splay between his shoulders as she silently asks me what's going on.

Mum and Dad are dead.

I have to say the words, but I can't, so Oscar hiccups them out, wailing them until tears are streaming down Willow's face. She's a porcelain doll now, so white I'm worried she might faint.

"Miss Hughes." The officer grabs my attention. "Is there someone you can call?"

"Uh…" The useless sound shudders out of me.

"A phone. Do you have a phone?"

"My phone," I whisper and then bob my head stupidly, my body somehow taking me to the table so I can grab my device and stumble back to the door.

I gaze down at the screen, struggling to read the reminder notification.

Call Stacey and Bianca.

"The twins," I choke, the phone slipping from my grasp. I catch it against my thigh and struggle to hold it.

My entire body feels like it's on the verge of breaking down.

Somehow, I make it back to the door and manage to ask, "Were the Freemans in the car too? Richard and Leanne Freeman."

The officers both nod, and another chunk of my composure rips away. I pull in a ragged breath and struggle to ask my next question.

"Do—do the twins know? Has someone called Stacey and Bianca? They're in Auckland at the moment. I don't know who they're staying with, but—"

"We have a couple of officers going to see them now."

I nod and blink, touching my thumb to the scan button and unlocking my phone.

Who am I going to call?

In an emergency, my parents are always my first thought. But I can't call them right now. I can't call them ever again.

The thought shudders through me, making my knees buckle. The male officer lurches forward, catching me and slowing my descent. I crumple within the door-frame, clutching my phone to my chest.

I'm struggling to think straight.

I'm struggling to breathe.

What's going to happen to us all?

Five children orphaned in one fell swoop.

It's devastating.

4

STACEY

O kay, so usually I love to shop.

But usually I'm with my girls who aren't anal about clothes having to be one hundred percent perfect before making a purchase.

I lean against the changing room wall while Bianca swivels from side to side, checking her dress in the mirror. I know what she'll be thinking in her head: does this sit right? What occasions will I wear it to? Does it go with anything else in my wardrobe?

Unlike me, she won't purchase anything that can't be mixed and matched.

I hold in my bored sigh, resisting the urge to give her my opinion, which is that the dress is gray and drab as!

If I'm a multicolored rainbow, Bianca is a pond of

pastel-colored water lilies. There's beauty in that, sure, but it's just nothing like me.

Her face is round; mine is narrow. Her hair is red—like carrot-top red, not that I'd ever dare say that—whereas mine is blonde with just a hint of strawberry. Her skin is pale and covered with these cute apricot freckles; I've taken after Mum with my skin being a little more on the olive side. I tan up real easy in the summer, whereas Bianca turns into a tomato unless she slathers on the sunblock.

Poor thing, she kind of got all of Dad's looks, but she got Mum's personality.

I'm the opposite combination, and I still can't decide who got the better deal.

"Come on, Bee," I mutter under my breath. She's now moved out of the changing room so she can check out the massive mirror at the end of the row of stalls.

I tip my head back with a soft groan. I can't give her my opinion, because she won't listen to it anyway. I don't understand why she won't let me give her a makeover. I could transform her dowdy look into something fantastic. She always hides her soft curves when she should be embracing them. I've tried telling her that she looks even bigger when she chooses tent T-shirts and dresses over fitted ones, but that just makes her eyes smart, and then she always tells me that not everyone is lucky enough to look like a supermodel.

It's sweet she thinks I look like a model, but that's not the point. Everyone has their own beauty, it's just a matter of letting it shine.

The piped music changes to a more upbeat tune, and I bob my head in time with the beat, counting up my bags and feeling that thrill run through me. I can't wait to get back to the house and lay out all my purchases. I'll send pics back to my friends in China, and they'll go a little green with envy. Here I am, soaking up the summer sun and stocking up my wardrobe for July, while they're still bundled up in the cold, although a few of them were heading overseas for a quick winter break. China doesn't really celebrate Christmas like we do, though, so some of them are stuck hanging out in the Suzhou snow. They'll flit off somewhere exotic at Chinese New Year.

I wonder what we'll be doing.

I hope Mum and Dad can at least afford to take us to Shanghai or something. It sucks when all your friends split on holiday and you don't have anything entertaining to do.

"Are you nearly done?" I check on my sister.

She's playing with the edges of the dress, holding it out like she's about to curtsey to royalty. "I'm just not sure."

"Well, if you can't picture yourself wearing it outside the store, then don't get it."

"I know. I know. I just... I like the color, and the way the fabric sits."

I press my lips together and stop looking at her.

Don't say anything, Stace. You're not the one who'll be wearing it!

My phone dings with a text, and I grab it for the distraction.

Michelle: You need to come home now.

I frown at the text. Michelle is usually way friendlier than that. I type back a quick *okay* and start gathering up my bags.

"Hey, Bee, Michelle and Carter want us to start walking back to the house."

We're sharing this cool Airbnb with them in Remuera. It's this old house that has been refitted with all modern stuff, and it's really flash. Michelle and Carter stay there whenever they visit Auckland. Thankfully they were coming back from China to spend Christmas with family and were happy for us to tag along. It worked out quite well, actually. Michelle teaches in the elementary section of our international school, and Carter's in the senior area. Thankfully, I haven't had him yet. They're our closest family friends in China, and it'd probably be really weird being in his class.

Bianca slips past me into the changing room.

"Are you gunna get it?"

"Don't know." She shrugs, unzipping the side of the dress and pulling it over her head.

I slip out of the changing room and wander back through the store, running my hand through the racks of brightly colored T-shirts, before stopping to check out a cute pair of denim shorts. I study the rips and frays with a smile and am about to go try them on when my phone dings again.

Michelle: Are you on your way yet?

I frown. What is her problem today?

She's so much more stressy than my mum. Maybe she feels the pressure of looking after someone else's kids or something. I have to say that her kids are way more motivated and well-behaved than I am. They're definitely stricter parents, but thankfully they go pretty easy on me and Bianca. We're not that much trouble. Especially Bee. She's a freaking angel.

Hustling back to the changing room, I call out, "Hey, Bee? They really want us back at the house, like pronto.

Not sure what's up. Maybe they're waiting to go out or something. Did you grab a key?"

"No." Her voice is so soft and mousy compared to mine. "I'm nearly finished."

"Do you want me to get the dress for you?"

"Nah. I've decided I don't need it."

I roll my eyes. When is that girl going to learn that shopping doesn't always have to be about need? She's probably got quadruple the savings I have. She could spend up large and still have money left over.

I nearly tell her that but change my mind when I spot a superhot guy cruising through the store. Hello, Biceps. My lips curl into a smile when he glances my way. I don't bother hiding my attraction.

He smirks and checks me out before turning into the men's section.

My grin grows even wider. He thought I was cute. I could tell. If I was here on my own, I'd follow him. I'm entitled. I'm a single lady again, thanks to Stefan's dick move at the Christmas party. It's actually kind of liberating.

I lift my chin and swallow, dodging thoughts of that stupid party. It was the night before we left for our New Zealand holiday, and it didn't turn out the way I'd imagined.

"I'm ready." Bianca appears beside me, adjusting the dress on the hanger before returning it to the correct rack.

"Let's go." I take the long way out of the store, catching one more glimpse of Biceps before leaving. He gives me another smile and winks, sending a different kind of thrill coursing through my body.

Bianca notices and gives me a weird frown.

I shake my head and pick up my pace.

She doesn't know about Stefan and me yet. I don't really want to tell her, because she'll want to dissect it all in a bid to help, but I don't want to talk about it. No dissection necessary. We're through, and when we get back to China in a week or so, I'll be a free agent. That is totes fine by me.

"Can you slow down a little?" Bianca struggles to catch up with me as I power up the hill.

I stop and wait for her. We're only halfway up the steep incline and she's already puffing. Yet another difference between us. I'm sporty and fit. She's… not. At all.

Music's her thing. She's an amazing pianist and has the voice of an angel. I'm pretty sure she can play any musical instrument she touches, but she'd deny it if I said that out loud. She always underplays herself. I don't get it. I'm more than happy for people to know that I'm a freaking queen on any court you put me on—

volleyball, basketball, netball. I play it all, and I'm good. Why not celebrate our successes?

Bianca probably thinks I'm boasting.

Yet another difference between us.

Honestly, I don't know how we're even sisters, let alone twins. It's like God was having a giggle when He put us in the same womb together.

Chalk and cheese—is that the expression?

My phone dings yet again.

Michelle: How far away are you?

I let out a confused scoff as I text back a five-minute ETA.

"Seriously? What is her problem today?" I tuck my phone into the back pocket of my jean shorts. "She should have just told us she wanted to go out."

"Do you think they want to take us with them this time?"

I cringe. The reason Michelle and Carter always stay in Remuera is because it's close to their Auckland friends and family. They've spent most of this vacation catching up with people, and Bianca and I have managed to avoid most of it.

Bianca puffs beside me, doing a little jumpy skippy thing to try and keep up with my pace. I slow down again to accommodate her, and she gives me a grateful smile.

Even though she bugs the heck out of me, she is a sweetheart. I do love my sister. We have nothing in common, and trying to understand her is sometimes impossible, but…we're family.

"Nearly there." I adjust my shopping bags.

"Oh, sorry, do you want me to take some of those? I should have offered before."

"It's all good." I smile at my sister, nearly laughing at the fact that she has one measly bag compared to my ten.

One powder blue T-shirt, I think that's all she bought.

Me on the other hand… shoes, earrings, leather bracelets, shorts, shirts, a light sweater, this cool cap. I can't remember what else I've acquired, but I'm looking forward to unpacking and finding out.

Swinging the little white gate open, we walk up the path and through the front door.

"We're back," I singsong, walking into the open-plan living area with a grin that immediately freezes and then disappears.

Michelle, Carter and the kids are sitting around the

dining room table. All of them have been crying. Michelle still has fresh tears on her cheeks, and Carter is devastated, his lined face pasty and drawn.

"What's wrong?" I end up snapping as my gut twists into a painful knot. I don't like tears, sadness, angst. They kind of work like a repellent for me, and my feet shuffle backward...until I bump into Bianca.

"Ouch," she whispers, shifting her foot out from under mine.

She looks scared, and I don't want to feed off her emotion, so I look away from her, but then I'm just facing Michelle again, who has now risen from her chair and is sniffling her way toward me.

"I'm so sorry," she weeps.

My forehead bunches with confusion; I can feel it tensing as she stops just in front of us and destroys everything.

"Your parents were killed in a car accident today."

"What?" Bianca breathes the word, her eyes instantly filling with tears.

I shake my head and force out a laugh. "That's not funny. You guys can prank better than that."

"It's not a joke, Stacey." Carter rises from the table, but I keep shaking my head anyway.

"They can't be dead. They're not dead!" I drop my

shopping bags. "They're coming back tomorrow. I'm going to pick them up from the airport myself! Two thirty-five. Flight NZ281. See? I remember." My voice is rising, cracking and splitting as my disbelief is shaken.

No one's laughing.

Bianca's now got tears on her cheeks too.

"No!" I shout and back away when Michelle opens her arms to hug me. "Stop this!"

"We can't." Michelle's lips tremble, her chin bunching as another round of tears breaks from her eyes.

Carter steps up next to her, hugging her against him while gazing at me with so much sorrow I want to slap him.

Stop looking at me like that! Stop making it real!

"Stace," Bianca whimpers, her arm gliding around my shoulders. She pulls me against her and rests her forehead against my cheek. She's a little shorter than me, and I automatically lift my arm over her shoulder while she drops hers to fit around my waist.

Her sniffles start to pierce me, breaking through the wall of denial, until my stomach shudders—one shock wave after another.

This can't be happening.

Mum and Dad are all we have.

"What's going to happen to us now?" Bianca's voice is wispy and weak, but Carter still hears it.

"We'll sort it out." He sniffs and blinks. "We'll make sure you have a home before we have to return to China."

"We can't just come with you?" I frown.

Michelle pulls out of her husband's embrace and shakes her head. "I wish we could take you, but without your parents, you… visa issues and…"

"We'd love to take you," Carter agrees. "We would in a heartbeat, but we just won't be allowed."

My chest caves, my stomach lurching again. My body wants to buckle, but I lock my knees and cling to Bianca.

"Don't worry." Carter tries to reassure us. "We're going to find you a home. Your parents will have a guardian listed in their will. We'll find out who that is and help you organize everything before we leave. You're not alone in this."

He keeps talking, but his words turn to sludgy custard in my brain.

This high-pitched kind of whine breaks through the muck, deafening me with a reality that makes me want to throw up.

Mum and Dad aren't coming back tomorrow. I'll never speak to them again.

My body jerks like I've just been struck by lightning. My brain does not want to compute that reality. I don't even think it knows how.

5

TANE

Gripping the rugby ball to my chest, I surge through the yard, aiming between Sione's massive sneakers. Cam's right on my tail. I can hear his puffing breaths, sense his hand reaching out to slap my back, so I flick the ball right, sending it spiraling back to Logan, who snatches it up and launches across the line in a dramatic try.

Rolling onto his back, he throws the ball in the air and whoops. I jump forward and catch it, laughing while Sione and Cam shake their heads and walk back to midfield.

Man, I'm glad they came over early. I've invited the entire rugby team and their girls, or whoever they want to bring, over for a New Year's Eve party, and anyone who's not away on holiday is coming.

But some of my mates showed up early, and we're

squeezing in a quick game of touch before we have to set up.

"That's five tries to two, Si-man. You want to quit while you're only three behind?" Logan grins while Sione tips his head and gives us both the finger.

Cam cracks up laughing, his huge smile taking over his face. He's got to be the smiliest, friendliest guy I know. We've been hanging out since we were ten, and he's my best friend. I hope we keep hanging out forever. He's the closest thing to a brother I've got. All these guys are, but Cam and me...we've got history. I know shit about his family that he won't tell another living soul. It makes you tight.

He's the only one who knows why my mum really left, and I trust him to keep it that way. Everyone else thinks she got a job opportunity that she just couldn't refuse. I left out the fact that she and Beck are over and it's not like she'll be coming back for weekend visits.

It doesn't make too much of a difference. She's not the type to get involved with my friends. Not like Beck, who coached most of us when we were still playing club rugby. He knows my mates. He loves them, and they love him.

I throw the ball to Cam and get into position for the next play but am distracted by a car coming down our driveway. Logan spots it the same time I do and immediately runs to the fence, vaulting it so he can open the door for Tameka as soon as she parks the car.

I don't know what he says, but she laughs and kisses him when she gets out of the car.

"Come help us unload this stuff," she calls over her boyfriend's shoulder, and we dutifully trudge to the car.

Logan and Tameka have been dating since they were fifteen. It's unbelievable that they haven't broken up yet. Teenagers are not supposed to be as in love as those two, but they've barely had an argument. I reckon they'll end up together for good… if Tameka's dad can get over the fact that his Indian-Fijian daughter is in love with a white boy. He tolerates Logan, but he's old-school strict about their relationship. It's weird. These days, you wouldn't think cultural barriers would be an issue anymore, but they still exist. Old, stupid beliefs passed down from one generation to the next, until you reach a generation that just isn't willing to accept it anymore.

Tameka's breaking the chain in her family.

Just like I'm gunna break the chain in mine.

Thoughts of my dad make me shudder. I flick them off and paste on a smile, grateful for Beck. He's my real dad.

"'Sup, Tim Tam?" I raise my eyebrows at Tameka, who

scored the Tim Tam nickname for a couple of good reasons: one, her flawless skin is the color of milk chocolate (some would consider that racist, but she's not offended by it) and two, she *loves* Tim Tams.

They are the best chocolate biscuit in the world, so it's understandable.

Cam reaches into the back and pulls out a box of drinks. "Your dad seriously supplying all of this for the party? How much did it cost?"

"He gave it all to me for half price." She beamed. "After some *serious* persuasion from my mother. I couldn't get any of the food on sale, though. Sorry, guys. Chips, dips, sausages and bread are all gunna cost ya."

"No worries," I tell her, grabbing the loaves of bread. "Just let me know how much we owe the illustrious North Ridge Four Square."

Tameka laughs while I lead Cam and Sione into our garage where we'll be hosting the party. I've already cleared the gym gear into one corner, and I laid out some chairs and beanbags. I figure most of us will be standing, so we should all be able to fit in, plus I'll open the doors so we can spill into the driveway if we have to.

Using my shoulder, I shunt open the old side door and laugh when Cam's surprised it hasn't fallen off yet.

"This place needs some major work." He places the

drinks down next to the pool table. "If I wasn't going away with my family, I'd offer to come over and repaint the thing for ya."

"Yeah, it's pretty bad." I wince, thinking about the peeling paint and holes that need patching. "We just haven't found time yet. I think it's on Beck's list for the summer, but being a worker down, it's not a priority."

"Why'd Grant leave again?" Sione asks.

Cam and I exchange a quick glance, and I try to keep my voice light. "Moving to be closer to his family."

That's not a complete lie. Grant and Mum are now living in his sister's granny flat until they can sort something out.

Tameka's laughing again as she and Logan carry in the rest of the supplies.

"I'll go into the kitchen and make up this dip." Tameka loads up with onion soup packets and reduced cream cans. Logan takes a couple off her and follows his girlfriend.

I watch them go and can't help that combination of joy for them and a slight pining for me. I've only had a couple of casual girlfriends since starting high school, but nothing sticks. I've never been in love. I think I want it, especially if I can have what Tameka and Logan have. They always seem so happy together. Like best friends, but with these huge benefits.

"You happy with the setup in here?" Cam looks around, tucking a straight lock of dark hair behind his ear. He's got one of those undercut things going—his head completely shaved except for this long bit at the top that flops all over the place unless he ties it back or forces it to comply with mounds of gel and hairspray. That's way too much maintenance, if you ask me. It'd drive me nuts. "You want me to move anything around?"

"Nah, I think it'll work." I survey the area, picturing everyone in here.

The wide garage door screeches up to reveal Beck. He gives Sione and Cam a silent greeting—the good old eyebrow raise.

"Hey, Beck." Sione raises his hand with a goofy grin.

Beck gives him a suggestion of a grin before crossing his arms. "You boys all set for tonight? Who's cooking the sausages?"

"I can do that." I half raise my hand. "Is it okay if I wheel the barbecue around so I'm closer to the action?"

"Yeah, of course, but I'm happy to cook them."

"Legend." Cam grins at our favorite father figure.

Beck's lips twitch with what could possibly be a smile, but it doesn't have time to form.

"Hey, Beck!" Logan calls from the front porch, holding up the phone. "It's for you."

It makes me smile that my friends feel at home enough here to go answering our telephone. I love the way Beck's just let them all in. *Me casa es su casa.* That's the way I want to be if I ever get my own home.

Beck walks across the drive and catches the phone Logan throws to him. "Hello?… Yeah, this is Beckett Connell."

I'd turned to ask Cam if he'll help me with the barbecue when something in Beck's tone makes me stop. Spinning back around, I'm just in time to see his eyes bulge with a look of shock that's kind of harrowing.

"What?" He runs a hand through his thick hair, his arm vibrating as he struggles to hold the phone. "When?… Ye-yesterday? Are the girls all right?"

He folds in half, struggling for air, and I rush toward him, resting my hand on his shoulder. "Beck?"

I'm not used to seeing him like this. He's the solid pine tree. He didn't even crumple after Mum left, just went really quiet. Whatever news he's hearing right now is killing him.

Standing back up, he grips his mouth before running his hand over his beard. "What… what about the Hugheses? Have you… have you heard from them?"

He glances at me, his expression a picture of agony I don't understand.

"Yeah," he chokes out. "Of course I'll be there. Do we have definite dates yet?"

He sways on his feet, and I step right up to him and support his back with my hand.

What the hell is going on right now?

I shoot a look at Cam. His blue eyes, usually so bright and playful, are now dark with worry. He moves closer to us, while Sione inches away. Unless he's playing rugby, Sione is the softest guy on the block. Even the *word* conflict makes him antsy.

Beck sucks in a sharp breath, and I spin to face him. "I'm what?… But that was years ago… I… I thought that would have changed." A shadow passes across his face, and now I'm even more confused than I was before.

What was years ago? What's he talking about?

"Yeah." He nods, puffing out a breath. "Yeah, I did agree. It was just a long time ago, though. So much has happened since…then." He whispers the last word and closes his eyes, swaying on his feet again. I grab his shirt to steady him. Beck's eyes pop open and he looks at me, sadness seeping out of him. "No. That's fine. They can… they can come here. Of course they can." Running a hand through his hair, he scratches the top of his head. "Yeah. Let's just, uh, get through the next few days, and then we'll talk details. I'll leave for Auckland first thing in the morning." He bobs his head, then lets out a heavy sigh. "Yeah, right. Thanks."

I hear the click and long tone of an ended call, but Beck just stands there holding the phone to his ear. I gently take it out of his grasp.

"Beck? You all right? What's happened?"

He blinks, his bottom lip curling down while he tries to swallow. His eyes glass with tears, and my lips part. I've never seen Beck cry before.

"Did someone die?" I whisper, not knowing what else to guess.

Beck sniffs and gives me a couple of small nods. "Yeah, mate." Gripping my shoulder, he struggles to speak but eventually manages to rasp, "I don't know what to tell ya, but our lives are about to change."

6

HARPER

My life will never be the same again.

I've managed to process that thought now. It's taken me eleven days.

The funeral is over. I barely remember any of it. I spoke, apparently. I don't know what I said, but I got through it without crying.

I've hugged a lot of people in the last ten days.

I think they keep expecting me to cry on their shoulders, but I don't have room for tears right now. There aren't any. I am dry like an arid desert. I can't afford to be anything else. Not when my brother's a thunderstorm. I think it took him four days to stop wailing. He's cried himself to sleep every night this week. He keeps calling out Dad's name in his dreams, bolting me out of what little sleep I am managing to capture.

Willow's the opposite. Everything about her is silent. Silent tears, stiff cuddles, no words.

Gripping the wheel, I listen to the sound of the car tires on the country road. Usually I'd have music playing, but I don't want anything distracting me. We've been driving since five o'clock this morning. Everyone was already awake, so I figured we'd leave early and make a couple of extra stops along the way.

We had breakfast in Palmerston North, but no one really felt like eating anything. I made them take the leftovers anyway—Mum always hated waste—and now the car reeks of stale McDonald's pancakes and cold hash browns.

My coffee cup was drained over an hour ago. I should have ordered two when we stopped for a toilet break at the petrol station in Turangi.

I shift in my seat, glancing at Oscar. He's staring out the window. I'd love to know what he's thinking, but I'm worried if I ask that he might start crying again, and it'd be good if we could arrive on the farm without snot and tears.

The farm.

Who knew that after everything we'd been through this new year, I'd also have to include a trip north. Nearly seven hours of driving because my parents want their ashes buried on the Connell farm.

Why?

I don't get it.

So Dad grew up near the farm. So what?

In the last eight years, I haven't set foot on the Connell property. Before the funeral, I hadn't seen Uncle Beck since…

I swallow, the nastiness of that day making me shift in my seat again. Gripping the wheel, I clutch the hard plastic, silently praying that *she's* not there. Uncle Beck didn't mention her when we were making plans for this burial service. Maybe we'll get lucky and she'll be away with her kid on summer holiday or something.

"In five hundred meters, turn right onto Marshmeadow Road toward Gordonton."

I follow the directions and try to think if I recognize any of this area. Since moving to Wellington, our lives have been kind of absorbed down there. Any trips we've taken have been to Australia or Fiji… or camping near Cape Palliser.

It's weird how you try to make your circle as small as possible. You find the quickest way to the supermarket, the most efficient way to school. You shop at the malls closest to your house, and the idea of leaving town for anything other than a very special occasion is almost unthinkable.

I guess this is a special occasion.

Not special.

Important.

Devastating.

Life-altering.

Tiredness tugs at me. I blink and hold the wheel even tighter, determined to get there in one piece. Ten and two. If I keep my hands at ten and two, I'll be good. I check my speed, my muscles coiling as I picture Dad behind the wheel. Was he holding the wheel correctly? Or did he have his arm perched on the edge of the window like he usually does, his other hand resting on Mum's leg?

Were they laughing when they came around the corner and suddenly came face-to-face with a tourist on the wrong side of the road?

What whipped through Dad's mind as he no doubt punched the brakes?

Did he know it was the end?

Did any of them know?

The police offered to go over the accident report with me, but I declined. I don't need details. Dead in a car accident is enough. Picturing it will only make it worse. All I really wanted to know was who was at fault. It wasn't my dad, which is a small comfort.

Anger for the tourist driver on the wrong side of the road keeps trying to stir within me, but I don't have space in my chest for that right now. Maybe it'll come. Maybe I'll be lucky enough to bypass it.

He's dead, so... my anger is pointless in a way.

"In one kilometer, turn right."

I glance at my phone and see that we're due to arrive in ten minutes.

Nerves attack me, swarming like panicked bees in my stomach.

I don't want to do this! But I have to. For my parents. Their ashes are in the back of this station wagon, expecting to be laid to rest. I can't let them down.

Plus, getting out of Wellington for a few days is a good thing. That's what Uncle Beck said. In his gruff, soft voice, he told me that distance might be just the ticket.

I guess he would know.

It's been twelve years since he lost it all, but I bet he still remembers it, and this whole thing will only unearth what he's no doubt tried to forget.

His voice shook when he offered to pay for our flights and said we could stay for as long as we liked.

"There's space." His voice cracked. "Plenty of space."

I swallowed and declined the flights. I want the car so I

can leave whenever it suits us. I'll need to stay at least one night to get the energy to drive back to Wellington, but at this stage, we've packed enough for one week. We'll see. I don't want to commit to anything.

"Turn right."

I follow the woman's gentle instructions, and we head down a road that is country all the way. Paddock after paddock of grass, neatly sectioned off. Cows grazing. The odd farmhouse popping into view, then disappearing just as fast.

"In three point five kilometers, your destination will be on the left."

I know this. Suddenly I remember.

Images from my childhood come flooding back. The key to that part of my life has been turned, and as the door in my brain is flung open, I'm met with the sound of my childhood giggles as I chase after Charlie and Matt.

"Wait for me, you guys!" I'd holler after them while our parents laughed behind us.

Aunty Abby was tucked beneath Uncle Beck's arm, her ceaseless smile and laughter shining over us as she watched her twin boys play with their cousin by choice, not birth.

A heavy sadness settles inside of me, pinching my

stomach and hurting even more than before. I need to shut that door and lock it up tight. I've lost enough. So many people are gone now. My family is being eaten away, one death at a time. All that's left are my siblings. Stacey and Bianca. Uncle Beck.

I turn into the driveway, no longer needing Siri to guide me. I know this place. The big white house to the left, the peeling old garage to the right. Matty, Charlie and I used to play pretend in that garage. On rainy days, Beck would pull out the cars so we could turn it into our castle. On sunny visits we'd play in the treehouse he and Dad built.

It was so long ago now, yet my memories are crystal clear. Flashes of joy that I've been hiding away, because it always inevitably hurts.

My throat burns as their ghosts haunt me for a moment. The sound of Mom's wail when she got the phone call. She was pregnant with Oscar, and I remember worrying about her large belly as she cried out and dropped the phone.

Gone.

Without warning.

"Gone," I whisper under my breath as a guy I don't recognize steps out of the garage.

He's tall and broad, with almond skin and the kind of

muscles that could make a girl's heart thrum. I blink, shocked by the flush of heat that travels through me. I look away from him and his tight contours, focusing on driving straight so I can park the car like I know what the hell I'm doing.

Which I do. I'm a good driver.

He stops walking, his beat-up sneakers scuffing on the packed dirt. Even his legs are muscly—shaped calves that look as though they could run for miles, solid thighs that flex as he stands there watching me park.

He has Maori blood in him. You can see the strength of a warrior, yet his eyes are pale brown, his nose narrow and just a little crooked. He must have some Pakeha blood running through those veins too.

Who the hell is he?

We all lurch forward when I hit the brakes too hard.

"Sorry," I mutter.

Oscar frowns at me.

I glance in the rearview mirror. Willow's slipping off her headphones, looking anxious as she glances around. She won't remember this place as well as I do. She was only three when Beck stopped letting us visit.

I swallow, flinching when I spot the mystery guy approaching the car.

Oh crap. Oh crap. Oh crap!

He pops my door open, letting in a gust of wind that ruffles my hair. I snatch at the long tendrils, bunching them in my fingers while the guy gazes down at me, his soft brown eyes gentle and kind.

"Hey, Harper." His lips rise into a sad smile, and I'm confused by his familiarity until a thought hits me.

Wait. No way.

The kid?

The skinny, sad-eyed kid from the picnic?

"Tane?" I whisper.

"That's me." He steps back so I can get out of the car.

I slowly stand opposite him, studying the way his black hair curls up around the edges of his cap. He smells like sweat, and judging by his shorts and lack of shirt, I wonder if he's been working out or something. Maybe hauling hay bales around the farm?

He's not even the same person he was seven years ago.

From skinny boy to buff man.

Tane.

That woman's son.

The one I was playing so nicely with at the picnic, until it all turned to crap.

I can't believe she and Beck are still together.

My stomach sinks as I glance toward the house and prepare myself to see her walk out the door and greet me.

7

TANE

Harper's face creases with worry as she glances at the house.

I study her profile, unable to deny my immediate attraction. She's gorgeous. The kind of face worthy of artwork. Is it weird to think that?

She's just got this period piece beauty. The angles of her face are smooth, yet strong. I can picture her on a canvas, surrounded by an illustrious frame that brings out the caramel highlights in her hair.

I'd love to say something to ease the anxiety wrinkling her forehead, but I've got nothing. I feel kind of useless as I stand there studying her, waiting for Beck to come and save the day.

He's taking his sweet time.

Shifting in my beat-up sneaks, I glance down and

notice Harper's black slip-on shoes. Her feet are so long and slender. Just like all of her is. Without meaning to, my eyes travel up her body, taking in the tailored skirt and the loose white button-down shirt that the wind is wrapping around her body. She's lean and wispy, like her highlighted hair that's dancing around her face.

She captures it again, forcing compliance with a shaking fist.

"It's windy today," I murmur, feeling like a complete idiot.

Stating the obvious, Tane? Just shut up, mate.

She glances at me, her eyes curious before turning to check on her sister. Willow slips out of the car. I'm trying to remember her but struggling. All I really remember from that picnic was playing with Harper, and then Mum turning into a drunken beast.

I internally shudder and step away from the car, set on entering the house and hollering for Beck to get his butt outside.

But the front door opens before I have to. Willow flinches. She's like a winter branch on the verge of snapping. I can sense it in her jerky movements and the way her eyes dart around the farm like she's just arrived on an alien planet.

Oscar's the opposite. He slams the car door and looks

around, giving me a baleful stare before Beck grabs his attention.

"Ozzy. Nice to see you, mate."

Oscar's shoulders soften as Beck walks down the two wide steps and lands beside him.

"Welcome back." The corners of Beck's mouth twitch. He probably thinks he's smiling at Harper and Willow, but it's not even close.

How can anyone smile right now? Tragedy hangs thick in the air; not even this summer wind can blow it away. It buffets our clothing, slapping at us, reminding us that this is no friendly visit.

"Tane, go get changed. The service will be starting soon."

"Yep." I nod and walk around to the back of the car. "Can I help you guys carry anything in?" I lift the boot and the first thing to strike me is the two black boxes tucked securely between the suitcases. They look like mini treasure chests, but they're not.

They hold treasure, but not in the form anyone around here wants.

We're after living, breathing flesh, not ashes.

My throat constricts as I gaze down at them, but I quickly snap out of it when Willow appears beside me.

"This your case?" I ask her.

She shakes her head and points at the other one. I grab it out and then take the navy blue bag next to it. She grabs one of the boxes, cradling it against her stomach like it's precious.

"Come on," I rasp, tipping my head toward the house. "I'll show you to your room."

She shuffles behind me and the others follow suit, Beck grabbing the last suitcase as we form a procession line into the house.

I sidestep the clutter. This house has always been over-full. Beck's parents were old, and his mum loved to keep things. Knickknacks and trinkets have been passed from one generation to the next, filling up the old farmhouse. There's a lot of history in this house, and I still remember the first time I walked in here and asked Mum if this was a museum.

She looked embarrassed and shook her head. Beck just laughed and walked up the narrow wooden staircase, showing me to my room.

I'm doing the same thing today. Walking up the dark stairwell, memories flood me as I show these new people to what could potentially become their home. By the looks of their luggage, they're not planning on staying too long. That's probably a good thing.

This house is used to small numbers, and right now, it's overrun. Although, it was built for big. The first of the

Connells to arrive in New Zealand built this place. It was designed for a family of ten. Ten!

Having been an only child, I can't even wrap my head around that.

Although I might need to.

We've suddenly gone from two to seven in under a fortnight.

I place Willow's bag on the bed by the window. She's standing in the doorway watching me, her hazel eyes big and curious, just like her sister's.

"Is this Oscar's bag or…?"

She points to the other bed in this room, so I assume it's Harper's and place it down.

"Thank you." Harper appears behind her sister. Her full, lush lips curve into a polite smile that lasts about five seconds.

"You're welcome." I hitch up my workout shorts and lament the fact that they came earlier than expected. I'd planned on showering up and being all ready to welcome them. My sweaty stench feels more powerful in this tiny room, and I make a quick escape.

Harper shifts to let me pass, and I catch a whiff of her perfume. It doesn't smell like flowers. I don't know what the heck it is, other than sweet nectar from the gods.

Shuffling down the hallway, I keep my eyes on my bedroom door in an attempt to hide the desire pulsing through me.

Don't desire her, you pervert! She's a grieving woman!

I can't resist one quick glance over my shoulder as I push my bedroom door open. She's watching me and jerks her head away just after our eyes connect.

Maybe it's best that they are only staying for a few days. Not sure I could handle living with a goddess like that only two rooms away from me.

"Harper!" Stacey appears out of her room at the opposite end of the hall, Bianca following in her wake.

Harper turns to hug them both and I slip into my room, my heart thumping wildly as my brain tries to adjust to the massive changes taking over the quiet old farmhouse.

8

STACEY

The sun is a glaring beast. I squint against it, wishing I'd brought my shades. It should be raining right now. Why is the sun out? Why is the sky blue?

It seems so wrong to be standing on this hilltop, a stunning view stretching out around us for miles. The Waikato plains—home to hundreds of farms and cows.

I can hear a distant moo, the wind carrying the sound right into my ear, before whipping my hair across my face. It's a taunting bully today, tugging out our clothing, making our hair dance when we should be listening to the minister.

His voice is getting sucked away from us and the wind is laughing. I can almost hear its mocking howl.

"Does anyone have any special memories or thoughts they'd like to share?" The minister holds his hand over the Bible he's just been reading from. The thin pages flutter and bend.

My insides coil when Bianca looks at me.

One of us should probably say something, but I can't! If I speak, I might cry. That's why I couldn't do the eulogy at Mum and Dad's funeral. I couldn't bring myself to speak. Bianca chickened out too, so Carter did it for us.

I don't want to think about that day. It was nothing but a full-blown nightmare.

Just like this is.

My head shakes without me realizing until the minister gives Beck a pleading smile.

Beck clears his throat and steps up. He plays with his beard while he speaks, running his fingers through the long black whiskers. There are a few ginger ones in there too, and maybe a couple of grays are starting to show. For as long as I can remember, he's always had a bushy beard. When I was a kid, I used to think he was a big teddy bear—furry and large. He gave the best hugs...until Matt and Charlie died, and then he started to get grizzly and sullen, pushing us away when all Dad wanted to do was help him.

I look to the ground and focus on a clump of grass at my feet, studying the vibrant green blades that curl over my shoes. Just beyond that clump are four little holes that have been dug with precision to fit four black boxes that will soon be buried in them.

It hurts to breathe.

Why?

Why did Mum and Dad want to be buried here? It's not like it's *their* farm, although Dad did always talk about this place with… I don't know, fondness, I guess. He'd tell us stories of the mischief he got up to with his two best friends. Even Mum had stories to tell about when she and Dad first got together and how they all used to hang out. Three couples, high on life and love.

Life.

That word seems to hurt now, like a dagger straight into my guts.

Tears drip down my face as Beck wraps up his speech and the minister gets to the part I've been dreading.

"We will now commit the ashes of Lance, Renee, Richard and Leanne to the ground."

He points at the boxes and silently shows us what to do.

I crouch down, grabbing Dad's box. Or is it Mum's? I can't read the label; my eyes are too blurry from tears. Bianca sniffs beside me, tears dripping off her chin as she nestles the box into the hole. I do the same and quickly jerk back to my feet, my gaze traveling to the large plaque behind Oscar.

. . .

Abby, Matthew & Charles Connell

Three bright lights who will forever be loved and missed.

I was five when they were killed in a car accident.

Another car accident. Huh. Maybe the universe is trying to tell us something. Or maybe life's just frickin' unfair.

Vague memories of loud, energetic twin boys skim through my mind but don't turn into anything solid. Mum and Dad would sometimes talk about Abby and her sons with these sad smiles on their faces. Now they're gone too. I wonder how long it will be before I start talking about my parents like they were just fictional characters in a story I once read.

The thought makes my stomach jerk and tremble. I sniff and pinch my nose, shoving the unhinging idea aside.

Taking Bianca's hand, I give it a squeeze. She barely squeezes back. She's frozen in place, like a tear-streaked photograph, staring at our parents' little gravesites. The wind blows her red hair, and the fiery tendrils dance around her. It's like a slow-motion movie scene, and I want to press Pause, Stop, Rewind, anything to make this nightmare stop playing.

Panic tries to seize me as I imagine life without Mum and Dad.

Who will make me laugh when I've had a shitty day now? No more lame Dad jokes? I always said I hated them, but the truth was I didn't. And now I can't tell him.

And I can't tell Mum how beautiful I thought she was, and how much I loved it when people said I looked like her. I always acted like it was so embarrassing, but it wasn't! It was a compliment!

My knees want to buckle; my body wants to fold like a freaking rag doll. My insides start to spasm and tremble, and it only gets worse when Beck takes a spade and starts covering the boxes with dirt. The first clump hits the lid with a definitive smack, and my brain screams for him to stop.

They'll suffocate! They need air, sun, water. You're killing them!

But they're already dead.

Clenching my jaw, I try to hide the panic riding through me. I need to rein it in, because screaming won't stop this nightmare. The only thing that can stop it is to pretend it's not happening.

Glancing past Harper, who is holding a sobbing Oscar, her eyes fixed on the graves at our feet, I gaze out to the blue sky, focusing on the brightness of it before scanning the fields. They are beautiful—different shades of green peppering the landscape. I focus on that, trying to count the various tones and colors. Anything to not think about what's happening right beside me.

I block out the noise by talking to myself, my head voice distracting me from the scoop and thump, scoop and thump. I need it to drown out Bianca's whimpering and Oscar's sobbing. Thankfully, Tane and Willow are quiet statues.

My eyes brush over them before turning to gaze at a different set of paddocks.

Talk, I say to myself. *Just talk.*

My head voice can sense what I need, my imagination giving me a bright smile before bolstering my spirits.

Okay, well, it's not the summer holiday you pictured, but the air is clean and fresh. Even this teasing wind feels good on your skin, if you change it from a stinging slap to a soft tickle. Sniff the air, Stacey. Do it.

I inhale and close my eyes, shutting out the graves and the cold reality of our future.

Lifting my chin, I feel the sun soaking into my skin.

We're just on holiday, Bianca and me. An interesting summer holiday at Uncle Beck's farm. That's all it is. There's nothing scary about that. Nothing scary at all.

9

HARPER

The grandfather clock against the wall ticks a steady rhythm. A slow, rusty heartbeat. Relentless in its mission.

Time is ticking by.

There's nothing we can do about it.

I swallow and curl my fingers, the hard wood of the teak table smooth against my knuckles. I wonder how many families have eaten around this table. Like everything else in this house, I wouldn't be surprised if it's been here since inception.

The farmhouse is like another planet compared to my home. Mum and Dad were both minimalists. They liked light, air, space. Mum couldn't stand clutter.

"It's just stuff I'll have to dust anyway. What's the point?"

In contrast, this place feels like a secondhand shop. Ancient reminders of the generations who came before —silver candlestick holders that need polishing, a china tea set gathering dust in the display cabinet, all surrounded by a dark wood that makes the living area feel more like a cave rather than an inviting lounge.

The lawyer opens his briefcase and pulls out a couple of files, arranging his paperwork and apologizing once again.

"Sorry I couldn't be here earlier. The day got away from me, but I promised I'd make it before sunset, and I have." He smiles a polite smile, then clears his throat when no one responds.

I glance into the kitchen, the only space that's had a renovation. I don't know when it was done, but cooking in there tonight wasn't so bad. Not that anyone ate my mac and cheese. I get it. I didn't exactly have much to work with. Plates of barely eaten food are piled next to the sink. No one had time to clean up before the lawyer arrived, and I can smell essence of hardening yellow pasta paste wafting into the dining area.

"Are we waiting for anyone else before starting?" The lawyer, what's his name again? He studied law with my dad, apparently. My exhausted brain can't conjure his name, so I let the idea pass. I'll just think of him as The Will Guy.

That's what he's here for.

I shake my head when he points at me and asks, "Are your brother and sister joining us?"

Oscar is watching a movie on his laptop. He was lucky enough to get his own room. Willow is up in ours, messaging her friends. She's still not talking and it's bothering me, but I haven't had time to do anything about it. I invited them to sit in on this meeting, but they both declined. They looked so miserable I couldn't fight them on it. Stacey tried to get out of it, as well, but Beck wouldn't let her.

She complied easily enough, so she probably knew she was entering a losing battle.

I'm curious to know what the wills say.

Tapping my knuckles on the table, I glance into the lounge. Tane's in the old olive green chair next to the fireplace. He's reading a sports magazine but is so obviously using it as a ruse to listen in. I'd do the same. A bunch of strangers moving into my house? I'd want to know every detail I could.

His mum's not here. When we were walking up the hill to the grave site, I casually asked. I wanted to know what I'd be facing after the service. Tane looked to the ground and mumbled, "She doesn't live here anymore."

That actually made me relax, although I felt bad about the sad anger in Tane's expression. I wonder what happened. I wonder why he's still with Beck. It's not like Tane's his son or anything.

"Okay, well, we'll get started, then." The lawyer places two files next to each other and is about to start when he pauses to look over the top of his reading glasses at us. "Harper's father wrote up the wills for both his family and the Freemans." He indicates Stacey and Bianca. "So, they're basically the same. Other than a few asset differences, they're a mirror of each other, so I'll sort of read the wills simultaneously. Okay?"

We all nod, and he begins, going through each point. In the case of both parents dying, all the money and assets are to be left to the children. My parents had life insurance, so the mortgage is being covered and the house is going into a trust, which will be managed by the lawyer, Beck and me.

The idea sends a chill racing through me. I'm not old enough for this!

All of my parents' savings are being transferred into the Hughes Family Trust, which we can access for education after high school. The same applies for Stacey and Bianca. Both families will also have a working account, which will be funded from the trust quarterly. This money can be used at our own discretion.

"Day-to-day living." The lawyer circles his hand in the air. I watch the tip of his pen go around and around. He looks at me, shifting his glasses down his nose. "It's enough to get by, but you'll want to use this money carefully. You'll probably need to think about getting a part-time job, just to give yourselves a little boost.

Unless you, of course, decide to sell the house in Wellington. You could then invest the money and live off the interest."

"But where would we live?" I whisper.

"That brings us to the next part." The Will Guy shuffles his papers around. "Guardianship."

The clock keeps ticking its steady beat, and I keep trying to align my breaths with it. If I don't, I might forget to inhale.

"Beckett Connell has been listed as your guardian. Both of your parents—"

Stacey slaps the table, a breath spurting from her nose before unleashing a little dragon. "We haven't seen Beck in years. No offense, but why is he our guardian? Did our slack parents just not update their wills?"

Flustered by her outburst, the lawyer adjusts his glasses to reread the paperwork while my hackles go up. I can feel the hairs on my neck bristling.

"My dad was an amazing lawyer. Meticulous. He wouldn't let stuff like this slide." I'm trying to keep my voice mild, but it's impossible to completely douse the snap in my tone.

"Okay." Stacey raises her eyebrows. "Fine. Then why did your brilliant father insist on keeping Beck as your guardian?" She glances at Beck. "No offense, you're cool and everything, but we haven't seen you since your girlfriend went psycho at that picnic and called my mother a lying slut. That was years ago!"

I glance into the lounge and catch Tane's eye. He gives me a shame-faced frown and goes back to reading his magazine, burying his nose between the pages. I feel this weird mix of pity and surprise. Surprise that he's not standing up for his mother, but that look of shame on his face... *break my heart.*

Beck clears his throat, shooting Stacey a warning look before softly saying, "Look, I don't get it either. I thought your parents wouldn't want me in that role after everything, but..." Beck shakes his head, his hand rising off the table before floating back down.

"There's a letter." The lawyer starts riffling through his paperwork again.

"Excuse me?" Beck shuffles in his seat while all eyes in the room ping to The Will Guy.

"The last time Lance updated his will, he included a letter." He hands it over to Beck, who unfolds it with shaking hands. With a thick swallow, he reads it to himself while we all wait to find out what it says.

Shuffling butts on seats. A sports magazine forgotten in Tane's lap. Bianca biting her lip like it'll make up for the dinner she barely touched.

I study Beck's face, my heart twisting at the way his lips tremble and the sheen of tears in his eyes. They collect on his lashes, a couple spilling free when he closes his eyes and scrubs a hand down his face. Sitting back with a sniff, he struggles to refold the letter while giving the lawyer a stiff nod.

"Well, what does it say?" Stacey snips.

Beck can't do anything but shake his head and stroke his beard. His wide mouth forms a wonky line and he sniffs again, shaking his head one more time.

Stacey huffs and I shoot my hand across the table, gently patting her wrist and whispering, "It's okay. It's..."

But it's not okay. I'm desperate to know what that letter says. Desperate for an explanation.

After his family died, Beck pushed us away, but Dad kept fighting and eventually he let us back in, only to side with his awful girlfriend when she was so obviously out of line. He didn't have to push too hard to keep Dad and Uncle Richie at bay after that. They could never understand why he stayed with her.

Stacey's fuming beside me, and Bianca's lip is going to be raw and bleeding soon.

I glance at the lawyer, hoping to wrap things up. I'm ready for this to be over. I need sleep. Oblivion. "So, is there anything else?"

"Well, yes." The lawyer clears his throat yet again and slides off his glasses. "You ladies all have a choice.

Harper, you're eighteen, which means you are old enough to raise your siblings on your own."

And the arid desert is back, filling my throat with sand and making it impossible to speak.

"What about us?" Bianca softly asks.

"You're both sixteen, so you also have a choice too."

"We can live on our own?" Stacey blinks, fear flashing across her face.

The lawyer gives her a reluctant nod. "Although, can I advise against it? You're both dealing with huge trauma right now, and it's important that you're supported throughout this process."

Stacey's eyebrows bunch together as she flicks her hand at me. "But Harper can go if she wants?"

"They have a life in Wellington. She may feel that a stable, familiar routine is best for her siblings." The lawyer's voice is so calm and even. The complete opposite to my raging insides. The sand has moved into my stomach, creating a choking storm that's making me feel sick.

"You don't have to decide right away," Beck murmurs, catching my attention with a little pat on the table. "You're welcome to stay here as long as you need."

I look at him. My eyes are burning. I can't say anything. I have no idea how to respond to this right now.

I mean, I think I knew that would be the plan. But I haven't had time to *really* consider it. Life has been funerals and survival. I couldn't think past the next day, but now I'm being presented with a future that feels too heavy to hold.

"I want to go back to China." Stacey stands from her chair. It scrapes against the wooden floor, making me wince. "Is there any way we can make that happen?"

The lawyer gives her a sad smile. "I'm sorry, but no. You need to get used to the idea that your life is now back in New Zealand."

"But we haven't lived here for like ten years!" She stomps her foot, desperation vibrating out of her.

"I know," the lawyer murmurs.

"What about all our stuff? Our apartment! Are we just supposed to leave everything in Suzhou!"

"We'll arrange to get it shipped here." Beck's lips curve just a little, like he's trying to smile but can't quite do it. "I can help you sort out all the details."

Stacey grips her mouth, pacing away from the table while Bianca nervously watches, then softly says, "Thanks, Uncle Beck."

"He's not our uncle!" Stacey spins back and slaps the table with both hands this time. "No offense, but you're not!"

"I know." Beck nods, again so calm and unruffled by this golden-haired dragon. Her eyes are blue fire. "But I'm the closest thing you've got to family."

"The only other living relative you have left is your grandmother in Australia," the lawyer interjects, checking his paperwork. "Ms. Adeline Cochrane."

"That's not an option." Stacey scoffs like he's stupid. "She cut my mother off years ago. She won't want us, and we don't want her. She's a stuck-up bitch. The last time Mum tried to reconnect, she piled on the guilt so thick and fast Mum was left crying for a week!"

I look to Bianca, who confirms it with a subtle nod. I didn't know any of my grandparents. Mum's parents died in England before she even moved to New Zealand, and Dad's both passed in my first couple of years. I wasn't old enough to remember them.

I didn't realize Aunty Leanne still had a mother. It's so sad that she's alive but not here. That seems wrong to me, somehow. As if this situation isn't broken enough already.

Beck shifts uncomfortably in his chair. "Look, Stacey—"

"We're not living with her. We're not!"

"Okay. Okay." Beck raises his hands. "You don't have to. You're welcome here."

"I don't want to be here." Her mouth trembles. "No—"

"Offense. Yeah. I know." Beck raises his hand with a sad frown. Not really a frown. More like compassionate pity that makes my heart want to fold in half.

"It's not fair," she grits out, her voice tiny as a tear slips down her cheek.

"No, it's not," Beck whispers.

She steps back from the table and looks around the room, breaths spurting from her nose in rapid succession. A meltdown is brewing; I can feel it. No one says anything, and now all I can hear is the clock in syncopated rhythm with Stacey's flaring nostrils and dragon puffs.

But then suddenly she sniffs, her back pinging straight and this weird emoji smile stretching across her face. Flicking her hair over her shoulder, she approaches the table like the director's just yelled, "Cut!" or something, and does this big fake yawn. "This girl needs her beauty sleep. I'm going to bed. I'll see you guys in the morning."

She glides away from the table while we all share perplexed frowns.

"Bianca?" Stacey's voice pitches when she reaches the stairs, her blue eyes flashing with panic until her twin rises from the table and looks to the lawyer.

"Is… is there anything else?"

The lawyer gives her a kind smile. "Why don't I let Beck know and he can tell you in the morning."

"Okay," she whispers, then bows her head and meekly follows after her sister, who is already halfway up the stairs.

The grandfather clock dominates the sound space again, and I'm not sure how much longer I can stand it. Flattening my hands on the table, I slowly rise, making sure my chair doesn't scratch against the floor. "I should probably go check on Will and Ozzy."

Beck looks up and gives me an understanding nod. "I'll finish up here."

"Thanks," I squeak and move around his chair.

I sense Tane's gaze on me as I walk out of the room, so I stop at the base of the stairs to glance back into the lounge. His gentle brown eyes are so full of compassion I'm worried I'll buckle into a sobbing mess on the floor, so I quickly look away from him and will my trembling legs to walk upstairs.

10

TANE

The sun is hot on my skin as I trudge up to the house from the milking shed. It's only eight o'clock, and already I'm sweating. It's going to be a scorcher today. Not that I don't love summer, but we need some decent rain. Not the few measly showers that have passed over us but a decent deluge that can fill the water tanks and green up the grass a little.

The bucket of fresh milk bumps against my leg as I carry it to the laundry door. A couple of dribbles hit my leg and soak into my permanently stained overalls.

I greet the chickens as I pass. "Morning, chooks." They squawk and crow at me, their crazy heads bobbing as they wander around their yard.

I glance at the fence, noting the cracked beam in the back section. We need to fix that up before it fully breaks and the chickens start running loose around the farm. We let them out for a wander every now and then, but their closed-in yard is really big anyway, so it's not like they don't have enough space, plus it saves me going chicken hunting when one of them doesn't come back when I want it to.

Beck's quad bike revs behind me, and I step sideways so he can park next to the house.

"We're going to need to put out some silage for the girls after breakfast. They need the boost. The grass in Paddock 32 wasn't lush enough this morning."

"Yeah, sure thing." I nod, walking up the back steps and placing the bucket of milk just inside the laundry door.

Using the edge of the step, I take off my gumboots and yank up my work socks before wriggling out of my overalls.

"I also need to resection Paddock 55—we'll put the cows in there after milking this afternoon. I need you to check the fencing in Paddocks 60 to 70."

"Uh-huh." I nod, internally groaning.

Bloody fencing. I wouldn't mind it so much if it wasn't a constant, relentless job on the farm. I don't know what Beck's gunna do once school starts for the year. He'll have to hire someone to help him out with the work-load. I kind of want to mention it but also kind of don't

—he's under enough stress—so instead I put in a bid for a little Tane Time.

"I'd also like to take Copper out for a ride today. She'll be pining for some attention since I didn't take her out yesterday."

"Yeah, you should have time to do that." Beck removes his gumboots, placing them neatly on the rack before whipping off his work socks and shoving them inside.

His large bare feet trudge past me into the laundry, and I follow him, quietly asking, "What about our house-guests? What are they going to do today?"

He stops and lets out a heavy sigh before glancing over his shoulder at me. "Let's just leave them to it. They can go for a walk or watch movies, play pool in the garage. They just need to relax. Recover. It is their summer holiday, after all."

I don't know if I agree with that, but I don't want to argue with him, either. Out of everyone in this house, I'm the only one with living parents. I haven't lost a wife, sons, nothing. I mean, I've lost, but it's not death that's robbed me, so I seal my lips and instead listen to the whine of the water pipes.

Beck looks up at the ceiling, his dark eyebrows dipping into a frown.

"Wonder how long they've been in the shower," he mumbles.

Again, I keep my mouth shut and head into the kitchen, sliding the internal door open and stopping short when I spot Harper looking in the fridge. I can't see her face or anything. All I can see is a pair of luscious long legs and long, elegant feet. Her toenails are painted red, and I can't help working my way up those slender toes and around her perfect ankles. Then my eyes start studying the shape of her smooth, tanned calves and I'm freaking undone. With a thick swallow, I try to drag my gaze away from her. Study the cream, speckled linoleum, check out the lines of the kitchen cupboards, something! Anything but—

She closes the fridge door and starts when she spots me.

"Oh! I thought you were still… How long does milking usually take?"

"Few hours," I murmur, not sure where to look.

She's in tiny boxer shorts and a singlet that's short enough to show off the bottom edge of her flat stomach. I can only assume these are her pajamas.

Are pajamas supposed to be that sexy? I feel like there should be some kind of law against how good she looks right now.

My gaze snaps to the floor, guilt singeing me. This is not the time to get a hard-on for Harper Hughes. She's just lost her parents, for crying out loud.

"Morning." Beck shunts me into the kitchen in order to

move past me.

"Hi." Harper raises her hand in a little wave, then crosses her arm over her body, gripping her shoulder and looking kind of embarrassed.

I swallow, giving her a closed-mouth smile and trying to act like sexy-ass pajamas in my kitchen is no big deal.

A toilet flushes upstairs and Beck jerks to a stop, looking up and frowning at the ceiling. I fight a grin. Beck is such a stickler when it comes to water usage, especially with the dry weather we've been having.

Harper fills the kettle and sets it to start boiling. She opens the fridge again. "There's not much in here. We need bread, eggs. Maybe some bacon. There's no fruit and only two carrots that I could tie into a knot they're so old. Oh, and we're out of milk." She shuts the fridge and looks at Beck, obviously expecting a response, but he's too busy staring at the ceiling. The toilet has just flushed *again*.

A low growl rumbles in his throat before he walks out of the kitchen and down to his room.

Harper stares after him. Even confusion looks pretty on her.

I swallow and point over my shoulder. "Milk's in the laundry."

"The laundry?" Her brow wrinkles even more. "You have a second fridge or something?"

I can't help a smile. She's so city. "Uh, no, it's fresh from this morning."

Her nose wrinkles. "Like, straight from the cow's udder?"

"Yeah." I chuckle and head into the laundry to get it.

She follows me. I can smell her behind me, this soft morning whiff. It's foreign and all female. Not sure if it's her shampoo or what, but she doesn't smell like she's just rolled out of bed. When she stops right next to me, it's hard to breathe for a second. Her long hair is touching my bare arm, her scent wafting toward me like a delicious fruit salad.

Apricot?

Maybe it's her moisturizer or something. Tameka, Kim and Melina are always slathering that stuff on. They smell fruity too.

"It's in a bucket." Harper states the obvious.

"How else am I supposed to carry it up?"

"Oh, no, it's just...how am I supposed to pour it into my coffee cup? And speaking of coffee, you guys don't have a machine. I could only find instant in the cupboard."

I cross my arms and smirk at her. "What's wrong with instant?"

"Nothing," she lies, her full lips stretching thin. "It's

just…not as nice."

"Well, I'm sorry you can't start your day with a latte, City Girl."

She gives me a dry look and then bends down to snatch the milk bucket. It must be heavier than she expected because she gasps, her balance thrown. I catch her arm to steady her. Her skin is soft and smooth, her bicep small within my grasp. It takes everything in me to stop my thumb from exploring the shape of it.

"You right?" I check her feet are stable before letting her go and bending down to grab the bucket handle out of her grasp.

Some of the milk sloshes out, splashing onto her leg and trailing white rain from her knee to her ankle.

"It's warm." She makes a disgusted face.

"It's fresh." I laugh and head to the kitchen. "And it tastes great in instant coffee."

She makes a face at my teasing, but then her lips twitch with a smile. Good. She can take a joke.

I throw her a damp cloth before pulling two sterilized glass jugs out of the cupboard. I usually only need one, but I got extra today. With all these new bodies in the house, we're gunna go through at least twice as much. Fresh milk like this only lasts three days, but I don't think we'll be throwing any out. I finish decanting the bucket, then pop them in the fridge.

Harper's finished wiping her leg and is now rinsing out the cloth while I grab the hanging pen on the fridge door and scribble the date on the 'milk and egg' notepad. You have to be careful with farm fresh products. Don't want anyone getting sick.

On the notepad underneath that one, I jot down all the food things Harper listed earlier, then add a couple of extras. Beck and I haven't really thought this through. I'm so used to small numbers; it's going to be weird filling this kitchen with enough food to feed seven people. I've hosted parties and stuff before, but I've always got Tameka and my boys to help me with quantities. I can't bring them into this. Not yet.

Everyone's too fragile right now. They need calm, peace, solitude.

My friends know what's going on, because they were here when Beck got the call, but Cam's the only one I've been texting about it. He's the only one I want visiting when he gets back from his holiday.

Thumping on the stairs makes me turn. A fresh-faced Stacey appears, her wet hair creating dark circles on her bright orange tank top.

"There's no hair dryer in the bathroom." She looks at me like I can somehow produce one from the back of my shorts, like I walk the earth packing one in my waistband.

"Um…" I blink at her stupidly.

"Don't worry about it." Bianca pats Stacey's shoulder. "She can survive."

The soft quip scores her a droll look from her sister, but she walks past it and stops by the dining room table, looking kind of lost as she wraps her fingers around the top of the chair.

Stacey steps up beside her, and I'm struck yet again by how different they are. They don't even look like sisters, let alone twins.

Stacey's a fresh orange, bright and energetic, her blue eyes sparking as she surveys the room and settles a pointed look right at me. Bianca, on the other hand, is playing with the ends of her long red hair, looking more like a cherry blossom petal as she stares out the window. Her white, freckled skin has soft, pudgy edges while Stacey's is tanned and taut. Beck mentioned she played a lot of sports. You can tell. She looks like a model in her short shorts. I can picture her on a Rebel Sports billboard. She'd be perfect.

Beck walks out from his downstairs bathroom, still drying his hands. "All right, which one of you kept flushing the toilet this morning?"

Willow appears at the bottom of the stairs, still in her pjs. Short boxers and fitted tanks must be standard bedwear in the Hughes family. Let's hope that doesn't apply to Oscar as well.

Willow starts running fingers through her hair, trying to

tame it into a ponytail.

Stacey looks her up and down before turning back to Beck. "What are you talking about?"

"We haven't had steady rain in a while. Water supply is getting low. You can't have long showers, and you can't flush the loo every time you use it." Beck looks around at everyone. "Remember this motto: if it's yellow, let it mellow; if it's brown, flush it down."

"Ew." Stacey's face contorts into a comical look of disgust.

"And as for showers, five minutes max. Two minutes is preferable."

"Five minutes?" Stacey flicks her arms in the air. "I can't even wash my hair in that time."

"Then switch it off in between."

Stacey crosses her arms and tips her head. "What's that supposed to mean?"

Beck frowns at her like she's stupid. "Wet your hair, turn off the water, put shampoo through it, then turn the water back on to rinse it out."

"This is unbelievable." Stacey pulls out a chair and plunks into it. "How is it possible that this place is even more archaic than Suzhou?" She looks at Bianca, who gives her a little smile and then shrugs.

Stacey lets out an exaggerated groan. "Anyway, what's

for breakfast? I'm starving."

"Not much." Harper winces. "We need to go shopping."

Beck huffs. "There's bread in the pantry, eggs in the chicken coop, fresh milk in the fridge. I'm sure you can put something together."

"Ch-chicken coop?" Bianca's round face contorts with worry.

I can't help a snicker. "I'll collect this morning, but Harper's right. We need to get some more food."

"I'd be happy to go and do some shopping," she chimes in. "Just let me know where the closest supermarket is." She actually looks kind of relieved by the idea of getting busy with a job, which again makes me wonder if Beck's decision to just let them do whatever they want is the right one.

Beck glances at me, then around at the girls, before nodding. "Yeah, all right. I'll get you some money. You girls can head off after breakfast."

He thumps out of the room, and I flash Harper a quick smile.

To my surprise, she returns it. Not sure if that's an automatic response or not, but I'll take it.

If confusion looked pretty on her before, her smile is enough to turn my knees to jelly.

11

HARPER

So, according to Beck, small shops happen at the Four Square near North Ridge High School, but since we're not doing a small shop, we have to head to Rototuna North. There's a big supermarket along with a bunch of other shops, everything from a hair salon to a pet shop, with Chinese takeaways and Subway scattered in between.

I drive between the petrol station and the KFC, finding a park near the massive New World supermarket.

It took us about twenty-five minutes to get here, and according to my GPS, we're in north Hamilton. This entire area is new. I can't believe how much Hamilton has grown from a country town into a country city, if that can even be a thing.

Grabbing the empty shopping bags out of the back, I trail the twins down the footpath. I catch a hint of fresh bread rolls from the bakery and my stomach growls. Even though I had fresh eggs and a piece of toast for breakfast, I could kill a croissant and latte right now.

Tane's teasing smirk flitters through my brain, and I can't help a little smile. He's way too good-looking. I already decided as I lay in bed last night, reliving the harrowing day, that no matter how handsome Tane may have grown over the years, it doesn't matter. My body might be attracted to the guy, but that's it. I'm not going to act on some lust-filled urges. And I'm not interested in a relationship of any kind.

Although, it would be nice to have Dylan around. He's been messaging me from London. He was in the air when the news first hit, and I didn't want to bother him with it, but Zoey insisted, and she messaged him for me. He called the second he touched down in Dubai.

I can't really remember what we said to each other, but he promised to stay in touch.

Zoey said he should have come back to support me, but no way. He's not my boyfriend anymore, and he's on his big trip. Him coming back wouldn't have changed a thing. It just would have been an extra pair of arms to hug me and potentially make me cry. I don't need that right now. I have to stay strong and in control. For Willow and Oscar. For me.

I just have to focus on the little things I can do. The normal things that don't make me feel anything.

Like grocery shopping.

Pulling the list from my pocket, I smooth out the paper against my shorts and struggle to read the first few items. Tane's messy scribble is almost illegible compared to my font-type printing. Even so, my thumb brushes over his inky scrawl. Watching him write a list made my stomach quiver with desire.

I'm so ridiculous.

I was standing there in my pajamas—so humiliating. I thought they were going to take way longer than they did. Beck told me they have four hundred cows on the farm. *Four hundred*. I assumed the milking would take most of the morning, which is why I didn't rush to get dressed.

So instead, I got busted in my jim-jams and then had to act like it was no big deal.

I snuck off and threw some clothes on while Tane was collecting eggs, but it still didn't make me feel any more confident when he walked back into the kitchen and all I could picture was the way his muscles flexed when he lifted that milk bucket and...

Oh, shut up, Harper! Stop thinking about him!

Being attracted to him is ridiculous. My hormones are obviously out of whack. I need to check my phone app to find out when my next period is due. It's gotta be something like that. I don't want to be attracted to some farm boy. Even if he is tall and strong and his olive hands grasping my arm this morning made me want to melt against his chest…

I snap my eyes shut and end up bumping into Stacey, who has jerked to a stop before crossing the road.

"What's the matter?" Bianca follows her sister's line of sight, searching the trail of people walking in and out of the supermarket.

"Hello, hottie." She nudges Bianca with her elbow and then points. "Check out blondie. Mmm-mmm."

Seriously. That girl could use a few lessons in subtlety class.

Bianca rolls her eyes. "Don't you already have a boyfriend?"

Stacey scowls, crossing her arms and giving her sister a haughty look. "No, we broke up before Christmas, but thanks for reminding me."

She powers off across the pedestrian crossing, leaving Bianca and me to chase after her.

Bianca manages to snag the back of her shirt before we enter the store. "When did you break up?"

Stacey looks away from her sister and murmurs, "At that party you chickened out on."

"I was sick. And you broke up *at* the party? What happened?"

"I don't want to talk about it." Stacey shrugs, flicking her high ponytail over her shoulder.

"Well, are you okay? Why didn't you tell me?"

"Because I was getting over him anyway. It was a mutual thing. It just... I'm fine. I'm not cut up or anything." The blond guy she was ogling ambles into the store behind her, and she waits until he's passed before checking him out again. "Especially when hot specimens like that are walking around."

I crane my neck to look at him. I don't see what the big deal is. His straw hair looks wild and reckless along with his sloppy attire—black, ripped-up skinny jeans, scuffed sneakers with the laces undone, an oversized T-shirt. When he turns to walk through the internal entrance, I catch a glimpse of his profile. Sure, his nose is nice, one of those straight, pointed ones. His face is angular, with sharp lines only a little rough around the edges.

I guess I can kind of see what Stacey likes, but beauty is so subjective. I'm more into tall, dark and handsome. Tane's face flashes through my brain and I blink, annoyed that it wasn't Dylan with his dark hair and blue eyes.

"Are looks all that matter to you?" Bianca tugs at the bottom of her shirt. "That guy could be a total jerk for all you know."

"It can't just be about personality, Bianca. You have to

be physically attracted to someone above all else. If there's no chemistry, how are you ever supposed to get something started? It all begins with that physical pull. That's what draws you to someone."

I'm inclined to disagree. Dylan and I started out as friends and then grew into a relationship with each other. He became better-looking as I got to know him. None of this shallow, flash-in-the-pan desire.

Nothing like the lightning I felt when I first saw Tane.

That felt dangerous, like one too many shots of tequila. It may feel good at the time, but it could potentially lead to a monster hangover. Not that I've ever had a monster hangover, but Alaina certainly has, and it's not pretty.

I need to stop worrying so much about Tane. Soon enough I'll be back in Wellington with my girlfriends, and he'll be nothing more than a memory. So what if I'm attracted to him a little bit? It's not going to turn into anything.

So stop worrying about it!

The list scrunches in my hand and I smooth it out again, about to tell the twins that we need to get on with the shopping.

But then I notice Bianca's expression. She's gone really quiet.

Stacey notices too and huffs, "Just say whatever it is that you're trying not to say. I won't be offended."

Bianca's delicate lips go wonky before she starts talking in a tiny voice. "I just think that you should get along with someone really well too. Like, what's the point of just dating a body? It'll be shallow and meaningless."

"You mean not a complete drag and super fun?" Stacey's ponytail swings like a pendulum as she tips her head to the side.

Bianca gives her a droll look. "You liked dating Stefan. You were together for like… a month?"

"Five weeks—not that I was counting—and it got old fast."

"Because he didn't have a decent personality." Bianca's eyebrows rise with an emphatic look. "At least the guy I was into was funny and sweet."

Stacey pulls a face and then swallows. "You talking about Riku?"

"Yes." Bianca's eyes light with a soft dreaminess before dimming with sadness. I bet it's just dawned on her that she's probably never going to see him again. Her shoulders droop a little.

"I don't think he was everything you built him up to be." Stacey shakes her head.

"What do you mean?"

"Just… I… he's probably just like all the rest. A horny guy who plays nice to get what he wants."

"He wasn't just playing nice with me. We were friends. We got on great."

"And never once did he try to kiss you."

"Only because he didn't know I liked him that way. He was a gentleman."

"Whatever," Stacey mutters and turns, bolting through the sliding glass doors.

Once again, we trail after her. Bianca glances at me, and I flash her a quick grin. All I can hope is that she's right and Stacey's wrong. I don't want sweet Bianca getting hurt. She's a kind angel, just like her mum was. A sudden sadness pierces me right in the chest as I grab a trolley and push it after the girls.

Just focus on picking decent food, Harper. Don't try and think outside of this one task.

Staring at the shopping list, I blink and will my logical brain to override any emotion trying to course through me.

Grocery shopping.

That's the plan.

Right now, that is the *only* plan, and nothing else matters.

12

STACEY

I rub my arms, warding off the chill of the supermarket air-conditioning. Seriously, are they housing penguins in here or something? I hate being cold more than anything. It always puts me in a foul mood. Although the conversation I just had with Bianca isn't helping either.

She has no idea what Riku is really like, but I can't go telling her that. She just won't get it.

Jiggling on my toes next to the mound of oranges, I keep rubbing my arms and nearly groan out loud when Harper lifts one to her nose to smell it.

Oh, come on! Just shove some in a bag and let's go.

This place is packed, swarming with weekend shoppers —families and couples getting the domestic stuff out of the way so they can relax for the rest of the weekend.

I tap my finger on my arm just as Bianca starts fingering apples, doing her best to find the crunchiest ones.

This is going to take for-freaking-ever. Why did I agree to come? I should have pulled a Willow card and softly said I'd rather hang out in my room. With everything that's going on, we can pretty much get away with whatever we want. I should take advantage of that.

An ugly feeling twists my belly into a painful knot. Rubbing my stomach, I bash the thought of ashes and dirt out of my head.

"I'm going to check out the rest of this place," I mutter, taking off before Bianca and Harper can protest. I can't stand next to the oranges and apples anymore. I have to move.

I walk past the wall of gluten-free products and sniff out the bakery for a few minutes. I'm nearly tempted by a freshly baked chocolate chip muffin but change my mind last minute and move toward the specialty dips and cheeses.

Man, shopping in New Zealand is so easy. You can get everything here…and all in the same place. One big store, instead of having to go to five or six little ones to gather everything you want. No wonder Mum got frustrated at times.

An image of her beautiful face scrunched with annoyance pops into my mind. Then Dad whispers something in her ear, a funny quip to melt the angst away and make her grin. He always knew how to get a laugh out of anybody.

My stomach aches and I blink, snatching a little jar from the refrigerated shelf.

Duck mousse. What the hell is that?

I'm about to read the ingredients when I spot a flash of blond hair out of the corner of my eye.

Instantly abandoning my mousse investigation, I round the corner and dash down the drinks aisle, wondering which way he went. I'm kind of stoked Blondie's still in the store. The second I spotted him, my entire body pulsed with desire. He's just the kind of guy I go for: tall, striking features, a confident, slightly cocky edge to him.

Ten seconds later, I spot the guy perusing the rows of chocolate bars and know if I don't do something to get his attention, I'll regret it forever.

Needing to play it cool, I saunter up behind him and use the excuse of an oncoming shopper to step sideways and bump him with my hip.

"Oh, sorry." I smile when he glances down at me.

He pauses, checking me out before his lips rise into an easy grin. "No worries."

Oh man, he is so much better-looking up close. Those eyes are magnetic, this russet color with a slight sparkle, like he's got a secret he's about to tell me. And those wide lips that tip up just a little more on the right-hand side…holy heck, he's hot!

I brush my teeth over my bottom lip, and his smile grows just a little wider.

"This place is always a madhouse on the weekends."

"Yeah." I nod. "Busy times."

Busy times? Seriously, Stace, you can do better than that.

I shove my hand into the back pocket of my jean shorts and dip my hip. I like the way he's checking me out, his eyes running up and down my body with an appreciative smirk.

"What school do you go to? I don't think I've seen you around."

"Oh, I've been overseas. Living in China, just got back." I turn my smile up to full beam, hoping to hide the truth of why I'm not currently on a plane bound for Shanghai. That's the way it should be. In fact, if life hadn't shat all over Bianca and me, we'd be starting school again on Monday.

Blondie steps a little closer, gently nudging me to the side so we don't get hit by an oncoming trolley. His hand is warm on my chilly arm, and I wish he'd leave it there. But he doesn't. Instead he rests his fingers on the edge of the shelf and continues studying me with his beautiful brown eyes. "You gunna be living here? In Rototuna?"

"Yeah, no, uh…" I point my thumb over my shoulder. "Kind of more near Gordonton and North Ridge."

"Nice." His eyebrows pop up and down. "Make sure your parents send you to North Ridge High and not some lame girls' school."

I giggle, not wanting to kill the moment by telling him about my parents. Instead I just nod and whisper, "I will."

"Nice." He winks, and my insides trill with pleasure as he snatches a Moro bar off the shelf and moves past me. Our bodies brush against each other for the briefest moment.

"I've gotta go, but…you have a name?"

"Stacey."

"Jonas." He lifts his chin at me.

I can't help a grin. He's so cute!

"See you later, China Girl."

"Bye." I wave at him while he walks away backward, not turning until he accidentally bumps into someone. He spins with a quick apology and says something that makes the older man grin and shake his head.

Swoon! He's good with the elderly. That just makes him even more gorgeous.

"What, you didn't give him your number?" Bianca's dry voice appears out of nowhere, making me jump.

I glance over my shoulder with a scowl. "He didn't ask for it."

"I'm surprised you're not shouting it out to him. You're such a reckless flirt." Bianca softens her reprimand with a smile, no doubt hoping to make it sound like she's teasing me, but I know she's really not.

We're so different in the boy department, and she'll never understand the way I function. I'm not just some reckless flirt!

A memory from the Christmas party flashes through my brain, but I swallow it down, hoping my stomach acid will burn it to dust. I wish memories *did* work that way. Or the past. Like you could just swallow anything you did that was maybe just a little bit slightly bad and it would disappear off your record.

I look out the store window and spot Jonas standing next to the glass. He's texting someone, but when he stops, he glances into the supermarket to find me. I know he does, because the second he spots me, he raises his chin with a grin before checking his phone again and then walking away.

I rise to my tiptoes, straining to see which car he's walking to, but Harper distracts me before I can. "Keep it moving, Stace, or we're going to be here forever."

I step around to the next aisle and grab a large packet of cashew nuts, dumping it in the trolley.

"How much are those?" Harper asks, scanning the shelf, then shaking her head. "No way. Too expensive. Put them back, please."

"Are you kidding?" I scoff.

"I'm sorry, but Beck only gave me so much money. I'm keeping a mental tally, and that will tip us over. If you want cashews, just wait until the end and if there's any spare change, you can grab a small bag of them, all right?"

"Forget it," I mutter, pulling the nuts out of the trolley and dumping them back on the shelf.

This is so painful.

In China, we never had to check the price of anything. Living was cheap over there. I guess good old NZ is a whole other story.

Man, I wish I hadn't even come on this stupid shopping trip. I rub the goose bumps on my arms as we near the meat section, which is set to Arctic degrees. The only thing to warm me is the thought that if I hadn't come, I wouldn't have met Jonas.

Oh man, I hope I get to see him again.

If anything is going to haul me through this nightmare, it's a guy like him.

114

13

TANE

I brush down my horse, my strokes even and smooth as I give her a little TLC. Copper was so happy to see me when I walked into the barn this morning. I took her out for a ride as soon as the girls left to buy groceries. We trotted past the cows, and then we cantered for a little before doing one full-blown gallop in the fields by the O'Neills' farm. I love that stretch between our two properties. But even more, I love that feeling of the wind hitting my face and the power beneath me as Copper shows off what she's made of.

After that, I let her amble back to the barn in her own sweet time. The sun was a warm blanket, coating us, taking us away from the tragic chill residing over the property right now.

"Beck was right about our lives changing," I murmur to Copper.

Beck's doing some accounting stuff and said I could squeeze in a ride before we spread out silage for the cows. I check my watch and figure I've got another twenty minutes before I need to go help with setting up the tractor. After lunch it'll be all about fencing, so I need to enjoy this time while I can.

I rest the brush on Copper's back for a moment. "I don't know how long they're going to stay. When the lawyer said they had a choice, I was kind of hoping they'd make it right there and then. Probably unrealistic." I resume brushing, watching the way the light falls over Copper's rusty flanks.

It's a soft, ethereal light in here, a complete contrast to the sharp brightness outside. I watch the dust fairies dance and keep chatting. "I don't envy any of them. I know what it's like to make the hard choice. It frickin' hurts."

I'm attacked by images of my mother's distorted face as she stood by the car and yelled at me. "Boy, you get in this car!"

All I could do was shake my head. I'd already used up all my words, explaining that I didn't want to go with her and Grant.

"You're my son! You come with me!"

I nearly countered that I didn't want to be her son but managed to catch the hateful words in the nick of time. Some days I wish I had said them, and other days I'm grateful I kept my mouth shut. It's hard to know what to feel sometimes. All I *do* know is that I don't want to talk to her right now. I don't want to see her. I don't want her explanation.

She cheated on Beck.

There is no excuse for that.

"I'd never cheat on my woman," I tell Copper. "Not that I have a woman, but if I did… I wouldn't cheat on her."

The ugly thoughts are shunted aside by a beauty that makes my breath hitch.

"You should see Harper, Cop. I'll bring her down to meet you one day. And you'll see. She's the most beautiful girl I've ever been around."

Copper whinnies, and I snicker, walking around to her head and clarifying, "The most beautiful *human* girl."

She grunts and snuffles like she understands me, and I scratch between her ears with a grin, feeding her a piece of carrot from my pocket. Her big lips tickle the palm of my hand, and I feed her a chunk of apple as well.

Her whinny of approval makes my heart swell. "You're a good girl."

Stroking her nose for a bit, I rest my head against her neck and am disappointed when my phone dings with a message. I want to ignore it, but it could be Cam or one of my mates, so I walk to the stable wall and grab it off its precarious perch.

"Shit," I mumble under my breath, shoving the phone in my back pocket without even reading the message.

It's Mum again.

We need to talk. Stop ignoring me…

The rest of the message is still waiting for me, but like all the ones before it, I'm not going to read them. I don't *want* to know her side. I don't want to answer her frickin' calls!

She's the one in the wrong.

Beck's the nicest man on earth. He didn't deserve to be treated that way. He put up with all her demanding shit for years, and then she went and cheated on him! She's an ungrateful hag.

I wince, the insult sitting badly in my gut.

No matter how I feel about her, she is still my mother, and calling her a hag or a bitch or any of the other nasties that have flown through my brain makes me feel a little sick.

But I'm pissed off!

Still.

Even after all these weeks.

With a huff, I throw the brush into the box and check on Copper's food and water supply. Giving her a quick kiss, I then check on Jax. She's all good too.

"I'll come by and brush you tonight, okay, darlin'?"

As usual, Jax gives me nothing. Unlike Copper, she's a quiet girl. Kind of like Bianca and Willow. Although, Willow takes quiet to a new extreme. I don't think I've heard her say one word since she got here.

I'm guessing she's mondo shy, but I haven't even heard her speak to her brother or sister either.

My heart twists uncomfortably, sadness sweeping through me in a bleak, cold wave. Those poor guys. How do you keep living when you've lost that big?

I'd be devastated if something happened to Beck.

Mum's gutted expression flashes in my mind, that brief moment just before they drove off when I silently said my final NO to her.

It hurt. Sure it did. But it was the only choice I could make. I wasn't leaving Beck alone, and like hell I was going with her and Grant.

Scratching the tender spot on my chest, I trudge out of the barn. The only thing to shake my mood is the sound of a car coming up the drive.

A smile tugs at my lips. Yes! The girls are back.

I shouldn't feel a thrill of excitement as I pick up my pace and crest the hill. Harper and I can't be a thing. My attraction to her is pointless, yet still I hurry to greet her. Hurry to offer my help. Hurry to—

I pause by the garage, my eyebrows bunching together when a rental car I don't recognize parks next to the house.

An older woman is behind the wheel, her prim lips pursing as she looks at the house, then spots me slowly walking toward her.

Her eyes narrow, making her look like a hawk about to swoop in on some prey.

Stopping in my tracks, I rest my hands on my hips. The only thought in my brain is *Who the hell is this?*

14

STACEY

The drive back from Rototuna is quiet. We're all lost in our own thoughts, which I find majorly unnerving, so I fiddle with the radio until something semi-decent is playing. Bianca's head bobs to the beat. I glance at her just in time to see her face bunch with disgust, and then she pinches her nose.

I sniff the area just as Harper swallows and looks ready to puke.

Silage.

I don't find it that bad. Compared to some of the smells we've encountered in Thailand, Laos and China, this is more like a sweet nectar. A weird, sweet nectar.

Okay, it's smelly.

I rest my finger under my nose until the worst of it

passes, then lean forward in my seat to check out the blue sky. It's a completely clear, cloudless day. Stunning. You don't get sky that crystal clear in China. There's always a mild haze of smog blanketing the pure blue.

As much as I'm struggling with the fact that I had to give up the life I know, if I'm going to be living anywhere, New Zealand's not a completely horrible choice.

The middle of nowhere North Ridge? Well, I'm still deciding on that one.

Although, if I end up in the same school as a hottie like Jonas, then I really can't complain. Bianca can take her spiky teasing about my flirty ways and shove them up her butt.

So I like guys.

So I get on well with them.

That doesn't make me a reckless flirt!

At least I know what I want, and I have the courage to take it.

The song on the radio changes to an upbeat number, a familiar tune that fires memories from the Christmas party straight into my conscience. I lean forward and change the station.

"Aw." Bianca frowns from the back. "I like that song."

"This one's better." I dial up the volume and Bianca doesn't complain, immediately humming along to the new tune.

She's an eclectic girl, which I kind of love about her. She'll basically enjoy anything I put on, which is one less argument we need to have.

Unfortunately, the song change hasn't pulled the Christmas memories from my brain. They settle in, playing out like a movie I don't want to sit through.

Stefan's hands squeezing Lorelai Johnson's butt while his tongue dove into her mouth like he was searching for golden tonsils.

Stupid asshole.

I wasn't going to let him get away with it.

He was cheating, which meant we were well and truly over. I wasn't gutted so much about that part, more about the way he handled it. You break up with someone *before* you get together with someone else. That's just basic relationship 101.

I walked up to them, tapped him on the shoulder and offered him a sweet, plastic smile.

"Uh... St-Stacey. I didn't think you were coming tonight."

"Oh, well, that makes it better." My cheerful tone was spiked with venom, but I managed to maintain the smile even while shooting a glare at Lorelai. "We're over, by the way. Just wanted to clarify that."

"Come on, Stacey." Stefan tried to reach for me, but I flicked him off with a look that was strong enough to make him retreat.

He took Lorelai's hand and moved away from me then. A flash of panic tore through me as I stood at the party, feeling like the only person in the room, a spotlight beam highlighting my humiliation. But then I was approached by the last person I expected.

I swear I never intended to spend the whole party with him. He just saw what happened and wanted to make me feel better. We spent most of the night talking, dancing, just having some fun.

That's all.

I didn't expect it to lead to anything beyond friendship.

I didn't expect him to be such a good dancer, or for his hands to feel so nice wrapping around my waist.

I tried to tell him that it wasn't the best idea, but he just smiled at me and…and…

Bianca's voice rises as she hits the high note, obviously forgetting her inhibitions as the music claims her like it always does.

She should have been at the party. If she had, I never would have…

I close my eyes with a sigh and focus on the fields passing by. We're nearly back to the house. I've never looked forward to distracting myself with unloading groceries before, but I am a keen jellybean today. Those groceries are going to get my full attention.

Harper turns into the driveway, and I'm reaching for my seat belt buckle as she slows to a stop behind a car I don't recognize.

"Who's that?" Harper murmurs, pointing to a woman in a blue suit. It's an old-school rich kind of style, tailored specifically for her pencil shape.

My eyes travel up her body and I lurch in my seat, slapping the car dashboard with a surprised gasp. "Oh, shitballs."

Bianca sucks in a breath. "Is that… Oma?"

"Yep," I clip. "Looks like the old bat's left her castle in Sydney."

"Please tell me you're not going to call her that when you get out of this car," Bianca murmurs.

"Of course I won't say it to her face." I roll my eyes, but don't rush to open the door when Harper yanks up the hand brake and we all stare out the windshield at the frost queen walking toward us.

I don't have too many memories of her. All I really remember is the one time Mum tried to introduce us to her, she made Mum cry. And I mean ugly cry. Poor Mum was a wreck, and not even cuddles from me or Bianca could ease her pain.

I tried to ask Dad about it before, but all I really got was "It's her way or the highway with that woman."

Ugh. You can tell by just looking at her. Even the way she carries herself is austere. She looks like the head-mistress from a hellish boarding school where skirt lengths are measured and cell phones are banned.

Tane's standing behind her, looking awkward, and I can only guess the tongue lashing he's already received.

Oma stops a few feet from the car, flicking her hand—a silent demand to exit the vehicle.

I glance at Bianca, who gives me a worried smile before opening her door and inching out.

What is she doing?

Dammit! Always has to be the good girl.

She approaches our grandmother, and they share a stiff hug before Oma kisses both of her cheeks. Holding Bianca's shoulders, she studies my sister, her smile too polite for a grandma.

"Are you gunna go?" Harper asks me.

"I don't want to leave this car."

"Don't think you're going to have much choice on that. She's flicking her hand again."

"I can see that," I grit out.

"Her eyes are starting to narrow. I don't think we want that to happen." Harper hides her exaggerated cringe by turning to look at me.

It almost makes me laugh, and I think maybe she's pulling this face to try and make me feel better.

It kind of works, but the second I click open my door, all the happy feelings disappear.

"Oma." I nod at her.

"Come here." Even those two words give away how posh her voice is.

It's not British posh. It's Australian posh, like she's descended directly from Queen Victoria but was accidentally sent to the colonies and just had to make the most of it.

I walk around the car and stop far enough away that she can't quite reach me.

"Stacey." She looks me up and down. "What are you wearing, dear?"

I look down at my outfit and shoot her a quizzical frown. "Last I checked, they were called clothes."

"Don't be rude," she snaps, pulling her shoulders back

and giving me a sharp look before glancing around us like we're all useless imbeciles. "Well? Is someone going to invite me in for a cup of tea?"

"Of course." Harper forces a smile and looks to Tane.

"Beck's on his way," he mumbles, then walks up the steps and opens the door for everyone.

We trail into the house, and Oma spots Oscar first. He's slouching on the couch, looking fat and lazy with his leg dangling over the arm of the chair and his computer perched on his lap. The screen shines on his face, and his eyes don't even deviate from whatever game he's playing.

"Oscar." Harper grabs his attention and tips her head at Oma, silently trying to warn him.

He jumps at her sharp tone, looking confused and maybe a little scared, so I lean down to whisper, "Escape while you can."

His eyes bulge, and he looks to Oma.

"Hello." She gives him a tight smile.

"Hey." He shuts his laptop and stands, tugging down his shirt.

Great, he's still in his pjs, and he just used "Hey" for a greeting. Here we go.

"Hey?" Oma bristles. "Is that really how you've been taught to greet people?"

"Um..." He glances at Harper, then back to the old hawk. "Hello?"

"That's better." She glances at her watch. "It's late morning. Can I suggest that pajamas are not appropriate attire for this time of day?"

"Uh..." He frowns and looks down at his rumpled clothing.

"Why don't you go get changed?" Harper tips her head at the stairs.

He shuffles between the furniture, throwing one more confused frown over his shoulder.

Behind Oma's back, Harper just shrugs, then mouths, "Hide upstairs."

He nods and takes off.

Lucky bastard.

I cross my arms and slouch on one hip, trying to figure out what the hell she's doing here. I mean, I'm smart enough to guess, but seriously? We haven't seen her for years, and now that Mum's gone, she just shows up. She cut her daughter off! And now she thinks she can just waltz into our lives again? She's delusional.

"Stacey, stand up straight. I know you're going through a harrowing time right now, but there is never an excuse to slouch." She pulls in a sigh and frowns once again at my clothing. Touching her chest, she shakes her head, looking heartbroken for a moment. If she had a string of pearls, I'm sure she'd be clutching them.

She sniffs and places a delicate finger under her nose. "Everything will be okay. I'm here now, and you won't have to stay…" She looks around the cluttered room. "In this… place."

My eyebrows dip together, shock rocketing through me. "Excuse me?"

"I'm here to collect you." She smooths down her jacket and inspects the couch like she's unsure whether or not it's worthy of her pompous ass.

"Collect us?" Bianca whispers.

"Yes, of course. I'm your only living relative. You belong with me. I would have been here sooner if someone had contacted me in a timely manner. Instead I had to find out nearly *two weeks* after my daughter's death. I missed her funeral." Her eyes are dark with accusation.

I share a look with Bianca, who bravely clears her throat and murmurs, "But we had a joint funeral. You cut her off for… Well, one of the reasons was for marrying Dad, right? So you probably wouldn't have wanted to be there anyway."

Oma struggles to compose herself, her voice straining out between tight lips as she tries to explain. "Things get said in the heat of emotion."

"You told her you didn't have a daughter anymore," I argue.

"I never thought she'd believe me."

"We haven't seen you in years. What did you expect her to believe?"

Oma points at me. "Watch your tone, young lady. There are things you were too young to understand."

"Yeah, well, we've grown up now." I try to stand tall, but it's kind of hard under Oma's withering glare.

The laundry door opens, and I slump with relief. Beck's here to save the day. Sort of. The second he walks through the kitchen, my hopes are kind of dashed. He looks as nervous as the rest of us.

Even so, he pastes on a closed-mouth smile and extends his hand. "Ms. Graf. Welcome to the farm."

She eyes his hand, her upper lip curling. He rubs his fingers together. "Just working on some machinery in the shed," he explains. "We're going to put out some silage soon, and…" He clears his throat and scratches the back of his neck. "Well, this is a surprise."

"Yes. So it would seem." Oma's voice is a cold spray of icy water. "No one thought to contact me about my only child's death."

I can practically see the icicles forming on the ceiling. Her draft is enough to freeze out a Yeti.

Beck looks to the floor and apologizes. "I'm so sorry for your loss, Ms. Graf. We're all hurting, and I should have contacted you. Or…uh… found a way to contact you. Sooner."

She nods once. "Let's not waste time on shallow apologies. I'm here to take my granddaughters home. They belong with me."

Beck glances at me and Bianca, his eyes wide with surprise before trailing back to her.

My insides are going nuts right now. I can feel my heart beating in my stomach, my head…even my fingertips are pulsing.

Beck, don't you dare agree with her!

"Actually, ma'am, I… uh, well, I've been assigned as their guardian. It's stated quite clearly in Richie and Leanne's will, and the girls are—"

The woman scoffs. "Their guardian? Are you honestly standing there informing me that my daughter chose a childless widow to raise her children?"

Beck's nostrils flare, while my skin flushes.

I can't believe she just went there. Oh, she better not know about the fact that he once had twins. Although she seems to know he was married before. She's such a bitch!

"Underqualified doesn't even begin to define what you

are," she snaps. "Taking in five children while running a farm. Do you really think you can manage that?"

His nod is slow to form, but it eventually comes, his eyebrows rising at the same time.

"Oh, I can see just how convinced you are," she mocks him. "I am offering you a valid solution to what is so obviously a very big problem." She points around the house. "Raising children in this kind of squalor. You are not cut out for this, Beckett Connell, and you know it!"

He swallows while the tension in the room rises to a breaking point.

Goose bumps ripple over my arms, and I wish I could think of something intelligent to say, but my thundering heart is the only thing registering in my brain right now.

"I will not have my granddaughters dragged up like pigs. It's bad enough they've spent most of their formative years living in Third World countries! Time is running out, and this is my only chance to teach them some decorum. If we're going to make ladies out of them, then you best send them to Sydney with me. I can offer them a better life than you can."

Scratching his beard, he then pats the back of his head and finally mutters, "The...um... The girls are sixteen." He swallows, then clears his throat, his voice growing in confidence. "They're old enough to decide for themselves. If they would like to go with you, I won't stop them, but they are more than welcome to stay here. The choice is theirs."

Oma rolls her eyes. "Good grief! They're sixteen! You can't expect them to make a choice like that when they're grieving." Spinning on us, she flashes her fangs and points toward the stairs. "Girls, go pack your bags. We'll travel up to Auckland tonight and catch a flight back to Sydney on Monday. That will give us plenty of time to get you organized before school begins this year."

I'm shaking my head before she's even finished. "I'm not going."

"Excuse me?" She looks completely shocked.

What is her problem? Is she blind, deaf *and* stupid?

She made Mum's life nothing but hard work, and she's expecting us to happily skip off to Sydney? Gimme a break!

"I am *not* going with you." I cross my arms and match her steely look with one of my own. "Mum kept her distance for a very good reason, and I am not moving to Australia so you can try and turn me into something I don't want to be. Growing up with you was misery. Why do you think Mum chose to live with her dad when you guys got divorced?"

The woman bristles, obviously humiliated that I would

bring this up in front of people she doesn't know. Her entire body is trembling as she spits out, "Young lady, what you need is some sound discipline, something your father lacked in spades." Her nostrils flare while she pulls in a sharp breath, then turns her glare to my sister. "Bianca, do you feel this way?"

"I-I..." My poor twin looks to me and then of course dishes out a wafty white lie. "We're grateful that you want to take us in and look after us, but if Stacey's not going, then neither am I. We have to stick together."

Bianca flashes her I-don't-want-to-offend-anyone smile, and Oma purses her lips, looking like she's just sucked on a lemon. She grips the strap of her handbag so hard, I'm worried her knuckles might pop through the skin, but her voice comes out low and even.

"Well, of course you do."

I didn't know a smile could look pissed off, but she beams one at us and then turns to Beck, shaking her head like she's disappointed in him.

Wrinkle lines appear on his forehead, but he doesn't say anything.

Pulling a card from her purse, Oma hands it to Bianca. "If you change your mind, which I'm sure you both will, here are my contact details. I'll happily pay for your flights and can make immediate arrangements. I can offer a wonderful life, but I won't take you kicking and screaming." She walks to the door, then turns to look at Beck. "You're making a big mistake. This situation has failure written all over it. I'll be hearing from you soon. I'm confident of that."

The front door slams shut behind her. Bianca flinches.

A hollow stillness follows her departure, and I'm desperate to break it. I'm going to suffocate in this stuffy silence.

The grandfather clock ticks loudly, reminding us that life still moves on. As a car speeds away from the house, I clear my throat and glance at Bianca. "Thanks for sticking up for me, Bee."

Her lips rise into a half-hearted smile, her pale green gaze sad as she quietly walks to the stairs and leaves the rest of us to recover from The Invasion of Oma Graf.

The rest of the day just kind of disappears somehow. I thought it'd be the longest day in the history of man, but I just got on with it, filling the space with groceries and messaging my friends in Suzhou. They wanted to know every detail about what went down over New Year's, but I told them I didn't want to talk about it and instead filled them in on Jonas and farm life. I tried to make it as entertaining as possible, and we ended with smiley face emojis and a couple of K-Pop gifs that made me laugh.

After lunch I disappeared into a movie with Willow—the quietest human being on the planet. Bianca isn't far behind her. She's barely said a word since Oma left, and I don't get it.

I feel like we dodged a bullet today. I'm so relieved Beck didn't suggest we go with that woman, so why did Bianca look so sad?

"Oma," I mutter, thinking about that stupid cow trying to mess everything up. As if things aren't bad enough right now.

Throwing my shirt on the floor, I pull on my pajama top and wait for Bianca to finish in the bathroom. I need to take my contact lenses out before bed. I don't like people seeing me in my glasses, so I try to take my contacts out just before I go to sleep, and I put them in first thing when I wake up.

Bianca's brushing her teeth. I can hear the tap switching on and off in between brushes. She's such a good girl. I bet she's only flushed the toilet once today, and I wouldn't be surprised if she set a two-minute timer for her shower as well.

I roll my eyes and figure I'll just always shower when Beck's out milking or something. What he doesn't know won't hurt him.

My phone dings with a chat message and I snatch it up, my eyes bulging when I see Riku's name pop up on my screen.

. . .

Riku: Just heard you're not coming back. Sucks. I was hoping we could pick up where we left off at the Christmas party. Best night of my life. You have the sweetest lips in the world, Stacey Freeman.

Oh crap!

A new message pops up underneath that one.

Riku: Oh, and sorry about your parents. Sorry. Should have said that part first. Totally sucks. I'm here if you need me. If I was there right now, I'd hold you tight.

What is he doing? If Bianca sees this, she'll freak out.

I wish I hadn't cleared the message. Now he'll know I've read it, but I don't have time to reply or delete it, because Bianca walks into the room.

I shove the iPad under my pillow and paste on an innocent smile.

Bianca stands in the doorway, her eyes narrowing as she flicks the towel off her shoulder and drapes it over the door.

"What?" I jerk my head back.

"Nothing," she mumbles, shuffling to her bed and slumping down with a heavy sigh.

I grab my towel off the end of my bed and am about to walk out, but then she starts playing with the ends of her hair *and* biting her lip.

I lean my shoulder against the doorframe. "Bianca, what is it?"

She shrugs, her green eyes starting to shimmer. "Today was kind of intense."

"Tell me about it." I look to the floor, silently begging her not to cry. Her tears tend to set off mine, and I just—

"Do you think…" She purses her lips to the side and starts creating a tiny braid at the bottom of her long locks.

"Do I think what?"

"Well, do you think we should have gone with her?"

"With Oma?" My eyes bulge so wide they almost hurt. "Are you kidding? No! That cow? I'd rather live with real ones that moo and poo on everything."

Bianca forces out a breathy laugh.

"Come on, Bee. Are you honestly second-guessing our decision? She's a demanding, horrible bitch! She wants to turn us into *ladies*." I put on a toffee-nosed voice, trying to get a smile, but all I get is an anxious frown.

"She's our flesh and blood, Stace."

"So? Mum and Dad formed a family with Uncle Beck, Uncle Lance and Aunty Renee. *They* are our people."

"*They* are all gone." Bianca's voice quakes, a tear slipping down her freckled cheek.

I swallow, summoning a little power into my voice as I walk across the room and take a seat beside her. "Not Beck. He's here. He wants us. He'll take care of us."

Bianca nods, but it quickly turns into a shake. "It's a lot of responsibility for him."

"We're all practically adults." I throw my arm around her shoulders. "It's not like he has to raise us. He's our roof and our food supply until we finish school, and then we can go to uni and stuff. This is just a means to an end. And some good things might come out of this place." Jonas's playful smile flashes through my mind, and I can't help a grin.

Bianca scoffs and rolls her eyes. "You're just thinking about that blond guy at the supermarket."

My lips stretch a little wider. "His name's Jonas."

"Whatever," Bianca mutters, nudging me off her. "I can't believe you. We just lost everything, and you're acting like it's no big deal."

I clench my jaw, getting off her bed and walking to the door.

"You can't pretend this isn't happening," Bianca says to my back. "Flirting with some stranger isn't going to change the fact that life will never be the same again. Mum and Dad aren't just away on some holiday. They are *never* coming back." Her voice breaks, and all I can do is cover my ears and run to the bathroom.

15

TANE

I crank the wire strainer, making sure the wire is nice and tight on the fence I've been fixing up for Beck. It's gotta be done right. Although Beck can be a bit of a slob around the house sometimes, when it comes to farm work, it's got to be as close to perfect as we can get it.

I don't mind. It feels good working out here, like this is what God put me on the earth for. That's what Beck told me once, and I knew exactly what he meant. So much so that I figured it applied to me too.

A couple of flies play tag around my head. I brush them away with a flick of my wrist, then take my cap off, wiping the sweat back with my arm.

It's blimin' hot today. With no cloud cover, the sun's a fireball. The cows will be struggling. Heat bothers them more than anything. Poor girls. They're all pregnant too. Seems kind of unfair that they've got to go through that in the hottest months of the year, but at least by the time they're nearly ready to pop, the temperatures will have dropped.

We need rain, and not just the odd scattering of showers that have blown through but a few days of really decent water. It'll revive the whole land…and fill our tanks. If we don't get some soon, Beck will need to call in a water truck for a fill-up. I know he doesn't want that expense if he can help it.

Rain might help ease the stress for him too. Beck needs all the help he can get in the stress department. The last few days have been bloody hard work. He hasn't said anything, but his silence speaks volumes.

Stacey and Bianca have been bickering endlessly. They seem to have differing opinions on nearly everything, and ever since the Iron Grandmother came to visit, they've been at odds and super tense. Bianca's words are always softly spoken, but they spark Stacey like she's being prodded with a hot poker.

Them sharing a room is not a great idea, and Beck will need to figure out new arrangements. If Harper heads back to Wellington on the weekend, which is her plan, then that'll free up a room. The idea of her leaving sucks, but I can't say anything. She's already extended her visit by a few extra days. I overheard her telling Beck that she was happy to stick around until things simmered down with the girls.

He seemed really grateful.

I don't mind. Having Harper around is... I don't know. There's something about her. She just quietly gets on. She tidies and cleans, organizes us without making a big fuss about it. We've had proper meals since she's been here. No more canned spaghetti or baked beans on toast. We're eating real food now, and mate, it's good. Her cooking outclasses anything I've ever tasted, and she makes it seem so easy, pottering away.

I've offered my help a couple of times, but I'm always too late. She gets to work while we're milking, and by the time we come in, dinner is practically on the table. Beck won't let her do any dishes afterward, and rightly so.

She probably would if he didn't insist she go sit down. Thing is, she doesn't seem to like just sitting down. She's a doer. If we're cleaning up the dinner mess, she can't help but start tidying the lounge, straightening cushions, picking up magazines, folding a sweater that's been left on the floor. It's kind of adorable to watch, although she'd probably be just as beautiful curled up on a couch reading a book too.

But I don't think relaxing is on her agenda right now. Maybe it gives her time to think too hard, and at the moment, I wouldn't want to be left to my own thoughts either. That can be dangerous territory when you're hurting.

"Hey, Tane?"

I whip around and spot Harper walking toward me.

An instant smile spreads across my face. Her hair is braided over one shoulder, and she looks gorgeous in a summer tank and denim shorts. Her long legs eat up the ground beneath her as she bustles toward me.

"Have you seen Willow?"

I shake my head, wishing I had a different answer. She looks worried.

"She said she was going for a walk, but I don't know which direction. I'm worried she'll get lost."

"It's pretty hard to get lost on the farm." I smile, trying to ease that look off her face. "I know it's a big property, but a road is never far away. Has she got her phone on her?"

Harper nods and pulls out her device, frowning at the screen. "I've texted her."

I nearly say that reception can be a little dodgy depending on where Willow might be, but I don't want to freak her out. "Fresh air's really good for the soul. Walking alone. Being out in nature."

"What if she's hurt?" The question spurts out. "What if reception's bad and she's lying injured and she can't get in touch with me? She's a ballerina, you know. She can't afford to get injured. She loves dancing more than anything. And she has to be careful. She can't afford to break an ankle or even sprain one."

Resting my tool on the back seat of the bike, I approach the gate and lean my forearms on the top.

So, this is what stressy Harper looks like. Fast, clipped words, agitated hand movements, rubbing her forehead like she's got an itch she can't quite find.

Weird how all that is still beautiful to me.

How the hell can I be gone so damn fast? I barely know this girl, yet everything she does seems to have a magical quality, like I'm watching her through a soft-focus lens or something.

"I have to find her. I just… I need to know she's okay. She's my respons—"

I lightly capture her flailing wrist, running my thumb over her racing pulse. She stares down at our connection for a beat before gently slipping out of my grasp.

She shoves her hand in her back pocket and gives me an awkward smile.

"Sorry." I wince. "I just wanted to stop the panic."

She forgives me with a short, wispy laugh. "I'm not usually this bad. I don't know what my problem is."

I hope the smile I'm giving her is kind enough. I know exactly what her problem is. She just lost her parents. She can't lose her sister too.

I keep the thought to myself and turn back to the fence I'm supposed to be finishing up. "Tell you what. I've got about two minutes left on this job, and then we'll take the bike and go look for her. Sound good?"

She glances at the two-wheeler and nods, then steps back and lets out a disgusted gasp.

It draws my attention, and I glance over the fence to spot her pristine white sneaker now lodged in a decent-sized cowpat. It's broken the crusted surface, and the runny poo beneath is oozing all over her shoe.

I can't stop the snicker from spurting out. "White sneakers? City Girl, you need yourself a pair of Red Bands."

"What are those?" She pulls her foot out and starts shaking it off.

I point to the rubber boots on my feet. "Gummies."

"Gumboots? They're in Wellington. In the garage. And they only come out when I have to watch Oscar play rugby on a Saturday morning." Gripping the fence pole, Harper starts sliding her shoe along the grass, cleaning off the worst of the muck.

"Might want to break that rule and pack them next time you visit." I force myself to wink and smile, wishing I didn't have to say the word visit. I want her to *stay*.

Quickly finishing up the fencing job, I pack my tools onto the back, then slap the seat.

"You coming?"

"I'll jump on out here." Opening the gate for me, she swings it back while I start up the bike and rev the engine. As soon as the gate is locked behind her, I pass her a helmet, and she straps it on before climbing on behind me.

Her long fingers rest on my waist, and I wish I could tell her to wrap her arms right around me.

I check myself, willing those thoughts away. It's not like that. It can't be that, even if I want it to be. I'm an idiot for dreaming.

Revving the bike, I set off down the dirt road, scanning the paddocks for Willow as I go. I decide to take my sweet time, using the hunt as an excuse to putter along slowly. I kind of like having Harper nestled up behind me. I could get used to this.

Stop it, you moron! She's leaving in a few days!

When we reach the end of the lane, I turn right and figure we'll start at the northwest side of the farm and work our way back to the house.

Harper slaps me on the shoulder and points.

"You see her?" I turn that direction.

"You've got horses!" she yells in my ear.

I put on the brakes, resting my foot on the ground so we can look at them for a minute. "Yeah, two of them. Jax and Copper." I point to the coppery mare and hate the way I'm yelling over the bike engine, so I kill it. "The taller one, she's my girl. Best horse in the world."

Harper grins. "Aunty Abby loved horses. I still remember the first time she let me ride hers. I was five. I wanted to be a cowgirl." Her short chuckle is tinged with sadness. "That memory is still so clear in my head."

I don't know what to say. I never knew Beck's wife or kids. There aren't even pictures of them in the house, although there's one of Abby in Beck's wallet. They're standing together in a field, and she's laughing while he kisses the side of her face.

"She was the best," Harper whispers. "I was only seven when she died, but I still remember the night Mum got the call. I will *never* forget the sound of her heartbreak. She dropped the phone and couldn't breathe, and Dad rushed in and—" Her voice cuts off, and I will do anything to stop the agony I heard in it.

She's not thinking about Abby's death anymore. She's thinking about her parents. Probably reliving that moment when she first heard the tragic news. I wonder how she reacted. Did she cry? Sob? Wail?

Nah. I bet she stood there stoic and strong while her siblings fell apart.

I grip the handles, waiting for Harper to start crying.

It's safe here. With me. I hope she feels that. If she needs to cry on my shoulder, she can go right ahead.

But she doesn't.

She just goes really still, gazing into the distance like she's searching for an answer she can't see.

When her phone buzzes, she actually jolts. Pulling it out of her pocket, she checks the screen and sags with relief. "It's Will. She's back at the house."

"Good." I give her a decisive nod and start the bike back up. "Come meet Copper, then."

Without waiting for an answer, I steer the bike toward the horses, hoping this distraction will be the perfect reprieve for her.

16

HARPER

I grip the side of Tane's shirt, thinking I should probably be holding the black handles just behind me, but leaning into the guy feels more secure. Who knew I was such a wimp when it came to riding a dirt bike? I've never been on one before, and as it bumps along the path, I hold my breath and wonder how long it'll take before my muscles actually snap.

When he parks the bike, I jump off and shake out my arms, glancing down at my pooey sneaker and frowning. Gross! Give me concrete footpaths and a poo-free yard.

Walking to the long patch of grass, I wipe my shoe through it, trying to get off a little more muck. I'm going to have to give them a thorough scrub back at the house. Ugh. I hope the shoes aren't permanently ruined.

It makes me miss Wellington.

I should be in a bikini right now, lying on the beach with Alaina and Zoey. We'd no doubt be debating if we should go into the ocean or head back to Alaina's pool. If the heat is as intense as it is today, we'd head for Alaina's pool and spend the afternoon talking about any and everything, dreaming about our year ahead and flicking through trashy magazines. It'd be freaking awesome.

But instead I'm here with sweat patches under my armpits, flies buzzing near my head, and smelly cow crap on my favorite pair of sneakers.

"Come on." Tane beckons me with a flick of his wrist.

I force a closed-mouth smile and watch my step, almost dancing toward the gate he's holding open for me.

As I jump past him, I can't miss the flex of his muscles and the sheen on his dark olive skin. He smells like sweat and hard work. It's weird how that aroma on him is kind of appealing.

My nose twitches and I turn away from him, focusing on the massive beast that is walking toward us. She looks taller up close, and I stiffen. The long grass tickles my legs, and I bend down to scratch my calf while keeping my eyes firmly fixed on the beautiful, but gigantic, horse.

"Hey, beautiful lady." Tane approaches her, his black gumboots clomping through the grass. The horse picks up her pace, obviously happy to see him. "How's my girl, ay?" He grins, stroking her nose and saying something soft that makes her ears twitch.

I hover near the fence line, flicking a fly away from my face and enjoying the show…from a distance.

"Come on." Tane tips his head at me. "Don't be shy. She loves people."

"Um." I scratch the side of my neck. "O-okay." I can't not go over. Not after I told him that story about Aunty Abby. I can't be that enthusiastic from a distance and then all pathetic up close.

Clenching my fists behind my back, I pick my way over to Tane, checking the ground for cowpats and horse apples. Stepping in either is disgusting. Even if I was wearing gumboots, I'd want to avoid animal droppings.

"That's it." Tane steadies my arm when I stand on an uneven patch of earth and tip sideways.

His hand is hot on my bare skin.

I force my attention to the horse towering next to me.

"Hey, Copper," I whisper, holding out my hand but jerking it back the second she leans toward it.

Tane chuckles. "She's only trying to sniff you."

"Her mouth is huge. Those teeth could bite my fingers off."

He laughs again, a loud, hearty sound that punctures

the air. Is it weird that he reminds me of Beck right now, even though they're not actually related?

"I thought you wanted to be a cowgirl?"

I wrinkle my nose at him. "When I was five. I haven't been around horses in years. I forgot how big they are."

"She's not gunna hurt ya." Grabbing my hand, he gently forces it onto Copper's nose.

His long fingers splay over mine as he flattens my palm against her broad nose. I swallow, trying to ward off the thrill curling through me.

Don't be insane, Harper. He's just a guy.

I bend my fingers, lightly stroking Copper's nose, and my lips curve into a smile.

"She's so soft," I whisper. "Like velvet."

"Yeah." Tane's grin is dopey and relaxed. There's something so endearing about it. The way his brown eyes are sparkling right now. They're soft and inviting, like they're throwing a welcome home party just for me.

I glance away and force myself to notice how blue the sky is, the gorgeous color of Copper's coat, the feel of the grass still tickling my legs.

"Want to go for a ride? We can saddle her up." Tane checks his watch. "I've got an hour before I have to round up the herd for Beck."

"Oh, it's okay." I'm shaking my head and backing away before the words are even out of my mouth.

"It won't take long. We can just do a little amble near the barn."

I shake my head again, taking one more step back. "No, I'm good. Really."

He studies me for a moment, his lips rising into a half grin that belongs on a model.

A model? Seriously, Harper, shut up! Just stop thinking!

"You're chicken." His smile grows, and I have to look at the ground.

Bobbing my head with a bashful grin, I agree with him. "Yep. Happy to admit it. That horse is huge, and I feel incredibly tiny and underqualified right now."

He laughs and scratches between Copper's ears.

"I'll win you over one day, City." He glances at me, and oh crap, am I blushing?

Does his sentence have some kind of double meaning?

No, of course not!

The idea of Tane liking me is ridiculous. The idea of me liking *him* is ridiculous!

He's a farm boy who I'm barely going to have anything to do with. As soon as we get back to Wellington, life will take over. I can't imagine us coming up to

Hamilton very often. I'll be busy with uni and my friends... plus there's Willow and Oscar to think about.

Flashes of my mapped-out future spike through me. Some of them are pleasant, but most of them are terrifying. I had a plan. A perfect, amazing plan, and I want to stick with it as much as possible, but now there's this great hulking alteration, and I don't quite know what to do with it.

I'm not going to be a carefree university student this year. I have extra responsibilities now.

Yanking the phone out of my back pocket, I check that Willow hasn't texted me again. Nothing. I hope she's still in the house and hasn't wandered off again without telling me.

"You know, I should probably get back to the house. Check in on Will and Ozzy. I need to get that boy off his computer."

I've let things slide this week, but I haven't missed the fact that Oscar and his new laptop are becoming one. Mum and Dad would not be impressed. I need to set up some screen time restrictions like they always had. I just haven't found the energy to deal with what will no doubt be a snippy argument.

With the amount of bickering the twins are managing, I don't want to bring any more tension into the house. We seriously need to do something about those two. I figured with the tragedy, Bianca and Stacey might pull closer together, but that's just not happening.

This morning I caught them arguing over how much milk was a reasonable amount for cereal. For goodness' sake! It's cereal! And it's not like we're in short supply of milk on the farm.

I huff and rub my forehead, grimacing at the slick sweat coating my skin.

"You all right?" Tane tips his head at me.

I shove the phone back in my pocket and frown at him. "What?"

"Everything okay?"

"What do you mean?" My heart stutters. The look on his face right now is so kind and compassionate, it's making me nervous. I focus on the sweat patches under his arms. It's unfair that they look so manly. Everything about him is manly and rugged. It should not be this appealing.

My tongue darts between my lips and I shuffle back, aiming for the fence line and a quick escape. I'm not exactly sure where we are in relation to the house, but I'm sure I can find my way.

"You don't have to talk about it or anything, but if you want, I'm a good listener." His words make me pause. "I guess I just want to know how you're *really* doing."

"I'm fine." My shoulders hitch with my automatic response.

His eyes narrow just a little, and for some stupid reason, words start tumbling out of me like he's hooked them with an invisible fishing line and is just reeling them right out of my belly.

"I mean, I'm not. How can any of us be fine right now? But what other choice do I have? I *need* to be fine. My brother and sister need me to be all good. To hold everything together."

His big gumboots trample the grass between us, and he stops close enough for me to get a whiff of him. *Eau de manliness* is impossible to describe now. Before it was hard work and sweat, but now it's something that makes my heart thrum.

I wipe a finger under my nose, trying to remind myself that it's sweat—an odor that should be repulsive. But it's mixing with whatever deodorant he's wearing, and it's—

"You're not alone." Tane's voice is soft and sweet, curling inside of me. "You don't have to be the glue all by yourself. Beck and... me. We're here for *you* just as much as the others."

"Beck's hurting." I shake my head and risk looking up at Tane. "He won't let it show, but he just lost his two childhood friends, plus he's been saddled with all of us. And no one really understands why. I can't burden him with my crap. He's got enough to carry."

Tane angles his body and points at his shoulders. "These are free, so load 'em up with crap anytime."

A snicker pops out of me before I can stop it.

"Come on." He grins and holds up his index finger. "Just one thing. Let one thing out."

I look out across the fields, pulling in a breath and about to deny him, when suddenly the words spurt out. "Willow hasn't spoken since we got the news. The only way I can communicate with her is through text."

My insides shudder; the enormity of even just that one thing feels too big to hold.

Tane scratches the back of his neck. "I notice she's pretty quiet."

"I mean, she's always been kind of quiet, but she's taking it to the extreme at the moment." Stress courses through me. "What if she never speaks again?"

"Give her time. Things like this can't be rushed, and everyone heals at a different pace." His words make so much sense, his smooth voice making them easy to believe, but still my head shakes.

He lightly touches my elbow. "She *will* heal. Don't lose faith in that."

I blink, trying not to be affected by how gorgeous he is.

161

How kind he is. I love the sound of his voice, smooth and deep, with just a slight gruffness around the edges.

"I, um… I…" Pointing over my shoulder, I berate myself for acting like a bumbling idiot. "I need to get back to the house."

"No worries." He disarms me with another one of his grins before waving goodbye to Copper. "See ya later, girl."

The horse whinnies, lifting her chin like she's waving back or something.

I slip through the gate and wait for Tane to start up the bike before jumping on behind him. We don't say anything on the way back to the house, and it's almost a relief. My emotions feel raw and tender. If we talked for too much longer or delved any deeper, I might have started to cry, and that's not something I can do right now.

I haven't shed one tear since those police officers showed up at the door. If people found that out, they'd probably think there was something wrong with me, but they don't know.

I can't cry.

I can't let that out yet.

I can't fall apart. Willow and Oscar need me to be strong.

Tane slows to a stop outside the house and is about to cut the engine when his radio squawks.

"Tane, mate, I need a hand in Paddock 21. You done with that fencing yet?"

"Yep," Tane replies. "I'll be there in a minute."

"Cheers."

Tane slips the radio back into his pocket and grins at me. "Better go."

I nod and scuff the hard dirt, my voice barely louder than the engine. "Thanks, Tane."

His smile tells me he heard me, and I can't help staying there for a moment, just to watch him drive away.

"You're ridiculous," I whisper, pulling in a breath and sniffing the country air.

I catch a whiff of something poo related. Yuck! Wrinkling my nose, I head to the back of the house and unlace my brown-stained sneaker. I am so not going to miss this place.

But I might miss Tane.

The thought rushes through me, a pleasant surprise and a warning.

Don't go there, Harper!

Pushing the laundry door open, I dump my shoes in the

sink, planning on coming back to them as soon as I check on my siblings.

But then I hear a feral shout from upstairs.

"How could you do this!"

I race through the kitchen and stop when I spot Oscar and Willow huddled on the couch in front of his computer.

They glance up at me, their eyes wide.

"What's going on?" I ask.

"I don't know." Oscar shakes his head. "But we're staying down here."

Fair enough.

I'm tempted to do the same thing, until I hear Bianca yell, "You're a selfish bitch!"

17

STACEY

I've never seen Bianca look like this before.

Her freckled cheeks are stained red, her green eyes vibrant with a sparking anger that's kind of terrifying. Where the hell did my meek, mild sister go?

I mean, I know we've been at each other this week, her quiet little barbs feeling like wire wrapping around my throat, but she's never shouted at me before.

This is insane.

I know we're under a lot of stress right now, but Bianca's inner dragon is scary as... especially when she's spewing her fire directly at me

I should have stayed downstairs. Oscar and I were watching Marvel YouTube clips. Not really my thing, but they were more entertaining than I thought.

Nothing wrong with watching hot actors doing heroic stuff on screen. I think I might just be a little bit in love with Chris Evans, although Chris Hemsworth is coming in a very close second.

Okay, they're tied.

Thor or Captain America—I'd happily have either of them.

If I close my eyes and tap my heels together, can I magically transport myself back downstairs? Back onto the couch next to Oscar?

Why did I need my phone anyway?

That's the reason I came upstairs, because I couldn't stand the thought of missing a message or a notification.

Damn my stupid addiction.

It brought me up here. Into the dragon's den. When I walked in, Bianca was standing there, holding her phone and breathing like she was on the verge of exploding.

"What's the matter with you?" I hovered in the doorway.

"You bitch!"

My entire body jolted with the insult. Bianca is not a swearing kind of girl. Her insults are usually sugar-coated with a sticky-sweet smile and easy enough to brush off, but outright name-calling? She's hitting a new level.

"What did you just call me?" My voice goes high with surprise.

"You got together with Riku at the Christmas party!"

I swallow. How the hell did she find that out?

She was never supposed to know. And I can't admit it.

I start with a lie, figuring there may still be a way out of this. She has no proof.

Crossing my arms, I jut out my hip. "Don't be crazy. Who told you that?"

"Ellen and Greta were there! They saw you!"

Shit! Were they? I didn't even see Bianca's friends there.

I hitch my shoulders, unable to look at the red dragon while I weave whatever story I can to save myself. "There were a lot of people at that party. And why are they waiting until now to make up these lies? They're your best friends. If I *had* done something like that, shouldn't they have told you about it the next day?"

"They didn't want to hurt my feelings!" She waves her phone in the air. "They were going to wait until we got back so that when I had to face your sorry, *pathetic* excuses, I'd have backup! How could you do this!"

Her insults make me bristle, my shoulders prickling with sharp spikes that sting and wound.

"Don't lie to me, Stacey. Did you make out with Riku at the party?"

I look to the ceiling, guilt trying to slice me in half, but I hate that feeling, so I shove it aside. I just have to make her understand. Throwing my hands up, I confess. "Okay. Fine. Yes, but he came on to me. I didn't initiate anything."

"Oh, so that makes it better? You knew how much I liked him! I'd told you about it!"

"I… I know, okay? And I tried to resist him at first, but we were having fun. He made me feel better over the whole Stefan thing. We were dancing, and I just got caught up in the moment. It was only a little kissing. I wouldn't have taken it further, and I definitely wouldn't have taken it past that night."

"So that's why he's sending you messages about your sweet lips?" Bianca's voice is trembling with the onset of tears, but I'm too shocked by her revelation to really soak that in.

"You touched my phone! How dare you! How'd you even know the password?"

"It's your birthday, you dumbass!"

"Don't call me dumb!" A red haze hinders my vision.

That's the one insult I really can't stand, especially from my brainiac sister who can't help but get an A+ on freaking everything!

I stomp to my bed and search for my phone under my pillow, but it's not there. Whipping around, I spot it on Bianca's nightstand and quickly snatch it. "Don't ever touch my phone again!"

"You're a selfish bitch!" Bianca spits right in my face.

I shove her away from me and give her the finger, not sure what else to do. I knew Bianca wouldn't get it. I was just proving to her that Riku wasn't worth her time. What kind of asshole flirts with a girl during class and then goes after her sister at a party?

"What's going on in here?" Harper appears in the doorway.

Bianca lets out a shriek of disgust and spins to face the wall. "I hate this place. I don't want to be here. And I can't live with *her* anymore!" She points an accusing finger at me, spinning around so I can get another taste of venom.

I hate the look on her face right now. It's ugly and broken. I can't see my sister in there at all.

Harper raises her hands and steps into the room. "Bianca, calm down. What's happened?"

"Nothing new!" She glares at me. "All you ever do is

think about yourself and what makes *you* happy. You don't care about anybody else!"

I scoff, doing my best to hide how much that hurts me.

"You don't give a shit about my feelings!"

"He doesn't even like you that way!" I retort. "So you flirted in class a little. That didn't mean anything to him! And that's not my fault. That Christmas party is just proof of what a jerk he is. If anything, I was doing you a favor."

"Shut up! Shut up!" Bianca covers her ears. "I can't do this! I can't keep fighting with you. I can't live with your mess and your constant disrespect!" Tears are building on her lashes now, making her green eyes shimmer like pale emeralds.

"Okay. That's...well, maybe we can work on a room swap." Harper's tongue darts between her lips. "Bianca, you're welcome to move in with Willow until we leave on the weekend, and then you'll have the room to yourself. I can sleep here for a few nights, that's no big deal. I'd be happy to—"

"I'm done," Bianca cuts her off, pointing at the phone in my hands. "That was it for me. You crossed a line. You betrayed your family."

"Bianca, come on." I roll my eyes, masking the fear ripping through me. "Don't be so dramatic. He's just some guy."

"You don't even get it!" Bianca's voice cracks, tears breaking free and rolling down her cheeks. "You don't get me. You don't see me at all."

What? Yes I do. I see her.

"I'm going to Australia." Bianca's soft voice rocks me sideways.

"What?" My response is laughter, of all things. "No you're not!"

"Yeah I am. Oma wants me."

Her steely response makes me believe her. Dread slices through me like a machete. "But... that's ridiculous! You're my sister. We have to stay together."

Bianca gives me a scathing glare. "Sisters love each other, Stace, and it's obvious you don't love me."

"Of course I *love* you!"

"You never act like it, and I don't have to put up with this anymore. I'm leaving. It's the only way I'm going to survive."

My lips part, shock rippling through me in merciless waves. "You can't be serious. We... You can't leave."

"Yes I can. And I will."

Slashing the tears off her cheeks, she slips past Harper, who has also been rendered speechless. We just gape at each other for a long, slow beat, like time has stopped ticking while we wrap our heads around this insanity.

My knees give out, and I land on my bed with a dull thud.

Bianca's leaving.

She's leaving me.

18

HARPER

The hum of the waiting engine buzzes inside of my head like a mosquito that I just can't kill.

This is unbelievable.

Bianca's actually doing it. She stuck to her word and called her grandmother straight after her massive meltdown. The woman was ecstatic, apparently, and she put all the plans into place pronto.

Two days later, and Bianca's now standing beside an airport transfer van. Her luggage is neatly packed in the back, and we're all standing outside the big white farmhouse ready—or completely not ready—to say goodbye.

Well, not all of us.

Stacey refused to come down.

I glance over my shoulder and up at the house while Bianca gives Willow a stiff hug. Stacey's probably standing in Tane's room, spying down on us behind the curtain.

She and Bianca haven't spoken since their big fight. The house has been eerily quiet, and even though Beck tried to resolve things between the girls, he couldn't even get them into the same room.

Bianca has spent the last two nights sleeping on the bed in the garage. She even refused to join us for dinner. This is so crazy. They're twins. Sisters. They should be fighting *for* each other, not running in opposite directions.

I wish I could find the perfect way to say that, but maybe the separation will snap them out of this somehow.

Although, it still feels wrong to me.

A warm breeze swirls around my skirt, playing with the hem like it wants to dance. It obviously doesn't get the seriousness of the moment. The chickens don't understand either. They're happily clucking in their yard, oblivious to the cold sadness seeping out of us.

Bianca steps up to me and wraps me in a hug. "Thanks for trying to help."

"Are you sure we can't change your mind?" I squeeze her, but she pulls away, shaking her head.

"This is for the best. I really want to go. Honestly. It'll be so much easier this way…for everyone." Bianca's voice catches.

"It's just… leaving things this way with Stacey, I—"

"I need time to cool off. We both do, and we can't do that around each other."

I can feel the sadness of my smile—my lips are pulling north, but my eyebrows are bunching together.

Bianca looks up at the window, her expression buckling before she spins and jumps into the van. We stand there, silently watching the van do a three-point turn before heading down the driveway.

I raise my hand and wave, but it's such a half-hearted gesture. As if we're not all sad enough anyway. This is just another blow to remind us how much life has changed.

And it's all happened so quickly.

Willow sniffs beside me. I rest my arm over her shoulders and kiss her cheek. "Glad you're not going anywhere."

Willow threads her arm behind my back and gives a little squeeze.

I smile at her. She kind of reciprocates, then pulls away from me and points to the path leading away from the house.

"Going for another walk?"

She nods.

I force a smile. "Text me if you need anything."

She nods again and shuffles off, her beat-up Converses kicking up billows of dry earth. The wind catches it and sends it spinning. Finally, something to dance with.

I close my eyes, feeling like I'm made of stone—the brittle, dry kind that could crack at any moment.

"You all right?" Beck lightly nudges me.

My eyes pop open as I rush to put my unaffected expression on. "Yeah. I'm gunna go check on Stace."

"Thanks." He nods, his voice gruff as he strokes his beard and looks around. "Where did Oscar go?"

I let out a tired sigh when I don't see him. "A thousand to one he's somewhere in the house on his computer."

"We have to get that kid off the screen."

"I know." I wince, burdened by yet another thing to handle.

Beck's lips twitch. "We'll make it tomorrow's problem."

"Okay. Thanks." I sag with relief.

We share another smile and I glance at Tane, who's watching me. He gives me a little wink before turning and heading after Beck—he's already on his way back to work.

I find Stacey on her bed. Tissues are balled up around her, soggy snowballs that only speak of pain.

"You need to talk?" I cross my arms and lean against the doorframe.

"No." She whimpers, bunching a tissue in her right eye. "She made her choice."

"I still don't follow exactly what went down, but I'm sorry it's happened. I'm sorry we couldn't help you fix it."

Stacey rolls onto her side, facing the wall and mumbling against her pillow. "That's life. It's unpredictable. Plans change. You just have to roll with it."

Her words sink into me, disrupting what I've always believed in.

You make a plan.

You stick with it.

Even when life tries to get in the way, you work around it, stay on course.

That's what my dad taught me, and I'm not willing to believe anything else right now.

That's why I'm sticking with my plan—uni in

Wellington with my friends. Sure, I have to manipulate the plan a little to make it work, but I'm not just going to throw my dreams away because life's not fair.

I wish I could somehow explain that to Stacey, but I don't think she's ready to listen.

19

TANE

The chickens cluck as I throw feed into their yard. I smile at their heads bobbing. The morning sun is glinting off their brown feathers, promising a stellar day. It'll be hot, but that blue, cloudless sky is pretty damn awesome.

I look up at it, my smile growing even more when I hear music starting up in the kitchen.

Harper must be up and getting breakfast ready.

"Nearly done?" Beck walks past me.

"Yep." I nod and hand him the bag of chicken feed. "I'll just grab the eggs."

"Cheers." He puts the chicken feed in the sealed crate, then starts taking off his gumboots. "I'm going in to wash up. After breakfast I want to go and take another look at that garage. It really needs a repaint. I might get you to head into town for supplies later. Mitre10 has a paint sale going on this week. We may as well take advantage of it."

"Yeah, no worries." I nod again, happy with the idea of getting out for a bit today. I wonder if Harper will want to come with me.

I picture us cruising into town. It'd probably be good for her to get away from her siblings for an hour or so.

They leave tomorrow. Unfortunately. After that, she'll have no reprieve until school starts up in a couple of weeks.

With a sigh, I lift the hatch and gather up six eggs. I don't want her to leave. Yeah, it's dumb. Like she and I would even be an option. But still. It's been nice having her around. There's something about her that draws me in. It's more than her physical beauty. There's a self-sacrificing kindness about her, a maturity that's nothing like the girls at school. She's one of those old-before-her-time kinds of souls, and I find it fascinating.

I even dreamed about her last night. Once she leaves, I'll no doubt spend my nights staring at the ceiling and wondering what she's doing, picturing her in Wellington, going to uni, studying, cooking for her siblings, trying to run a home. It's gunna be hard work. I wish I could support her. I wonder if she'll take my number. I need to offer that to her before she leaves in the morning. A "call me anytime" type deal.

With a light scoff, I shake my head.

She probably won't, mate.

Shoving the disappointment aside, I kick off my gumboots and shuffle through the laundry in my thick farming socks. The smell of bacon hits me before I push the sliding door open. Yum! My mouth starts to water, and it only gets worse when I see Harper standing in front of the stove in bare feet. Her long, elegant legs are on full display, shining with freshly applied moisturizer. They look so smooth and luscious.

She's in a pair of tailored shorts that barely reach midthigh, and the loose T-shirt she's paired it with slips off her shoulder when she reaches into the fridge for the milk jug. Tugging it back up, she places the milk down and spots me staring at her.

"Morning." She smiles.

"Hey." I clear my throat and hope she can't hear my heartbeat as I approach her. "Fresh eggs."

"Perfect." She takes them off me, lining them up carefully behind the chopping board so they don't roll onto the floor. "I'll scramble these up once the bacon's done. Are you hungry?"

"Always." I grin, then sense Willow's eyes on me.

I flash her a warm smile, but she just turns back to unloading the dishwasher.

Harper lets out a little laugh and moves around her sister to put the kettle on. Her shirt slips again while she's filling the jug, and I can't help studying the curve of her smooth shoulder. Man, I'd love to know what her skin feels like.

I curl my itching fingers into a fist and force a friendly smile when she returns to the stove.

"You okay?" Her confusion is sweet, and my head bobs like a jackhammer.

Willow eyes me again and I clear my throat, taking a step back.

"Yeah, I'm all good." I rub the back of my neck. "Actually, I have to go into town later, and I was wondering if—"

"Where's my computer?" Oscar's shout reverberates through the house, his feet thundering down the stairs like a tsunami.

Harper stiffens, shooting me an edgy look. I nod at her, sending whatever waves of silent encouragement I can. We had big chats with Oscar and Willow last night. It was mostly for Oscar's sake, but we figured it'd feel less like an attack if Willow was in on the conversation too. Beck explained about how too much screen time was bad for everyone and they needed to ease off a bit. Oscar twitched throughout the whole conversation, hugging his computer like he couldn't live without it.

"So, tomorrow, you're having a screen-free day. Got it?"

Oscar and Willow nodded. Harper smiled with relief.

But not anymore. All smiling is off the table when Oscar stomps into the kitchen and yells, "Where is it! Did you sneak into my room and take it while I was sleeping?"

Spinning around, a pair of tongs clutched in her hand, Harper calmly explains, "Yes, because I told you I would. We talked about this yesterday. Remember? You're having a screen-free day. It'll be good for you. You can explore the farm, get outside. You can—"

"I need my computer. Give it back to me."

I'm kind of annoyed at his pissy tone right now, not to mention the fact that he just interrupted Harper midsentence. Like she needs this shit.

I frown at Oscar and seriously want to put him in his place, but I don't know if that would be helpful for Harper, so I press my lips together and bide my time. But if he keeps shouting at her…

"I took it off you for a reason." Harper's jaw quivers, but she stands strong. "You've been on it nearly 24-7. It's not healthy. A screen-free day isn't going to kill you."

"I want my computer!"

Harper flinches but responds calmly. "Well, I'm sorry, but you can't have it."

He lets out an angry growl, fisting his hands. "You don't have the right to take it off me. Mum and Dad gave it to me for Christmas. It's mine!"

"I'm trying to protect you, Ozzy!" Her voice pitches high. "They wouldn't want you on the computer all the time. We've always had screen restrictions. You were only ever allowed two hours max on the iPad."

Oscar fists his hair and fights obvious tears. "Give it to me, Harpy!"

Willow gasps behind me, but I'm too focused on Harper to look. Her nostrils are flaring, a tendon in her neck stretching tight.

Yikes. Harpy. I'm guessing that's a full-blown insult by the look on her face.

I'm about to open my mouth and tell Oscar to watch his mouth, but Harper points the tongs at him and starts speaking before I can.

Her voice is firm and adamant, in spite of the slight trembling in her arm. "No. You can have it back tomorrow. I'll give it to you for an hour on the drive home."

"I need it now!" Oscar's voice breaks as it rises from a shout to a bellow. He stomps into the kitchen, puffing like a bull ready to charge. "Give it to me!"

I shift position so I'm standing just a little closer to Harper, ready to jump in if he lunges at her. He's seriously looking feral right now. His nostrils are full on flaring and his glassy eyes are dark with anger.

Harper swallows, her voice kind of raspy as she makes her final stand. "I can't do that. And if you can't accept it, then—"

"Arggh!" Oscar spins his back to her, snatching the milk jug off the bench and hurling it at the wall.

It shatters and milk spurts everywhere, along with a shower of glass that hits every surface it can, bouncing off the walls and skittering across the floor right around Harper's bare feet.

She curls her toes and I act without thinking, lifting her onto the kitchen counter. She gasps and looks at me with wide eyes. A teardrop of milk is dribbling down her cheek, not to mention the splattering all over her shirt and legs.

She's trembling, and I steady her with my hand before firing a black look at Oscar.

He's glaring at Harper like the spilled milk is her fault, his hands curled into fists, his nostrils still flaring. I swear he's about to go rage when a shout from the hallway stops him short.

"Oi!"

Oscar jumps and spins around, his eyes no doubt bugging out as a pissed-off looking Beck thunders into the room.

He jerks to a stop when he spots the milk, the glass and a twelve-year-old kid who won't look at him.

"Get outside," Beck growls, pointing at the front door.

All the fight drains from Oscar, his red skin going white as he leans away from Beck like he's expecting a punch to the face or something.

Beck pulls in a breath, closes his eyes and says more softly, "Just... follow me, and don't throw anything on your way out the door." Beck starts walking through the dining room and lounge.

Oscar looks to Harper, silently begging for support, but she's looking just as surprised as he is. She opens her mouth, but I'm not confident any words are gunna come out.

"Let's go!" Beck barks from the doorway, and Oscar flinches before bowing his head and shuffling after the grizzly bear.

"What's Beck doing?" Harper grips my shoulder, obviously intent on jumping down to see what's going to happen with her brother.

I scoop her into my arms and carry her over the milk and glass minefield. My socks are hopefully thick enough to avoid the little shards digging into my skin.

I don't put her down until we're well past the war zone and standing next to the lounge window. Pulling the net curtain aside, I point to Beck's ute. He's standing by the back of it, saying something to Oscar, who is looking at the ground like it's going to open up and save him.

I can't help a grin as memories flood through me.

"Don't worry," I whisper, breathing in her scent without meaning to. She washed her hair this morning, and it smells so unbelievably good, even mingled with the splattered milk.

I hunt for the tissue box and pull one out just as Beck hands Oscar a hammer and tugs him around the side of the house.

"Thanks." Harper takes the tissue, totally distracted as she heads down the hallway that leads to Beck's area of the house. She stops in his office to look out the window.

Leaning against his desk chair, she wipes the milk off her face while watching Beck point at the fence. One hand is on his hip, and it's like freaking déjà vu watching him.

"What's Beck saying?"

I step up behind her, using the excuse of quiet conversation to get as close as I can. Her intoxicating scent nearly throws me, so I shuffle to the right a little and cross my arms. "Well, if it's anything like what he said to me when I first started living here, it'll be something along the lines of 'I understand that you're angry, mate, but there are better ways to express yourself. Now if you need to hit something, you might as well make it something useful.'" I lower my voice, probably not sounding like Beck at all, but his words still ring in my head.

I was a scared, bratty fighter when I first arrived in this place. I was used to men yelling at me, cuffing me around the ears and telling me I was stupid, never handing me a hammer and telling me to bash a nail with it.

I sense Harper's gaze on me and glance down, caught off guard by her hazel eyes.

She's so beautiful it's hard to breathe for a second.

It's not until she turns back to watch Oscar do a piss-poor job of hammering in his first nail that I find my voice again.

"Beck gave me a hammer and got me working on the fence for a while. It was just like this." I point out the window. "The fence didn't really need that much work, but… Beck knew what he was doing. The next time I lost it, he got me shoveling horseshit, and the time after that I had to scrub the green scunge out of the bottom of the shower. And the time after that…" I tip my head, looking up to the ugly, old light shade on the ceiling. "You know what, I can't remember the order. I just know that I worked my bum off my first year here."

Harper swallows, looking worried.

I touch her shoulder, hoping to make her feel better. "It was a good thing. He worked the anger right out of me. You need to trust Beck. He's a really great dad."

I want to say more, like *You should stay. You need the support, and we can be that for you. Don't drive back to Wellington tomorrow!*

But all that tumbles out of my mouth is a soft "Come on, let's be kind and go clean up the kitchen. I doubt Ozzy will feel like doing it when he comes in for breakfast."

20

HARPER

I scurry back to the kitchen, liking Tane's suggestion of cleaning up before Oscar gets back inside. Even though he was being a total shit, yelling at me that way, I still want to help him. I could sense the fear beneath his rage.

He's obviously linking the computer with Mum and Dad, using it as a way to stay connected to them. But it's not healthy. They'd be disappointed in me if I just kept letting this slide.

But how am I supposed to do this?

With a heavy sigh, I walk into the dining room and am hit by the pungent smell of burning bacon, but I don't have time to do anything about it, because all I see is Willow standing by the sink with tears coursing down her face.

"Will? Are you okay?" I go to rush into the kitchen, but Tane snatches my arm, pulling me back.

"You need to put some shoes on, or I'll be picking glass out of your feet for ages."

I step back. He's right, but I need to get to my sister.

Tane dashes up the stairs while I bob on the balls of my feet. "Willow?"

She turns to face me, slashing tears off her cheeks with the edge of her sleeve.

"Are you okay?"

She nods, then shrugs.

"Beck's just getting Oz to do some hammering. Keeping him busy."

Her lips twitch with a relieved smile.

"Everyone's fine," I reassure her.

She nods again.

"But the bacon's burning." I wince, pointing to the stove.

Willow gasps and lurches toward it, quickly turning off the element.

I wave a hand in front of my face, disturbing the smelly air. "We're going to need to open some windows."

Willow starts unlatching every window in the kitchen and pushing it out so a little breeze can come in. I move to the front door and prop it back with an old iron that looks like it's been here since the late 1800s.

Staying crouched on the floor, I run my fingers over the hard metal and wonder again how I'm supposed to do this.

I've been hoping that routine will save us. When we get back, Willow will return to ballet classes, Oscar will get busy with his friends and cricket. But what if he loses it again? I've never seen him like that before. When he was two, he was the king of the tantrum, and yeah, I've heard him yell at Dad before, but he's never smashed anything.

He was freaking feral.

What if he does that when it's just me and him alone?

What if I can't get him out the door to school one morning?

What if Willow goes back to school and refuses to say anything to anyone?

I'll have to deal with her teachers.

Panic curls my stomach, and I press the back of my hand against my mouth.

Shit, I'm going to have to go to parent interviews now.

I'll be a uni student *and* a solo parent.

Bile swirls in my stomach, threatening to lurch up my throat. I breathe deep and stand up, smoothing down my shirt as I struggle to pull myself together.

Leaving's the right thing to do. It's the plan, and I have to stick to it, but the idea of doing this on my own is…

And what about Beck, Tane and Stacey?

She's been so quiet and mopey since Bianca left. Quiet, but also resolute. She won't admit to anyone how much she's missing her sister.

Bianca texted to let us know she'd arrived safely. But she didn't text Stacey. She texted me. It was pretty awkward, and I swear I heard Stacey cry herself to sleep last night.

Tane's feet on the stairs distract me, and I turn to face him as he pops into view. He holds up my pair of black slip-ons.

"Thanks," I murmur, shoving them on and wiggling my toes until they sit right.

"Sorry, I had to go into your room to get them."

"That's okay." I put on a brave smile, hoping I hadn't left any underwear on the end of my bed or anything. Thankfully I'm dressed for the day, so my room should be tidy. I like to leave it that way before coming downstairs.

Willow sniffs as Tane helps her out of the kitchen. She's in jandals, but still, little shards could catch the edges of her feet. His biceps curl as he easily lifts her over the worst of the glass, and I'm struck by his strength. Willow is light and delicate, but still, he plucked her up like she weighed nothing. He made me feel the same way when he lifted me off the floor earlier.

If I hadn't been so horrified by Oscar's outburst, I would have appreciated it a lot more.

You're not supposed to appreciate it! Tane is not an option. You have bigger things to worry about than romance.

I thread my fingers together and squeeze as he gives my sister a kind smile and steadies her. "You right?"

She nods and then walks to the stairs. As she ascends, he throws me a glance, his eyebrows rising as if to say, "Well, this has been a dramatic morning."

My lips lift into a smile before I can stop them.

"I'll get the broom." He jumps over the glass, but I still hear a crunch when his battered sneakers hit the floor near the laundry. "We've got a pretty big area of debris here," he calls from the laundry. "There are even shards by the washing machine!"

I sigh and gingerly make my way through the kitchen, figuring I'll start in the corner by the sink and work my way toward Tane.

Snatching the paper towel roll, I crouch down and start pushing the glass inland.

We work quietly, the sound of the radio hosts keeping us company. They're giving away tickets to an upcoming Pentatonix concert in Auckland. I wonder when the next time will be that I get to go to a concert. I can't imagine dancing and feeling that kind of joy right now. It's hard to even muster a genuine smile these days.

The thought depresses me, adding to the weight that's already too heavy.

"You don't have to do this on your own," Tane murmurs.

I pause and slowly look up at him.

He's picking at the end of the broom handle, gazing down at me with those kind eyes of his.

"You don't have to leave tomorrow, or the day after. You can live here for as long as you like." His tanned cheeks tinge red and we break eye contact, both looking to the floor. "That's what Beck would say, anyway. I know it is. You're family to him, so this house is yours too."

I shake my head, kind of liking the sound of it but also rebelling against the idea.

"What about school, and cricket, and ballet, and rugby,

and friends and uni? I'm already enrolled at Victoria. I'm going to study business and marketing. There's a plan in place."

"Yeah, of course there is." Tane nods, resting the broom against the oven and bending down to open up an old newspaper so we can wrap the glass up safely.

He looks disappointed for reasons I can't begin to understand.

We've basically taken over his house, disrupted his quiet life. I would have thought he'd be pleased to see the back of us.

"Nothing's set in stone, though," he murmurs. "People can't live that way, because life doesn't play fair. It's unpredictable."

I huff, irritated by that. I don't want life to be unpredictable!

"I like having a plan," I mutter. "It makes me feel secure."

"Okay." He places the larger pieces of glass into the middle of the newspaper, blinking a few times like he's trying to word his next sentence carefully.

I wait it out, curious.

"How about this, then?" His tongue darts between his lips before he presses them together and nods a couple of times. "Why don't you at least stay until the end of the summer holidays? School goes back beginning of Feb for me. I don't know about Willow and Oz, but that'd give you nearly two more weeks here. Help. Support. Maybe Beck can work some magic and knock the aggro out of your raging brother before you leave."

His smile and joke are hard to resist, and before I can think straight, I'm actually asking, "You don't think Beck would mind?"

"Nah. He'd be stoked."

I swallow and look to the floor, focusing on the milk-sodden paper towels. Bunching them up, I plop them into the middle of the newspaper, my brain whirling with possibilities.

I could delay the plan, I guess.

I mean, I've already pushed back our departure once. I suppose I could do it again. It'd give me a few more days to get my head straight, but...

I'm just not sure.

Staying here only puts a hold on the inevitable. I have a life in Wellington, and I want to get back to it. I'm a city girl. I want my friends, my latte, my shoes clipping over concrete footpaths. I want to go to the beach during the day and attend parties at night.

But that's the thing...

The real problem is, I want to get back to the life I was *supposed* to have, not this new version that involves way too much responsibility and a future so overwhelming I feel like I'm facing a wall of water that's going to bowl me right off my feet.

21

STACEY

Something's burning.

My nose wrinkles as I step out of the bathroom. The steam from my shower swirls out the door, evaporating behind me as I walk to my room.

Dumping my pajamas on the bed, I straighten my tank top and suck in a breath. I really don't want to go downstairs and face everyone, but I can't *not* know what that burning smell is. Plus, there was some major yelling going on before, and I'm kind of curious to find out what that was all about.

So, I turn out of my room, ignoring the empty bed beside mine and the even bigger cavity in my chest.

I can't believe Bianca left. I fluctuate between hating her and missing her.

In my stronger moments, I'm pissed off that she would

just abandon me on this farm when we've only got each other left. But in the darkness of night when the more-pork bird hoots outside my window, I can't deny that sinking sadness. It settles over me like a cold, wet blanket.

I hate that feeling so much. Sunrise can't come quick enough.

It's actually good that I'm heading downstairs. I can distract myself with these people. They can help me forget.

"Gross! What is that smell?" I pinch my nose when I reach the dining room.

"Burned bacon and spilled milk." Tane stands with a newspaper bundle in his hands.

Harper rises from the floor as well, rubbing her hands together before turning to deal with the crispy frypan.

"And what was all that yelling before?"

"That would be Oscar losing his rag." Tane raises his eyebrows at me. "Beck's got him outside, working off the rage."

"O-kay." I bulge my eyes at him and walk into the kitchen to get myself a drink. "Anyone want a coffee?"

"Yeah, me," Tane calls from the back door.

"I guess so," Harper mutters.

Tane reappears with a snicker, nudging Harper in the back with his elbow. "Coffee snob."

"Instant isn't coffee," she throws back. "It's an excuse for coffee, and you would know that if you'd ever tasted real coffee before."

Tane grins at her while I lean back and watch with a smirk. Are they flirting right now?

How cute is that?

I hadn't noticed it before, but maybe there's some chemistry between these two. That could be entertaining. Chemistry is a great way to forget the bad stuff, the ugly life keeps throwing at me. It makes me want to see Jonas again.

Oh man, I hope I do.

And it'd be great to see him before school starts too.

School.

Without Bianca.

A shudder rips down my spine and I spin, grabbing three mugs and dishing out a teaspoon of coffee into each.

I've changed my mind; I can't stay down here today. I'm going to take my coffee back up to bed and distract myself with a movie. That always works like a charm.

The kettle pops, and I pour boiling water into each mug

just as the back door flings open and Oscar stomps into the house.

He scowls at Harper but mutters a half-hearted "I'm sorry."

Harper gives him a dry look but doesn't say anything.

"A proper one, mate." Beck lightly squeezes his shoulder.

Oscar huffs, then tries again. "I'm sorry." He seems slightly more sincere, especially when he looks around the kitchen and whispers, "You cleaned up."

"Just wanted to help you out," Harper murmurs, taking the frypan to the rubbish bin and throwing out the bacon ash.

"Well, that was bloody nice of you. Wasn't it, Oz?" Beck nudges Oscar between the shoulder blades.

He kind of stumbles forward and bobs his head, then mutters, "Thank you."

"You're welcome," Harper clips. "You should thank Tane too."

Oscar's cheeks scorch red as he turns to glance up at Tane and whisper his gratitude.

"We're all good, mate." Tane musses up Oscar's hair— probably male-speak for *I forgive you*.

"Right. Well, that's done. Sort of." Beck cocks an

eyebrow at the sullen boy, looking like a gigantic bear towering over his naughty cub. "Now, get yourself some breakfast. Something hearty, like Weet-Bix. You're gunna need the energy."

Oscar's upper lip curls as he wrenches open the cupboard and pulls out a cereal bowl. I inch past him, aiming for the fridge and some fresh milk. Hopefully there's still some left. I'm relieved I don't have to have my coffee black when I open the door and spot a full jug, nice and chilled from a night in the fridge.

"Can I have that after you?" Oscar mutters.

"Of course." I force a smile and finish up the coffees while Beck hollers up the stairs.

"Willow, get down here, please. It's time for a meeting."

Ugh. A meeting? This can't be good.

Willow skips down the stairs on her fairy feet. (Every time she moves, I swear wings are about to pop out from her back. She's just got this whimsical grace about her, like she was born to walk on her tiptoes or something.) She stops next to Beck, looking kind of confused and worried.

"Sit." Beck points at the table. "Everybody."

We all shuffle to the table, looking reluctant and wary. Tane takes a sip of his coffee and leans back, resting his arm on the top of the chair. He must be the only relaxed person at this table. It's easy for him. He's been living here for years. He's used to Beck's gruff voice and bushman beard.

The seat next to me is achingly empty. I tuck my foot under my butt, failing to ignore the fact that Bianca's not here.

"I've made a decision." Beck taps the table with his knuckles. "Harper, Willow, Oscar—I think you should stay for another week. I have a big job I've been putting off, but many hands make light work. That's what my old man used to say, and he's right. So, after breakfast, you lot need to go get yourselves kitted out with gumboots and overalls. Oz can borrow some of Tane's old gear, so he's gunna stay here with me, and we'll come up with a list of stuff that needs doing."

His decisive words leave no room for argument, but my brain is still trying to form one anyway. I frown, glancing at Willow, who is nibbling on her thumbnail.

Harper's jaw works to the side, and then she manages to stammer, "I… well… we kind of planned to go back tomorrow so I have time to get organized before school starts."

"It's only one week." Beck holds up his index finger. "You'll still have plenty of time to get ready for school. I need your help."

I can sense Beck's playing a card that Harper will struggle to turn her back on.

Someone needs help?

Harper seems the type to always give it.

And then he goes and lays down one more reason to seal the deal. Swiftly glancing at Oscar, then back to Harper, he murmurs, "A little hard work is good for us. We need it."

Harper's expression crumples and she glances at Oscar, who is inhaling his Weet-Bix like he hasn't been fed in three days.

Tane's sitting up straight now, his face practically begging her to say yes.

Oh yeah, he's into her big-time.

I hide my smirk behind my hand, and finally Harper's head bobs up and down. "Okay. Yeah, I guess we can stay. If you need our help, then you know…" She drums her fingers on the table, and Beck gives her a broad grin.

"Right. Done. Excellent." He stands tall, his chair scraping on the wooden floor. "Tane will drive you into town. I need him to pick up some paint and supplies anyway. Why don't you all grab yourself some food, then head off. I want you all back by lunchtime." He claps his hands and rubs them together like his master plan is falling into place perfectly. "Let's go, everyone!"

22

TANE

The Base shopping mall is busy today.

I stand near the curb outside The Warehouse, waiting for Harper to get back from using the bathroom. Willow and Stacey are already inside the behemoth shop. They'll no doubt come out with purchases. It's hard not to. The Warehouse is stacked with cheap stuff—everything from shampoo to garden tools. They carry a pretty good line of T-shirts too. I always buy my workout gear from here.

But not my farming stuff.

I'll take them to Mitre10 after this. I have to get the paint anyway, and they can get some decent overalls and gumboots at the same time.

I'd actually rather take them to the Hunting and Fishing shop. They have the best gear, but it's pricier. And since they're not staying long-term (dammit), then they shouldn't have to shell out for the highest-quality stuff.

Scuffing my jandal on the ground, I watch clumps of people weave up and down the outdoor walkways, bags swinging from their arms. Children squeal and giggle from the playground in the center of the grass square while parents rest against the red fence and take a moment to breathe.

A mother and tween daughter scuttle past me, arguing over cheap shoes versus quality and how money can be saved or wasted. I turn my back on them, scanning the row of shops for Harper. What is taking her so long?

"Where are the girls?"

Her voice makes me jump, and I spin around to find her behind me. How the hell did she sneak past? I was facing the direction of the toilets basically the whole time.

I notice a disposable coffee cup in her hand and narrow my eyes at her. She snuck past me to buy a latte?

"I know what you're thinking." She gives me a cheeky grin. "What is that delicious smell?"

She passes the takeaway cup under my nose, and I get a decent whiff of some pretty mouthwatering coffee.

But I'm not about to admit that to her, so I just nod and raise my eyebrows.

"That, my friend, is *real* coffee." She takes a sip, looking far too sexy for her own good as she tips her head back and moans in ecstasy. "Real, delectable coffee."

I want to kiss her neck. I want to feel that smooth skin beneath my lips.

Ducking my head, I stare down at my black jandal straps instead. She's in jandals too, her long, narrow feet and painted nails looking delicate next to my broad Goliath feet. I try to focus on my big toenail— surely that will help me hide the attraction pulsing through me—but then she laughs. It's just a soft, short giggle, but it's enough to lose the war.

I look up, drinking in her pretty face and sparkling eyes as she holds out the coffee cup.

"Would you like to try some?"

Unable to resist, I take the cup and place my mouth over her lipstick mark, forcing myself to focus on the coffee. I take a decent sip, and man, it's so bloody good.

"You like it?"

"Yeah." I shrug, handing the cup back. "It's all right."

"It's freaking delicious and so much better than that crappy instant stuff you call coffee. Admit it."

"I don't know." I tip my head, enjoying the game. "We buy the special roasted blend. It's pretty good."

"Mmm, special roasted with warm cow's milk."

Sarcasm drips from her mouth and is only made funnier by the way she sticks out her tongue and shudders.

With a quick laugh, I snatch the cup out of her hand and down her entire coffee in one go.

She gasps. "I can't believe you just did that."

I hand the empty cup back and wince. "Yeah, burned my tongue too." I stick it out, trying to air my scorched taste buds. "Crap, that hurts."

She laughs and gently slaps my shoulder. "You are such an idiot."

"I prefer to think of it like a man determined to prove his point."

"Oh, because that's so attractive."

"Is it?" I grin, probably looking way too hopeful.

She rolls her eyes. "What point were you trying to prove exactly?"

"I'm not sure, but I got you to laugh, so…" I stick out my tongue again and point at it, my words muffled as I speak with my tongue hanging out. "Worth it."

She shakes her head and snorts.

Aw, she's a snorter. That's cute.

Her cheeks flush red, and I can sense her clinging to her dignity as she pushes me toward the Coffee Club cafe.

"Just go buy me another coffee. Latte with a shot of vanilla."

I shoot her a dopey grin and she gives me a wide, unchecked smile.

It's all kinds of beautiful.

"I'll go find Stacey and Will." She laughs again and walks away, her long hair swishing across her back as she shakes her head.

Oh man.

My beating heart skips with pleasure, and I seriously have to check myself as I head into the cafe. My legs are itching to skip, jump, tap my heels together. It's ridiculous. A little flirtation over coffee should not be making me feel this good.

No other girl has ever made me feel this giddy before.

I kind of like it.

23

STACEY

I stand in the shoe aisle, assaulted by the smell of cheap rubber. I mean, I'm kind of used to it. I've spent the last four years living in China. Ninety percent of the stock in The Warehouse is probably *made* in China.

Snatching up a pair of rubber boots, I check the sole and nod.

Made in China.

Wrestling them back onto the overcrowded shelf, I wander down the concrete aisle, kind of hating the fact that I'm here to buy a boring pair of gumboots. I'd much rather be shopping for clothes or jewelry. Something pretty and fun to wear.

A kid starts crying behind me.

I glance over my shoulder as his father pulls him away.

"I told you to stay with the family! You can't just run off."

The boy wails a little louder, so his dad picks him up and walks a little faster.

I swipe a hand across my mouth, dodging the memory of being carried by my dad. I used to wrap my legs around him so tight he could let go of me and I'd still be holding on.

"My little spider monkey," he'd chuckle.

I scratch my neck, wondering if gumboots will seriously be enough to ward off the ugly sadness.

But then I spot something that definitely will.

My breath hitches.

Jonas?

No way.

It's meant to be!

Racing to the end of the aisle before I lose sight of him, I duck past a trolley loaded with bedding supplies and weave around a kid holding a massive box of Lego.

"Jonas!" I call, just before he disappears into the maze of men's clothing.

He spins, and the second he sees me, a huge smile lights his face.

"No way." He touches my shoulder when I stop in front of him. "I really wanted to see you again. I felt like such a dick after I left you last time. Why the hell didn't I get your number?" He looks to the ceiling, slapping a hand over his eyes. "Idiot move."

My insides flutter as I dip my hip and smile at him. "You want my number?"

"You better believe it." He pulls out his phone and snaps a pic of me, then programs my number in.

Thank God I know it by heart.

I watch his screen, stoked when he remembers my name without me having to tell him.

Sliding his phone into his back pocket, he looks me up and down, so obviously appreciating the view.

It makes me feel like a million bucks.

"You gunna use it?" I point at his battered jeans, trying to indicate the phone he's just put away.

"Your number?" He smirks. "Be a bit of a waste if I didn't."

"How long you gunna make me wait?"

He leans toward me with a playful grin. "Enough time not to make me look as desperate as I feel."

I can't help a giggle. He's so adorable! And he wants me. I love how unsubtle he's being about it.

Brushing my teeth over my lower lip, I tip my head at him, deciding to be just as bold with my flirting. "Well, that doesn't have to be very long. And when you text or call me, make sure it's with plans to take me out somewhere."

His eyes spark with approval. "A girl who knows what she wants. I like it."

"Well, it'd be nice to start North Ridge with a friend or two." Bianca's face flashes through my mind, but I don't want it killing this moment, so I desperately try to shove her away.

"You going to North Ridge?"

I nod.

I asked Tane the day I got back from first meeting Jonas what school he goes to. I tried to be really stealth and casual about the whole thing, like I didn't really care, but I was more curious than anything. It was an effort to hide my glee when he mentioned North Ridge High and said that's where Bianca and I will no doubt go as well.

I didn't want to ask Tane if he knew Jonas or anything. I don't know why. Maybe I was worried he doesn't like Jonas, and I don't want to hear anything bad about the gorgeous guy who's just taken my number.

"What year will you be in?" Jonas asks.

"Twelve."

"Same as me." He runs his hand down my arm. "I'll make sure you have the best start. No newbie worries for you. I'll have your back."

I'm about to reply with some witty quip about having more than my back, but his phone interrupts me with a loud ding.

He snatches it out and reads the text. "I gotta cruise."

"I'll hear from you soon?"

He just grins at me, wiggling his eyebrows before sauntering off. I watch him swagger away, studying the shape of his tall, lean frame. He is owning his grungy look. He could totally be a rock star. That's the kind of vibe that pulses out of him. I love it.

"He has my number," I whisper under my breath, then let out a little squeal. Spinning like a ballerina, I head back to the gumboot aisle, feeling a million times better about life.

Jonas is the perfect distraction. He's going to save me from the ugly.

"Stace!" Harper calls.

I flinch and turn to find her.

She's standing with Willow and pointing toward the checkouts. "You ready to go?"

"Nearly. Just got to buy one thing."

"Cool. We'll meet you out front."

I give her a thumbs-up and dash back to cheap gumboot town. My phone chirps like a bird, and I pull it out of my pocket to check the message.

0225988160: Is this too soon? Or can I at least use the excuse that I'm just trying to get my number onto your phone? Jonas

I giggle and quickly program in his contact details before replying.

Me: Never too soon. Number is now programmed in. Don't make me wait too long for those plans. I'm the desperate one. Desperate for some fun.

Jonas: Fun? That I can deliver. Will text you as soon as I've sorted something for us to do.

I reply with an excited gif. I know it's old-school, but the Carlton dance is one of my favorites. As soon as I've sent it, I worry that Jonas will think it's stupid, but he replies back immediately with an *Elf* gif that makes me laugh.

Yes! We have the same sense of humor.

This is perfect.

A smile plays on my lips as I head back down to the gumboots and bypass the ones I was considering, instead snatching a pair that is more fitting of my mood.

Shoving one on, I check that it fits and then hurry to the checkout.

I'm loving this smile that just won't leave me alone.

Oh man, I hope Jonas doesn't make me wait too long. I really need him right now.

24

HARPER

The sun is hot as we stand there in the paddock behind the garage. Swirls of heat rise off the fence, giving it a blurry edge. I'm glad I made everyone slather on the sunscreen. It's going to be a scorching afternoon, and New Zealand sun can turn even the most resilient skin crispy in less than twenty minutes.

I've put two and two together and figure Beck's going to get us scraping paint, sanding wood and then repainting the garage.

Glancing over my shoulder, I wrinkle my nose at the old structure.

It definitely needs a little TLC.

Tugging at my new overalls, I wriggle my toes inside my Red Bands and have to smile. I clomped through this paddock without even looking at my feet. Animal poo be damned, I was completely protected in my new gummies.

Is it weird that I kind of like them?

Yes, it's weird!

I clear my throat and steal a glance at Tane. He's standing tall and gorgeous beside me, flicking a fly away from his face while he waits for Beck to give us some instructions. His cap is on backward, the bill covering his neck while a pair of wraparound shades hides his eyes from me.

I love that he burned his tongue just to make me laugh this morning.

I shouldn't love it, but I do.

Flirting with Tane was fun. I don't know what came over me, or why I chose to do it. I feel light for some reason. I can't even explain why.

"All right." Beck claps his hands together and gives them a rub while he inspects his troops.

Without even being told to, we've lined up like soldiers in Beck's army.

It's kind of funny.

He scans the row, inspecting our new purchases, his head jolting back when he gets to Stacey and points at her feet.

"What are those?"

She looks down. "Gumboots."

"They're pink!"

"Yeah, so?"

"Gumboots aren't pink."

"Well, these ones are."

"But…" Beck looks comically incredulous. "They're pink!"

I bite my lips together, trying not to laugh. Tane's quivering shoulders are so not helping. He's fighting the snickers as well.

Stacey spreads her arms wide. "Hey, I'm just trying to make the best of a situation where I have to wear rubber boots."

A snort pops out of me before I can stop it. I slap my hand over the embarrassing sound. Tane glances down at me and his own laughter starts up, a smothered chuckle.

Beck looks completely perplexed. "They're going to get poo and muck and paint all over them."

Stacey's expression buckles with disgust, but then she sucks in a breath and lifts her chin. "They're rubber. I can wash them off."

Beck pinches the bridge of his nose, and I glance at

Willow, who is also fighting a grin. Seeing my sister actually smile—her real smile—makes the joy bubble right out of me, and I let out a loud laugh that Tane joins in on.

Beck snickers and shakes his head. Stacey gives him a triumphant grin, and I nudge Oscar with my elbow. He lets out a little snicker as well. I wish it was more, but I'll take it.

"Oh, all right, you lot, listen up." Beck scratches his beard. "I've got a big job for you, and I figure if we all work hard, then we can get it done by the end of the week."

He points behind us, and we all turn to study the decrepit-looking garage while he explains exactly what we'll be doing.

"I know it looks as though it's on its last legs, but she's solid and still has a lot of life in her. She just needs a spruce-up."

He hands out scrapers and sets up a couple of ladders. Tane and I take the top while the others all start working on scraping paint off the bottom panels.

It doesn't take long to work up a healthy sweat. I wipe my forehead with the back of my hand and glance down at Willow. Her eyebrows are bunched in concentration, the tip of her tongue sticking out the side of her mouth. Oscar's the same. It's a family trait, the whole tongue thing. Dad used to do it all the time.

Oscar grunts and attacks a stubborn clump of paint, leaning into it.

Good man.

This is so healthy for him.

Staying was the right decision.

Thoughts of Zoey and Alaina at the beach tease me for a second, trying to rob me of my happy. I grit my teeth and focus back on the paint. They're going to laugh their asses off when they find out what I spent my day doing. I'm just going to have to tell them that I'm building muscle while they're acting like beached whales. That'll shut them up.

My eyes travel over to Tane, who has already finished scraping his section and is now sanding back the wood. The electric sander is loud and drowns out the buzz of cicadas, but I don't even notice it. I'm too busy checking out the way his shoulder muscles flex, the yummy shape his biceps are making.

About an hour ago, he stripped off the top half of his overalls. They're now dangling down by his thighs and all I can see is delicious almond skin, barely covered by a loose-fitting singlet.

He's so strong and masculine. It's impossible not to be attracted to him.

I should definitely mention that to my besties. If the beached whale thing doesn't put them in their place, knowing I can spend my day checking out Tane will make them green.

I haven't told them about him yet. Every time we talk, I just fail to mention him.

I don't know why.

I should tell Mum, though. We always talk about my love life.

I mean, I *wish* I could tell Mum, because we always *talked* about my love life.

Thinking about her in the past tense is brutal.

And knowing I can never call her again is even worse.

There will be no more big chats about my future or my heart. No more monster hugs. No words of reassurance to spur me on.

All I'll get from either of my parents now is silence.

The thought slices right through me, obliterating whatever joy was warming me before. I suddenly feel untethered, like a balloon tossed in the wind that could end up anywhere, or spend the rest of its life flying on an uncontrolled breeze.

25

STACEY

I rub my aching shoulder, squinting at my iPad screen and trying to look as though I'm listening. Michelle called without warning, and I stupidly answered it.

I wish I hadn't.

I don't want to FaceTime.

I don't want an update on things in China.

It just reminds me that I'm not there. That this dream I'm trying to live in is actually my reality.

Squeezing my tender muscles, I try for a mini massage as Michelle harps on about something to do with school and my transcript.

After a day and a half of scraping down that stupid garage, I am so not in the mood to talk about education. I'm done.

Thankfully Tane is like a freaking ox, plus he works fast too. So he's like a cheetah ox or something. He's managed to get through three times as much as the rest of us. When Beck hasn't been doing other farm chores, he's pitched in too. At this rate, we should be ready to start painting the thing by Tuesday or Wednesday.

Thank God. I can't wait for this job to be over.

I mean, I'm getting a nice tan and all, and it's probably good for my muscles, but right now they're screaming at me.

I need a shower. A long one.

My lips pull into a resentful frown. Stupid five-minute rule.

"So, we've packed up the apartment, sold off any furniture I'm sure you guys didn't want or need, and the rest is being shipped back to New Zealand." Michelle's eyes suddenly start to water, and I clench my jaw.

No tears. Please, no tears. I want happy. I need happy!

Michelle sniffs and gives me a watery smile. "Sorry. It's just been really hard boxing up your stuff. It makes me miss your parents so much."

I nod, my throat swelling so fast that words are impossible.

"But everything has gone smoothly. The school has been so helpful in working everything out money-wise, and the shipping company has been great too. They assure me your stuff should be there by April at the latest. I've emailed Beck with all the details."

"April?" I whisper. "That's months away."

"I know, but it has to go through customs, and that always takes forever. You might get lucky with a March delivery. I know you're probably desperate for your stuff."

I shake my head, not sure if I actually am. Opening those boxes when they arrive will only remind me of everything I've lost.

Glancing at the empty bed in my room, I swallow and turn back to the screen. I can't look at that bed. I tried covering it with my discarded clothes, but it didn't work. Bianca would hate it so much, so for some weird reason, I've kept her side of the room neat as a pin. Whenever we've had to share, she always needed that invisible line. It was fine. No big deal.

But now, I can't forget about that line and how it's still there, even though she's not.

"So…" Michelle wipes at her tears and forces a smile. "How are things? Where's Bianca?"

The question's a punch in the gut, and I respond the only way I know how. "She's in the shower."

"Oh. Okay. Will she be long? I'd love to say a quick hi. I

have a class starting in a couple of minutes, but I can stick around until the bell rings."

I shake my head. "We've been working outside today, so I think she's having a good soak. I'll make sure I pass it on, though."

"Thanks." Michelle looks disappointed, and her voice starts to wobble. "We really miss you guys. The students at school have all been asking after you. We're holding a memorial service for your parents on Wednesday."

Now my insides feel tender too, swollen and raw. I don't know how to respond. Do I say that's nice? Do I show gratitude when all I want to do is smash my iPad against the wall?

My phone dings and I glance at the screen, spotting Jonas's name.

Yes!

Desperation courses through me. It takes everything in me not to snatch my phone and kiss it. Jonas will save me from this. He'll take the ugly feelings away and make me smile. He'll help me forget.

"Hey, Michelle, I've gotta go, and I know you have a class. I'll talk to you later?"

"Okay, hon." She gives me a motherly smile that hurts because it reminds me of Mum. "You take care, sweetie."

"Yeah." I force a quick smile, then end the call, dropping the iPad facedown on my bed. Gently nudging it away with my toe, I grab my phone and hold it like it's precious.

Jonas: Got something fun planned for you, China Girl. Can you make it out tonight?

A smile spreads across my face while tears I didn't even know I was holding slip out of my eyes. I slash them away, annoyed that my vision is getting blurred.

The phone vibrates in my hand again.

Jonas: We're going to Hamilton Gardens for dinner. Meeting there around 6:30. There's live music and food trucks. You can meet my friends.

I don't love the whole friends part. I'd rather hang out with just Jonas, but it would be good to meet some more people before school starts.

With a decisive sniff, I quickly reply.

Me: Parents should be cool with it.

. . .

Jonas: We can pick you up.

Me: No, I'll meet you. I've got my restricted, so I can drive.

Jonas: Okay. Do you know where to go?

Me: Maps will guide me. Where exactly should I meet you?

Jonas: I'll wait for you near the main parking area. You'll see me.

Me: Sweet! See you soon.

I jump up and scramble to get my stuff ready, pulling out clothes and making quick decisions. It's a first date, yes, but it's also a date with his friends. I want to get my look right. It needs to be a little sexy, but also casual, like I've thrown stuff on without really thinking too hard about it. Like I look gorgeous without really trying.

Running for the shower, I'm relieved to find it's free and for once don't have to fight the length. Six thirty is not that far away, and I don't want to be late.

Applying a little makeup, I step back from the mirror and adjust the shoestring straps on my orange top. It hugs my body perfectly, showing off my shape. The jean shorts I've paired it with sit low on my hips, and you can see just a little of my stomach.

"Yeah, good." I nod and spin to find the new sandals I bought in Auckland.

Slipping them on, I do one more quick appraisal, happy with my choice to leave my blonde locks long and wild. They tickle my bare shoulders, and I kind of love that feeling.

Creeping to the top of the stairs, I pull in a breath and run through the speech I worked on while showering.

Mumbling it under my breath, I walk down the stairs and pop into the living area with a bright smile. Willow's sitting on the couch, her feet tucked under her as she watches the news with Beck. Tane and Harper are in the kitchen. They're not really talking, just quietly working side by side. The smell of frying onions and freshly barbecued sausages tickles my taste buds, but I ignore my hunger and waltz into the lounge.

"Can I borrow the car, please?"

Beck's eyes shoot toward me. "Why? Where are you going?"

I dip my hip, oozing out the casual vibes and hitching

my right shoulder. "I met some people in town yester-day. They've invited me out."

"Some people?" Beck pauses the TV and turns to face me properly. "Who are they?"

"Uh, this guy called Jonas and his friends. They go to North Ridge High."

"Tane?" Beck calls into the kitchen. "You know some guy named Jonas from North Ridge?"

Tane saunters past the dining room table, drying his hands on a tea towel. "Uh, yeah, maybe. Jonas Kerrig-an?" He looks at me.

I shrug. "I don't know his last name."

Beck scoffs. "But you're going out for dinner with him? When you don't even know his surname?"

"You don't exchange surnames when you meet some-one, Beck."

"I do."

"Yeah, well, you're like fifty."

His eyebrows bunch together. "I'm forty-seven."

I start picking at the frayed edge of the couch and mumble, "That's nearly fifty."

Tane snickers and tries to help me out. "I'm pretty sure he's Year 12."

"He is." I nod.

Beck's still frowning. "He trouble?"

"Not that I know of." Tane shakes his head, then flashes me a quick wink.

My lips flirt with a smile, and I think I love Tane more than I ever have. He's like a cool older brother or something. I could seriously bear hug him for helping me out on this one.

"Hmmm." Beck scratches his beard, staring at the paused TV. "So, it's a group of you, then?"

I nod, hope starting to tingle in my rib cage. "I want to get to know some people before school starts. I'm assuming you'll be sending me to North Ridge?"

"Yeah." Beck frowns as if this has only just occurred to him, yet another thing to have to organize. "And where are you meeting them?"

"Hamilton Gardens. There's live music and food trucks or something."

"Gourmet in the Gardens," Tane murmurs. "I keep meaning to go check it out. It's supposed to be pretty cool."

"Well, do you want to go with her?" Beck points between us.

My eyes bulge and I throw a look at Tane. I'm hoping it says, *No offense, but don't you dare say yes.*

I might love him for backing me up, but that doesn't mean I want him chaperoning me.

Tane's lips twitch and he shakes his head. "Nah, I'm too tired to drag my ass out tonight. She'll be okay, won't she?"

Beck finally nods after a heavy sigh, then points to the stairs. "Well, you better go get changed, then."

"What?" I look down at my carefully selected outfit. "No, I'm ready, I just need the keys."

Beck's eyebrows rise slowly, and for a moment I wonder how high they'll get before they stop. His forehead is completely bunched when he points at me. "You're not going in that."

"Yes I am. What's wrong with this? It's shorts and a T-shirt."

"Those are not shorts!" Beck stands up and waves his finger at them. "I can see the pockets hanging down past the hem thingy."

"That's the fashion." I tug at the hem, trying to make the shorts just a touch longer.

"If you bend over, I'll see way more than I want to. Your butt cheeks are basically showing!"

I roll my eyes, having had this conversation with my parents on a few occasions. Old people. Honestly. They just don't get it. "Would you relax. This is what I wear."

"I doubt Richie would be happy with me sending you off like that."

My nostrils flare, hating that he's bringing Dad into this. Gritting my teeth, I try to keep my voice calm. "He let me wear whatever I wanted. You're not my dad, Beck."

A thick pulse of tension beats through the room.

Willow's staring at the TV with wide eyes, and there's no longer a clatter or sizzle in the kitchen.

I refuse to turn around and find everyone staring at me, so I train my eyes on the big bear. I'm not backing down on this one. If I have to, I'll run out that door and call Jonas to come get me. I can start walking for Hamilton Gardens if I have to.

Beck's shoulders suddenly sag, and he mutters something under his breath while running a hand over the top of his head. "Fine. I'm not your dad, but I *am* your guardian, and I want you home by ten. You've just got your restricted license, right? Let me see it." He holds out his hand, and I'm forced to pull it from my back pocket and show him.

I took the test the day after we got back to New Zealand. Bianca and I both passed easily. Dad was pretty proud. I can still see his chuffed grin in my head. He had worked us hard in Suzhou, taking us out most days to make sure we were ready.

Beck studies the newly acquired license carefully, and I start to groan when he takes too long. "I'm gunna be late."

Handing it back with a grunt, he gives me a steely look. "Ten o'clock. And no passengers in the car."

"Yeah, yeah, fine. I'll see you at ten." I shove my license into my pocket and click my fingers for the keys.

Beck heads to the kitchen and grabs them out of the bowl for me. "This is for the little run-around, not the ute."

I nod, grateful when I finally curl my fingers around the keys.

"Go slow on the country roads." Beck's voice cracks, and I look up with surprise.

His forehead is still wrinkled, his brown eyes swirling with concern. He's worried about me. That's actually kind of sweet.

I swallow, not wanting to feel anything other than excitement for the evening ahead.

Forcing a smile, I assure him, "I've been learning to drive in China. If I can survive that, I should be able to drive anywhere."

"Country roads are different. You have to take it easy."

"I will. I promise."

He swallows. "See you at ten, then."

"Okay." I skip out the door, feeling truly liberated. I'm about to escape it all.

Jonas and his friends know nothing about my parents, my sister, the fact that I now live with a guardian. I can be whoever I want tonight. I can be the girl I was in China—carefree and living life to the max.

26

TANE

The treadmill hums beneath my feet, and I increase the pace for my last ten minutes. I try my best to keep up my fitness levels between seasons. Working on the farm helps, and so does the touch rugby, but Coach has already hinted that he wants me for team captain this year, which means I need to put in my best performance.

It's my final year of high school—Year 13—I've already been made a prefect and being captain of the First Fifteen would be the icing on the cake. Students are going to be looking to me for direction, I'm not going to let them down by slacking off.

Pumping my arms, I keep my breathing even, enjoying the rhythmic, steady beat of running. It's so automatic and gives me a chance to think about other stuff. This gym I've been setting up in the garage for the last couple of years is my sanctuary.

Beck suggested it when I got into the first fifteen Year 11. I was one of the youngest players on the squad, and Beck wanted to give me every advantage he could, so we started searching on TradeMe for secondhand gym equipment. Cam pitched in too, and we were soon working out together four times a week. Then, of course, we just kept adding stuff. There's now a pool table, a drinks fridge, a long couch. It's our pad and the first place Cam and I will hang out when he comes over.

He's usually here about four or five times a week, and I kind of miss him. He's due back from his holiday any day now. He's the only friend I don't mind stopping by.

I've kind of kept my other mates at bay while we've had guests here. They were here when Beck got the call on New Year's Eve. They know what happened, and others have been texting me after hearing the news. They seem to understand that I can't really go into detail (I'll give them the low down when school goes back) and they've all been cool when I've said I can't hang out.

I'm needed here right now. Beck will never hold me back, but I think he quietly appreciates the fact that I've basically become his farmhand since school got out.

He's going to have to hire someone new before February, though. There's no way one man can run this farm single-handedly. He can get in a relief milker for a while, but permanent would be better. The old cottage is empty thanks to Grant being an asshole, so it's ready and waiting for someone new.

I'm pretty sure Beck's looking into it, but he's got a lot on his plate right now. Poor guy. The look on his face when Stacey waltzed out of the house in those short-shorts. I almost felt bad for helping her out, but I could sense how much she wanted to go.

If she's sticking around, which it seems she is, then I really need to get her onside. I can imagine she's a dynamite when she's pissed. She needs an ally in the house, although I don't want to go against Beck either. I'll just have to negotiate the ground carefully, be the friendly bridge over tense waters.

My lips dip into a frown as I wipe the sweat off my forehead and up the pace again.

Harper's been tense the last two days. I don't know what happened.

One minute we were flirting over coffee and laughing about pink gumboots, and then it's like a light switched off and she shut down.

I wish she'd talk to me, but she's gone into a mode of polite smiles and shallow conversation. When I tried to push her this morning, teasing her just a little, she actually snapped at me.

I backed off after that and gave her some space. I've learned from my mother that you don't go messing with a woman's moods. I hate myself for thinking it, but maybe she's, you know, in that time of the month or something. Maybe she has a headache or a sore stomach and is just too embarrassed to say anything.

Or maybe it's everything else piling up around her. Like the fact that she's heading back to Wellington with two siblings she's probably not ready to look after. I mean, she can cook and clean and look after a house. That's obvious. And it's like she *needs* to do it too. That girl cannot sit down and relax, always pottering, but is that because she's dodging a case of the unhappies?

Like if she stops for a moment, it'll all catch up with her and she'll be hit full force with the weight of her future.

Shit, I wish she'd just stay.

We could help her through this.

But she won't stop talking about how they're leaving for Wellington soon. It's like she wants the world to know she's got a plan and she'll be damned if life is going to get in the way of that.

I don't get it.

Wellington just sounds like hard work to me. Why leave a support network?

She's probably got support in Wellington. You're not the only person in her life.

I scowl at the thought and keep pushing, my chest getting tight as I sprint the last kilometer.

Just when I think my legs are about to give out, I slam the Stop button and quickly ease from a run to a walk. The machine is just winding to a stop when my phone starts ringing. I answer it without checking the screen and immediately regret my decision.

"Oh, so you are alive, then." Mum's sharp voice makes me wince. "Finally. You're finally going to hear me out, ay?"

I don't know what to say, so I just breathe into the phone and consider hanging up, but that would be so harsh. Even though I'm pissed, I still can't bring myself to do it.

"Why are you puffing?"

"Just been on the treadmill." I step off it and head to the mini fridge, pulling out a cold water bottle.

"It's nearly nine at night. Why are you running now?"

"Because I needed to." I swipe a droplet off my lip and punch the cap down. "I like to keep my base fitness up so it's not such a killer when the season starts."

Mum makes a noise of approval. "How are things?"

I frown and run a hand through my sweaty hair. "What do you want, Mum?"

"To find out how my boy's doing," she snaps. "Is that a crime or something? You're my son!"

I sigh and perch my hip against the pool table. "I'm good. Life's busy. We're repainting the garage."

"Oh, yeah, good. That needed doing."

I nod and try to think of something else that doesn't involve me saying Beck's name.

"When are you coming down?"

"Mum." I squeeze my eyes shut. "I told you. I'm not moving to Upper Hutt."

"You belong with me."

"No!" I hit the eight ball, watching it smack into the yellow one before rolling to the edge. "This is my place. My home! I'm not leaving it just because you got horny and crossed a line."

"Hey!" she barks at me. "Show some respect."

"Respect? You want to talk about respect? The way you treated Beck was unbelievable!"

"You don't know the whole story, boy. Don't go judging me without all the facts."

"You were having an affair! Cheating on Beck, who saved our lives. How could you do that to him?"

"He's not as perfect as you think! You didn't see it all. You don't know the whole story."

"Whatever, Mum," I bark, anger roaring through me. "You hurt him."

She scoffs. "I doubt that."

The hot anger freezes halfway up my throat. It's replaced with a cold blast of confusion. What the hell does she mean by that?

Of course she hurt him. He's been sad.

Is she seriously implying that her affair didn't touch him?

She's full of shit.

I nearly tell her but catch the words just in time and manage to mutter, "I've gotta go."

"Tane, please." Mum's voice is firm. "I'm your mum. You can't stay mad at me forever."

"Watch me," I grit out before hanging up and slapping my phone onto the green felt.

27

STACEY

Finding Hamilton Gardens is a cinch, despite the fact that the country roads are way more intimidating than I thought they would be. I was supposed to be going 100km per hour, but I ended up puttering along at around 80. I'm used to driving the streets of Suzhou, which are chaotic with e-bikes and pedestrians who never check before crossing. You have to be alert in a whole different way. Country roads are quiet, but they're fast, and you never know what's around the next corner.

Maps leads me through Gate One, and as soon as I drive down the steep slope toward the parked cars, I spot Jonas standing on the corner of the grass embankment, just like he said he would be.

I grin at him and then follow the parking warden's pointing finger. I'm directed to a patch of grass about three rows back. It's busy. The car park is completely full, which is why I had to park on the grass. By the time I check my appearance in the rearview mirror, Jonas has run over to open the door for me.

"Hey, China Girl."

Squee! I love the way he says my nickname, drawing it out like it tastes sweet.

"Hi." I grin and lock the car.

"Easy drive?"

"Yeah, sweet as. Didn't get lost once."

With a gorgeous smile, he takes my hand and weaves me through the cars until we're walking up the grassy slope and then down toward a pond.

I can hear music in the distance, and my insides start to kick with pleasure. Jonas is still holding my hand, his strong fingers curling around mine. It's like we're a couple. Anyone passing by us will assume it, and I kind of totally love that.

Jonas is hot, and I need a hand to hold right now. I'm aware I barely know the guy, but I shove that hesitation away, determined to be in this moment.

"Turtles," Jonas points out as we walk across the bridge.

A bunch of them are perched on a log, stretching their necks out to the evening sun.

"They're cute." I laugh and we stop to count them, spotting five altogether.

"Oh, and one in the water." Jonas points.

"Good spotting." I nudge him with my hip.

He bites his lower lip, his eyes gleaming with what I think is appreciation. He's totally into the way I look tonight.

Yes! Outfit choice is a success.

"Come on," he whispers close to my ear and gently tugs me over the rest of the bridge. As soon as we touch the other side and start up the hill, the music kicks in way louder and I grin, bobbing my head to an acoustic version of an Ed Sheeran song. I can't remember what it's called, but Bianca loves it.

Man, she'd love this whole thing. Live music. Delicious food.

The smells from the various food trucks tickle my taste buds, and I can picture Bianca and me walking up this hill, both excited in our different ways. Me jumping like a rabbit, her shy smile and affectionate green gaze. She thought I was nuts, but she loved me.

Not anymore, though.

My shoulders tense and I swallow, gripping Jonas's hand and fighting off the fist inside of me. The one that's squeezing and hurting.

Gazing around, I take in the awesome atmosphere. Picnic blankets and camping chairs dot the massive green. Everyone from toddlers to grandparents is spread across the expanse. Even a few happy dogs are lying in the center of their family circle. Bordering the crowd is a long line of gourmet food trucks. A plethora of ethnicities is represented, and my mouth starts watering as I wonder what I'll eat tonight. Sushi? Or maybe a Turkish kebab, or oooo! French pancakes!

"There they are." Jonas points and we wind our way through the crowd, stopping next to a large blanket littered with five teens, all cut from the same cloth as Jonas. Ripped jeans, wild hair, casual smiles.

I like it.

"Guys, this is Stacey." Jonas introduces me, and I forget names as quickly as he says them.

"Hey." I wave at everyone.

"'Sup?" The guy in the back corner raises his eyebrows at me before sharing a quick look with Jonas.

Leon, was it? Or maybe Leo.

I have no idea what they're silently saying to each other, but I hope it's something good.

The sweet girl tucked under his arm gives me a kind smile. I reciprocate and take a seat when she pats the blanket next to her.

"Luka," she reminds me, and I give her a grateful smile while Leo… Leon?… hands me a Coke bottle.

"Thanks." I take a big gulp and immediately start coughing.

The guys next to Jonas chortle while Jonas pats my back.

"Sorry, should have warned you. Leon never hands out straight Coke."

"Rum?" I rasp.

"My favorite." Leon wiggles his eyebrows at me.

Not wanting to look like a muppet, I take another swig, just to prove I can handle my liquor.

I haven't ever been full-blown drunk before, but we bring beers and mixers to our parties. Rum's not my favorite. I'm more of a lemon and vodka girl, but this is fine.

Everything's fine.

I'm happy.

Life is good.

"So, China Girl…" Leon smirks at me. "What's your story?"

The fist inside me bunches, but I try to play it cool. "What story?"

"Aw, come on. Why are you now in the Tron?"

"The Tron?"

"It's a nickname for Hamilton," Luka explains, tucking a dark wave of hair behind her ear. "I don't even know where it comes from, but Hamilton. Hamil*tron*. I don't know. The Tron."

I grin. "The Tron. I like it."

"So, why you here?" Leon licks his glistening Coke lips and gives me a pointed look.

I'm not sure how I feel about this guy. He's strong in this quiet, slightly sinister way.

Sinister seems too strong, but there's just something…

I focus on the black lines of tartan blanket beneath me and shrug. "Family moved back. My parents used to live here when they first got married and stuff. So, here we are."

"To the armpit of New Zealand." The guy directly opposite me raises his bottle, while the girl next to him laughs and gives him a little shove.

Dee. Her name's Dee.

"Nico, it's not that bad."

"It's boring as. I can't wait to get out of this dump."

"Oooo, and go to the big city?" Dee rolls her eyes, then winks at me.

I smile back, enjoying the banter around me. These guys are obviously tight. Hopefully I can fit in without a hitch and start the new school year with some friends. I wouldn't mind sharing lunch with this group each day.

"So, it's just you and your parents?" Leon asks.

"And my sister."

Shit! I shouldn't have said that.

"Is she the redhead or the tall brunette?" Jonas rests his hand behind my back, drawing his face close to mine. "I saw you with them at the supermarket."

My heart trills as his breath warms my neck. "The…the redhead. She's not here right now. She's in Australia."

Double shit! Why am I saying this stuff?

"Aussie. Nice." Leon raises his eyebrows. "Why didn't you go?"

My nose wrinkles as I scramble for something to say. "Oh, she's just staying with my grandmother, who is a complete cow. I refused to go."

"But your sister went? Is she a sucker for punishment or something?" Nico laughs.

I bite the edge of my lip, wondering how much to say. "We're opposites. We drive each other crazy. She got over sharing a room with me and decided to spend some time in a different country. I don't get her. At all." I force out a laugh but can't ignore the niggle of guilt for shedding Bianca in such a bad light. I'm making it sound like her leaving has nothing to do with me.

I wish it didn't.

Why'd she have to react so freaking badly?

Riku's just some sleazy guy. She should be grateful I made him show his true colors before he hurt her even more.

"What do your parents think?" Leon keeps up this so-not-awesome interrogation.

I swallow, distracted by my inner argument which doesn't seem as powerful as it did the day she left. Shit, Mum and Dad would be gutted about how things have gone down.

That's the first time I've actually let thoughts of their reaction factor into my thinking. I've been so busy trying to push them out of my mind.

Pull it together, Stace! They asked you a question. If you cry, I'm gunna kill you. Be cool!

I tip my head up to the blue sky and scoff, "They always side with her."

"Hearin' ya," Nico spits. "I hate my stupid sisters, and my perfect little brother. I stay away from home as much as possible."

"Totes! Family sucks!" Dee tinks her bottle with his. "Same for you, right, Jonas?"

"Abso-frickin'-lutely." He snickers. "My family's insane. I can't do one thing right for my dad. Ever. And now that my sisters have left home, it's even worse, because all the attention is on me and what a letdown I am." He shuffles closer and swings his arm around my neck, pulling me against him and kissing my hair. "You're in good company, China Girl. We've got your back."

I smile and relax against his body. He's so freaking fine.

"Who needs family when you've got friends." Leon smirks and raises his bottle. Everyone cheers and I join them, smiling as I immerse myself fully into this moment.

Slugging back my drink, I feel myself start to relax even more as we talk about other stuff. I listen mostly and pitch in when I have something useful to say. We share laughs, and then it's food time.

Jonas has to borrow money off Leon, because Jonas's dad is a complete tightass.

"I have to earn every frickin' dollar he gives me, and it's barely shit," he grumbles. "Two days a week at his stupid law firm filing documents. Boring as hell, and he doesn't even give me minimum wage."

"You know I've always got you, man." Leon dishes out two twenties and we saunter off, Jonas holding my hand again and treating me like his girl.

We share a plate of loaded fries, and then I offer to shout everyone an ice cream.

"You da best, Stacey girl!" Nico shouts at me while I line up behind the frozen yogurt truck.

Leon and Jonas come with me, Jonas holding out one of Leon's pre-mixed Coke bottles.

"Thanks." I take it but am stopped by Leon's hand on my arm.

"Aren't you driving home?"

"Oh, shit, forgot." Jonas snatches the bottle out of my hands and gulps it back.

He gets through nearly half of it before letting out a satisfied burp and grinning down at me. "Can you drop me home after this?"

"Of course." I laugh and shake my head. He's too cute.

His arm comes around my shoulders again, and the happiness continues.

I know I'm technically not supposed to have passengers unless I'm accompanied by a fully licensed driver, but as long as we don't get caught, it'll be sweet as. I'm just dropping him home, not driving him up to Auckland.

After ice creams, we head for the playground and mess around on the swings and jungle gym. The guys act like idiots, pretending to be superheroes as they dangle off the equipment and yell stupid stuff into the night air.

It's nearly completely dark now. The sun set about half an hour ago, and I should probably think about heading home. I told Beck ten, and I shouldn't be late if I want any chance of borrowing the car again.

"I'll save you, Dee!" Nico hollers, launching off the top of the jungle gym and landing with an "Oof."

Dee giggles, swaying over to him and dropping to her knees beside him.

"Kiss me," he groans. "It's the only way you're gunna save me."

"As if." She slaps his chest and rises with another laugh. "Weren't you supposed to be saving me?"

"Oh yeah." He sits up, scratching his head and letting out a dopey chuckle.

Aw, man, I really don't want to leave. I want this happy, giddy idiocy to last all night, but...

"Hey, we should probably go. The gates get locked at nine thirty." Jonas swaggers over to me, perching his arm on my shoulder. "Okay, see ya later, losers."

"'Night, asshole." Nico salutes him while the girls giggle and wave at me. "Nice to meet you, Stacey."

"Same." I laugh and wave to everyone, smiling at Leon, who smirks at me.

I swallow and turn away, still undecided on the guy.

He oozes out this weird vibe that I can't figure out. I mean, he must be nice because he stopped me from drinking and driving. I'll be sweet after that Coke from hours ago, but I wouldn't have if I'd kept downing the drinks like Jonas did.

But I don't know. There's something about his intense stare that's really off-putting.

"So, what'd you think?" Jonas presses his forehead on the top of my head as we saunter along.

I wrap my arm around his waist. "That was cool."

"Yeah, my friends are pretty awesome."

"How long have you guys been hanging out together?"

"Me and Leon go way back. We used to live next door to each other, and when we moved, I still saw him at school, so it was all good. I hang at his place as much as I can."

"So, his parents don't suck?"

"His parents are checked out. They're so busy making money, they're barely ever there. He basically has the house to himself. You'll see. We'll end up there soon enough."

"Nice," I whisper, not sure if I really mean it.

Jonas sighs, his body swaying against mine as we make our way through the dark park, "I really like you, China Girl. You're hot. So freaking hot."

I giggle. "Thanks."

"And I like your laugh, and your smile. And you were nice to my friends."

"Tick, tick, tick?"

He chuckles and pulls us both to a stop on the bridge. The moonlight glints off the water, trailing a path toward us. I glance away from it when Jonas rests his hands on either side of my face.

"Big ticks all 'round." He smiles and I grin back, my heart picking up pace as he slowly leans toward me.

His thumb brushes the edge of my cheek while his fingers lightly curl into my hair.

Oh, this feels so good and his lips haven't even touched mine yet.

I'm practically floating as our breaths mingle together. His nose slides against mine, pausing for just a moment before closing the gap.

The second our lips connect, I lean into him, gripping the edges of his shirt and rising to my tiptoes so I can deepen the kiss.

He moans in approval and my hands glide up his back, suctioning our bodies together. Tipping his head, he invites me in with a little flick of his tongue. I eagerly seek out his sweet taste, loving the rum and Coke flavor coating my mouth.

And he thinks I'm so hot.

He has no idea.

I move my arms to wrap around his neck as his hands glide down my body. He gently cups my butt before sliding his hands back up to wrap me in a secure hug.

I need this.

I so need this.

I have no idea how long we kiss for, but when he pulls away and smiles at me, I feel like I've been thrown into the heart of a romantic movie.

"This year is going to be a thousand times better because of you."

"Ditto," I whisper and lean back in for another mind-blowing, totally distracting kiss.

28

TANE

Beck's pacing, his large bare feet thumping across the wooden floor by the dining room table.

It's 9:50 p.m.

Stacey's got ten minutes. I'm pretty sure if she doesn't walk through that door on time, Beck's gunna take the ute to Hamilton Gardens and start hunting.

Poor guy. I hide my smile behind my hand and try to focus on the cricket game. I'm not really a cricket guy. Rugby's more my thing, but New Zealand is playing Australia, and I'll pretty much watch any sport there is.

Oh man, I hope we win.

Losing to Australia sucks. I don't know why, but of all the teams in the world, they're the hardest to lose to. I guess it's just a Tasman rivalry thing.

Trent Boult runs in with a fast ball. It's a pretty good

delivery, but the batter still connects and manages to sneak between the fielders for a four. I wince as the Aussie crowd goes ballistic.

"Come on, boys," I mutter under my breath, quietly cheering the Black Caps on.

Turning back to Beck, I figure I'd rather watch him pace than us lose. At this stage, the game could go either way.

Maybe if I don't watch for a while, we'll get a wicket. Turning the volume down, I shift in my chair as Beck passes the bottom of the stairwell. My thoughts immediately shift to Harper. She escaped up there about thirty minutes ago, feigning exhaustion. At least I think she was pretending. We have been working pretty hard, but I couldn't help thinking it was an excuse to get away from me.

She's pulled ever further away today, and I have no idea what to do about it. It's weird, but it makes me think of my mum and how far I've pulled away from her.

I'm kind of a prick for doing that to her, but I'm pissed off!

What did she mean about me not knowing the whole story? About Beck not being as perfect as I think he is?

The big guy mumbles something under his breath.

"What?" I ask.

"Richie always wanted daughters. When we'd talk about the future, he always wanted to raise girls. He was so stoked when they were born. Me? I wanted boys. I got my boys." His voice cracks, but then he clears his throat as if he's ramming thoughts of Matt and Charlie to the back recesses of his mind. "I don't know what to do with girls. I couldn't even keep them together! I still don't know if I should have let Bianca go. She says she's happy, but is she really? Twins should stay together, right? They're family!" His hands fly up like wings before thumping back down against his thighs. "And those shorts. Aw, mate, you saw those shorts, right? With the pockets flapping out?"

It was hard to not notice them. With Stacey's tanned, toned legs, a guy would have to be blind not to appreciate how good she looked. Maybe I shouldn't have tried to be so helpful in getting her out the door.

"She said it's the fashion." I quietly try to make it better, then wonder if that's even helped.

Beck scrapes shaking fingers through his hair. "That Jonas kid better have watched his hands." He checks his watch. "Richie's gunna kill me. I shouldn't have let her go. I should've—"

The sound of a car coming up the drive makes Beck jump, his eyes popping wide as he rushes to the window and pulls the curtain aside.

"Thank God," he whispers.

He sags against the wall and Stacey opens the door, humming her way into the house.

She jolts to a stop when she spots us both staring at her.

"What?" She looks between us.

I just smile. "You're home."

She pulls out her phone, glances at the screen and looks at Beck, kind of bewildered. "On time. You said ten."

Beck pats his chest, then points at her, trying for a smile. It's hard to see within his beard, but it's there, subtle yet relieved.

Stacey rolls her eyes. "Please tell me you haven't been pacing. For one, I have a phone. You can text anytime to check in with me. Secondly, I'm not dumb enough to break curfew the first time you let me borrow your car."

Beck nods and stands tall, crossing his arms like he's trying to hold his composure. "Have a good time?"

She tips her head with a dreamy grin. "I had an amazing time."

"What does that face mean?" Beck points at her, his composure cracking. "You didn't make out in the back seat of his car or anything, did you? You said you were with a group. I wouldn't have let you go if it was just you and him."

She holds up her hands. "Beck, I didn't make out in the back of his car."

I narrow my eyes at her, noting the slight blush on her cheeks. Oh, she made out somewhere. I need to check this Jonas guy out. I wonder if Manu knows him. He's a teammate, already pegged for one of the wing positions this year. He's faster than the Flash and a damn good rugby player. He's also in the same year as Jonas. I'll give the guy a text tomorrow, see what he knows.

Beck's studying Stacey too, looking kind of worried when he softly asks. "But you were... you know, good?"

She giggles. "Of course I was."

Her flirty wink makes me wonder, but I don't say anything as she skips for the stairs.

"You're going to make my hair turn gray, aren't you?" Beck calls after her.

She laughs again and calls back, "I'll do my best!"

Beck flops onto the couch adjacent to me and throws me an agonized frown. "I don't know if I'm cut out for this, mate."

With an encouraging smile, I lean forward and slap his knee. "You're the best dad I've ever had. I know you say Richie was a legend and it'd be way better if he was here, but he's not. You are." My words make Beck shudder, but I keep going anyway. "You're gunna be enough. You taking charge the last couple of days... that's worked. Lance and Richie kept you in their wills for a reason. You're the best guy I know."

His brown eyes light with a grateful smile. He doesn't say anything, just squeezes my hand and sniffs.

Another roar goes up from the TV as the Aussie batter hits a six.

I groan and tip my head back. "Seriously? I'm going to bed."

Beck forces out a chuckle. "Just turn it off, mate. We'll find out the score in the morning."

I grab the remote and put a stop to the agony.

"'Night, then."

"See you at five thirty." Beck holds out his palm, and I give it a slap as I walk past.

Mum's full of shit.

How can anyone not adore Beckett Connell?

How can she possibly not think he's perfect? Especially when you compare him to my real dad.

My muscles coil as a memory tries to eat me alive, but I snap my eyes shut and will it away.

Gripping the railing, I glance back into the lounge. Beck's unaware that I'm watching as he pulls a letter from his pocket and carefully opens it.

I wonder if it's the letter the lawyer gave him. I wonder what it says.

Beck pinches his nose and then sniffs as though he's fighting tears. I quietly leave, figuring he's probably after some privacy.

Creeping up to my room, I sneak past Stacey's door and notice her light is still on. She's humming, and I'm happy for her that she had a good night. She'll no doubt be gunning for another one soon.

Hopefully it'll get easier on Beck.

His mates are asking a lot of him, but surely they wouldn't have kept him as a guardian if they didn't think he was capable. Although, they probably never expected to have their lives cut so short either.

But even so…

I don't know what the hell Mum is on about.

She's deluded. Beck is the best man in the world.

I refuse to believe anything else.

29

STACEY

I manage to hum the entire time I'm stripping off my clothes and getting into my pajamas. I hum as I brush my teeth, smile at myself in the mirror, remembering the thrill of Jonas's tongue in my mouth, his heady taste, his wandering hands.

It is kind of fast, I guess. One date and we're already groping each other.

But it felt right. Addictive. Completely distracting.

And I need that right now.

I hope he texts again soon. If not, I might have to text him for a Jonas fix.

The idea makes me giggle, goose bumps rising on my arms as I relive his hands gliding up my back and into my hair.

He's something special.

I know it even after only one date.

I don't think I've buzzed this hard after making out with a guy before.

Slipping beneath my sheet, I roll onto my side and stare at the empty bed. The buzz inside of me rapidly fades. The covers of Bianca's bed are pulled military tight, not a wrinkle in them. I can picture my sister making it. I can picture her lying in it, rolling over with a sleepy smile and softly asking, "How was it?"

"It was great," I whisper. "Jonas's friends seem cool, and he is such a good kisser." My soft laughter falls into the empty room but is quickly sucked into the black shadows over Bianca's bed.

I miss her.

The pain sears through me, burning holes in places I don't want to be feeling.

Reaching for my phone, I open WhatsApp and stare at Bianca's name. We'd always text each other through WhatsApp. Sometimes during school, I'd text her when I was bored in class, or we'd send a message to each other at home when we wanted to say something we didn't want Mum or Dad to hear.

I flick through our last thread, remembering it clearly. We were sitting in Shanghai airport, waiting for our flight to board. Dad was playing GardenScapes on his phone, Mum was flicking through a fashion magazine and Bianca sent me a message.

B: PINEAPPLE!

That was our code word for whenever we saw something crazy funny. It happened a lot in China. I sat up in my chair, scanning the people around me and struggling to hold in my laughter when a short guy in skintight leather pants, a mink coat and aviator shades strolled past.

Me: Oooo - he thinks he is so hot right now.

B: Look at the boots!

I bit my lips together, my insides quaking with laughter as I took in his shiny red boots with the pointed toes.

Me: Personally, I'm loving the frosted tips.

Bianca giggled, her thumbs typing furiously as she sent me a reply.

And that's how we spent the rest of our time until we had to board the plane.

My eyes burn at the abruptness of the ending. Mum would have told us to hurry up and put our phones away while gathering all the hand luggage and making sure no one forgot anything.

She would have asked Dad to check under the seats, and I can't exactly remember, but I probably shoved my phone away and that was that.

I didn't know we wouldn't be WhatsApp-ing again.

I was clueless to what awaited us in New Zealand.

Maybe if I'd known, I would have treasured that moment more. I would have hugged Mum a little harder when she left for their South Island trip. I would have let Dad kiss me on the cheek instead of telling him I was too old for that now.

I wouldn't have made out with Riku at the Christmas party.

Gritting my teeth, I flop onto my back and stare up at the ceiling, trying to conjure that joy from just hours ago. I want to go back to the tipsy laughter, the goofing off on the playground, the romantic make-out session by the pond. But none of the memories seem enough.

I want to shout, "Screw family! I just need these new friends!"

But still…it won't be enough.

Tears build inside me, slowly rising until my stomach is trembling with the effort to fight them. With a soft whimper, I curl onto my side.

Bianca was always there at the end of any date, ready for me to dissect each moment, softly smiling at my loved-up swooning, laughing at the funny way I'd retell each detail.

But now, after having one of the best dates of my life— having made out with the hottest guy I've ever known, having had this ultimate, amazing experience—she's not here to share it with.

I could text her, but she doesn't want to know me right now.

Because I screwed up.

I squeeze my eyes shut against the acknowledgment.

I don't want to be a bad person. I don't want to hurt my sister. I don't want to live without my parents.

The truths scratch at me, making sleep impossible to capture.

All I can do is cry into my pillow and pray for oblivion to take the uglies away.

30

HARPER

The sky is overcast and gray today. No blue, just a bleak, shadowed version of the sun.

It suits my mood, I guess.

My frown seems to be permanently in place at the moment, and I wish it wasn't, but I don't know how to change it. I hate feeling this unsettled.

I don't want to be here.

A chicken struts past my foot, bawking and pecking the ground as I throw grains into the yard. I also brought out some stale bread, which they're happily devouring.

I'm feeding chickens.

I sigh, my shoulders feeling heavy as I try to shake off a bad night's sleep. I would have been fine if Alaina hadn't texted me just after I turned the light out.

It was a photo of her and Zoey, dolled up and heading out to a club. They looked gorgeous, and jealousy ripped through me like a toxic virus. I tried to roll over and go to sleep, but I obviously didn't really mean it because I kept the phone in my hand and it vibrated throughout the night.

New texts and pics. A short video.

"You should be here with us, Harp! We miss you!"

"I miss you too," I'd whispered, yearning to be transported off the farm and back into the life I was supposed to be having.

Instead, this week has been all about scraping, sanding, painting, cooking, washing—acting like a mother to a family I never even asked for!

After my reckless flirt with Tane, the realization dump that followed was brutal.

Mum will never be a phone call away again. She's never going to *be* here again, and I have to rearrange my life. This isn't just some holiday on a farm. This is my new reality. When I leave this place and go back to Wellington, I still don't know if I can head out clubbing with my girls. I'll have two siblings to look after. Sure, I can leave them at home on their own now—Willow's old enough to babysit—but I'll take them with me in my mind.

They are *my* responsibility now.

How can I possibly entertain something with Tane, act like I'm some carefree girl when I'm not? I'm the furthest from carefree I can get. I don't have the right to a summer fling. I don't want a fling. I'm not that kind of girl. I don't flirt without thought, but Tane brought it out of me the other day, which is why I've had to back off.

It sucks. I can see that he's kind of hurt by it, but what am I supposed to do?

I'm not a country girl. I belong in the city.

Besides, it'd be weird to fall for someone who's still in high school. Yes, I've only just finished high school myself, but still. I'm moving into a new phase of my life. University, adulthood, the big future.

My shoulders droop, burdened by the fact that a thought that used to make me so excited now depresses me.

Laughter catches my attention, and I glance over my shoulder in time to see Beck and Oscar walking side by side. Beck scrubs the top of Oscar's head, and my brother smiles. Like actually smiles.

"You did great, mate. Those cows love ya."

Did he help with milking this morning?

What the hell?

Oscar continues to grin up at Beck as they head into the

house, chatting away like friends, and completely not noticing me.

"Morning, guys," I mutter darkly after they've walked inside, then throw out the last of the grain. The chickens go nuts chasing after it, and all I can do is stand there staring at them.

My forehead wrinkles as I think about leaving on Sunday. The long drive back is going to be painful, and I doubt Oscar will smile like that as we head home.

But we need to.

School is looming closer, and I have to get them organized. I haven't checked if Oscar's uniform still fits, and I need to find out when Willow's ballet classes resume.

There are school supplies to purchase, and I should probably start looking for a part-time job.

An image of us arriving home to a big empty house scorches me. Dad won't be in the kitchen, messing around with the blender as he comes up with some new smoothie concoction he found on the internet. Mum won't be humming to herself as she flicks through a glossy food magazine. The fridge won't be full of fresh produce.

That's my responsibility now.

Shit, I'm going to have to budget, to shop, to feed my siblings. School lunches.

Ugh! Do I have to make those? Or can I force them to do it? Mum always monitored that kind of stuff.

My muscles feel tight, my brain stretched thin as the myriad of tasks piles on top of me.

The phone in my pocket dings, and I pull it out. Zoey's sent me a picture of Alaina, who is completely out for the count. Her hair is a tousled bird's nest and her lips are a blurred, smeared mess of pink lipstick.

I let out a dry snicker and wish I had something witty to type back, but humor is off the cards for me today. And maybe every day for the rest of my life. How am I ever supposed to laugh again?

I want to go home.

I want to be with my girls!

I know these texts, this contact, is supposed to make me feel loved and missed and thought of, but all it does is either incite jealousy or make me want to jump in the car and just take off without my siblings.

The thought is a little tempting.

Mum and Dad *did* leave Beck as their guardian. I'm kind of within my rights to leave them here.

But I can't. How can I abandon them to go and live my life?

I'd be plagued with guilt.

No, they have to come with me. We're family. We need to stick together.

Rubbing my aching forehead, I walk to the coop and clear out the fresh eggs, cradling them inside the bottom of my T-shirt, which I've turned into a makeshift basket.

There are eight really big ones today.

No doubt everyone is expecting me to fry them up, feed the troops. Resentment stirs in my belly, and with a huff, I stomp out of the yard, managing to land my jandal in a healthy clump of chicken poo.

It squirts onto my foot, and I suck in a gasp. Biting my lips together, I feel the torrent of curse words bounce from one side of my brain to the other.

Will I seriously never learn? Why the hell didn't I shove my gumboots on?

Now my foot is splattered with poo, and my pretty white jandals with the sparkles on the straps are just as stained as my sneakers.

"Argh!" I scream and hobble back to the house.

Kicking off my jandals at the stairs, I lose my balance and manage to crack two of the eggs that are tucked inside my shirt.

Slimy egg whites and yellow yolks sink into the pale

pink cotton, sticking the shirt against my belly, feeling cold and disgusting.

"Shit!" I spit out. "Bloody chickens!" I drop a couple of F-bombs and Willow, who I didn't notice was standing in the laundry, lets out a shocked gasp.

Swearing wasn't permitted in our house, and Willow's obviously not used to hearing it spurt out of me.

I close my eyes and suck a breath in through my nose. Pushing past her, I dump the eggs into the kitchen sink, feeling a bizarre sense of satisfaction as they all break apart on impact.

Willow's staring at me, completely gob-smacked, but all I can do is scowl at her and thump up the stairs, not caring one bit if I end up leaving chicken poo tracks in my wake.

31

TANE

Rain's coming. I can smell it in the air.

I haven't checked the weather app today, but I never find it that accurate, so I'm going with my senses. With long, quick brushes, I try to finish up the last coat of paint on the garage. It's been drying really nicely, and if it can set before the rain arrives, then Beck will be happy.

It's been cool working on this project, having everyone out here pitching in.

It would have been better if Harper wasn't so grumpy about it. I want to go back to flirting over coffee, but I can't see that happening anytime soon. Especially after this morning.

My lips want to smile, but the expression becomes a grimace instead.

It's probably for the best that she's set on heading back to Wellington this weekend. She doesn't want to be here. That much is obvious.

What's the point of falling for a girl I can't have?

Man, romance is complicated. I'm not even in love and I know this.

All I have is a mild crush... or maybe a slightly intense crush. If I could just get her out of my head, I'd be fine. Once she leaves for Wellington, it'll be easier. I won't have to see her.

My cheeks heat with color, and I'm glad I'm out here alone.

Without her around, and then school starting, I'll get busy and distracted with other stuff. She'll eventually fade out of my mind.

My insides rebel against the idea, but I mutter a quick affirmation of "Get over it, man."

Slapping some more paint on the wall, I try to shake off her pull on me.

Unfortunately, that only opens up space in my brain for Mum. And that's something I *really* don't want to think about. I haven't told Beck I spoke with her a few nights ago. I definitely don't want him to know what we talked about. I don't want to bring up that shit like I'm calling him out or something.

He didn't do anything wrong.

At least I don't think he did.

With an irritated huff, I dump the paintbrush into the bucket and climb down from the ladder. Stepping back, I survey the last of my touch ups and am satisfied it'll do.

The garage is looking pretty fantastic and now matches the white farmhouse again. We did good.

A smile tugs my lips but doesn't genuinely form until I hear the rumble of a car engine and spot Cam bumping down our long driveway.

Finally! Some relief.

Grabbing the paint can, I walk up to meet him, actually giving him a hug when he steps out of his car.

"Whoa," he chuckles. "Bro, are you okay?" He slaps my back a couple of times.

I step back and nod. "Yeah, just good to see ya." His eyes narrow at the corners, but I shake my head and avoid the unspoken question. "So, how was the beach?"

With a slow nod, his eyebrows lift. "Yeah, good."

"And your dad?"

He tips his head with a light snicker. "He wasn't himself."

"So, better than good, then."

He laughs with me. "Yeah, it was pretty awesome. Peaceful. Bizarre."

His confused expression makes me laugh again, but he wipes out the sound with his next question.

"How's it going here?" His serious gaze tells me I can't get away with a dodge this time, so I hitch my left shoulder.

And then I sigh.

And then I tell him the truth.

"It's been shit, with a sprinkling of hope every now and then, but it always inevitably lands back on shit."

Cam winces with a light hiss.

"Yeah." I take my hat off and scratch my black mop. I need to get it cut before school goes back. I like it short, back and sides. The curls on top can do whatever the hell they want.

"Sorry it's so rough, mate. I guess you knew it would be."

"Yeah." I blow out a breath, not sure I knew it'd be this challenging.

An image of cracked eggs in the kitchen sink flashes through my mind.

"What happened here?" I'd asked Willow.

She just gave me an awkward cringe, and I knew it was

pointless trying to get anything out of her. She doesn't talk!

So I headed upstairs to find out if Oscar had thrown another hissy fit, but instead I bumped into a half-naked Harper, who was storming out of the bathroom. Her long hair was wet and tousled, draped over her bare shoulder. I jolted to a stop and that's when she saw me, letting out a little yelp before covering her sexy blue bra with the bundle of clothes in her hand.

"Shouldn't you be milking right now!" she yelled at me.

I was struck dumb, my eyes burning from the small but luscious curves I'd just witnessed. I probably looked like a complete idiot, trying not to get another peek at her body.

In the end, she just huffed and pushed past me.

I stumbled back a little and bumped into the wall, stealing a glance at her bare back and the way her hair swished against it as she retreated to her room, slamming the door behind her.

"Garage is looking good." Cam distracts me, and I'm grateful for the topic change.

We chat about it as I walk to the outside tap and rinse out the paintbrush. Resealing the paint can, I store it away and then invite Cam for lunch.

"You sure?"

"Yeah, mate, of course. You're always welcome here." I grin at him and slap his shoulder before heading into the house.

My stomach jitters with nerves as I follow him into the house. I've only given him brief descriptions of the new guests and have avoided any mention of Harper's beauty.

"Hey, Cammy boy!" Beck chuckles and gets up from the couch as soon as my best mate walks in.

"Hey, Beck." They shake hands and talk polite for a couple of minutes.

"The waves were pumpin'. Got some good rides in."

"And family time?" Beck's question was loaded. Cam hasn't been able to hide his family grief from the entire world, but I don't think he minds Beck knowing.

He gives Beck a serious smile and nods. "We had a good time."

Beck's eyes smile. "Glad to hear it. Stay for lunch?"

"Yeah. That'd be great. Thanks."

Stacey appears at the bottom of the stairs, and I start the introductions. As usual, Cam's completely unfazed by her flirty smile.

Girls love Cam.

He's tall, handsome and kind. It's like the ultimate

combo, apparently, and girls are always nipping at his heels. For some weird reason, he never takes advantage of it, though. He's had the odd crush and dated a couple of girls, but things never seem to last. I guess they soon realize that Cam's not about to let them in and they give up on him.

He seems happy enough… probably because he hasn't met the girl worth fighting for yet.

I glance into the kitchen, my voice deepening as I introduce my best mate to my best crush. I wonder if she's worth fighting for.

Tane! Shut up, man! She's leaving!

"Hi." She nods at him, obviously flustered by the idea of having to prepare food for an unexpected guest. At least, I think that's what she's thinking.

I'm not about to let her feel that way, so I step into the kitchen, offering my help.

Cam picks up the vibes and eases back into the lounge, plopping onto the couch to chat with Beck and Oscar.

As usual, he's soon engrossed in an easy conversation, even getting a smile out of Oscar.

"Sorry if I was rude," Harper mumbles as she butters some extra bread. "I'm not great with the unexpected. I like to know what's coming, and I never did well with people just popping over unannounced. I wish I was more like Mum. She was so good at just flexing and making room for change."

I can't help feeling like she's talking to herself, so I keep my voice quiet. "You need all kinds to make the world function properly."

She lets out a hard, breathy laugh and shakes her head.

I figure it's a good chance for me to clear the air after this morning.

"Hey, um, I'm sorry about this morning. You know… seeing you, I just—"

"Wasn't your fault." She shakes her head but refuses to look at me.

I'm tempted to tell her she has fine taste in underwear, but I doubt that'll go down well, so I just smile at her.

She looks away from me, burying her head in the fridge and unearthing a few tomatoes. "Slice these, please?"

"Sure." I get to work while she continues puttering around and putting together a stunning platter of cold meats and vegetables. It's a rainbow of health and yumminess.

"Wow." I grin at her. "It's like eating at a five-star restaurant every day."

She gives me a skeptical frown. "You don't eat out much, do you?"

"Come on." I lightly nudge her with my elbow before stealing a slice of cheese. "You're a great cook."

"Not really." She shakes her head, rearranging the cucumber rounds so they sit in a perfectly straight line.

"Well, it's the best cooking I've ever had, and I really appreciate the fact that you've been looking after us all."

She goes stiff beside me.

What did I say?

I want to ask her, but she shunts her way past me, carrying the platter of food to the table. Grabbing the bread, I follow her, trying to catch her eye, but she refuses to look at me.

"Wow. This looks awesome!" Cam grins at her, taking the seat beside mine.

Beck nods. "Harper's amazing in the kitchen."

"You want to be a chef or something?" Cam asks.

"No." She shakes her head, a short, sharp movement that doesn't invite further conversation.

Cam and I share a quick glance, but he doesn't say anything, instead diving into creating his own salad sandwich like everybody else.

Beck gets a light conversation going, talking about the farm and the garage project. Cam, the friendliest guy I know, responds with ease, and thankfully the meal passes with this light happy tone.

Until he turns to Harper and tries to engage again. What can I say, the guy loves a challenge.

"So, are you going to be going to school with us, Harper?"

"Uh, no, I'm supposed to be going to university this year." She shifts in her chair and places her sandwich down like she's suddenly not hungry.

Cam goes on, oblivious to the shift. "Awesome, which one?"

"I'm enrolled at Victoria University, but everything's kind of up in the air and I... I don't..." Her eyebrows bunch together. "I'm not sure... I...." She shakes her head, rubbing at her frown lines with trembling fingers. "Sorry. Excuse me, I need to go, uh... check on the... chickens." She bolts from the table, and we all gape after her.

"The chickens?" Beck frowns.

Cam winces, mouthing an apology at me. I brush the air with my hand and glance over my shoulder, flinching when the back door slams shut.

Beck scratches his beard, staring into the kitchen with a worried frown.

Cam tries to redeem himself. "So, what about you, Stacey? You coming to North Ridge?"

She nods and swallows down her mouthful. "That's the plan."

"And what about your sister? Tane said you've got a twin. Is she around?"

Stacey's smile disintegrates. Glancing at her plate, she pushes the crumbs around with her index finger and drops the last quarter of her sandwich. "She's in Australia right now. I don't know when she'll be back."

"Oh? Are you moving to Australia too, or…?"

I close my eyes, wishing I'd given my mate more of a heads-up. Shit!

Stacey's face bunches with a scowl. "No. I… It's kind of complicated. I…" She huffs and stands up. "I gotta go check on the cows."

Beck's eyebrows rise with surprise as she stomps away from the table. The front door slams shut behind her, and my eyes dart to Harper's uneaten sandwich.

I should tell Cam I'm sorry for not preparing him better, but he speaks before I can. "So, Oscar, Willow, is there anything I can say to make one of you go check the horses, or can I remove my big fat foot from my mouth now?"

Willow starts fighting a smile, while Oscar hitches his shoulder and mutters, "Chicks, right?"

I roll my eyes. What would he know?

Cam snickers quietly and looks to Beck. "Sorry about that."

"Don't worry, mate. Things are a little…tense right now. Big emotions, you know?"

Cam nods, and I just sit there gazing at the two empty seats and wondering what the hell we're supposed to do about the big emotions.

32

HARPER

I can't see my gumboots sitting outside where I thought I left them, so I grab Stacey's pink ones and shove them on, stomping away from the house.

I don't know where I'm going, and I don't even care.

Willow walks around this place all the time, and she never gets lost.

I just need to get away.

Away from those annoying questions and my uncertain future.

My mind is telling me that Victoria University is a go. But it's not that simple.

It won't be uni the way I want it. It'll be this compromised version where I'm trying to study and be a parent. I'm worried about the crap we're going to face down in Wellington, but I don't want to stay here either.

I'm not a farm girl!

My family needs stability, and Wellington is that. We have friends down there. A life!

But no family.

The thought makes me shudder, and I try to boot it out the back door.

Beck's not my family either!

That thought is so isolating that I want to curl into a ball.

I've never felt this lost or untethered, and I hate it.

Wrapping my arms around myself, I trudge down the bumpy dirt road for I don't know how long. I pass neat rows of paddocks, a herd of cows munching on grass. They're kind of clumped together today. I'm not sure why. Shaking my head, I ignore them and keep going, turning one way and then the other until I reach a creek I have to jump across. Finally, I'm thumping up a hill until I find a lone tree stump that I can perch on for a while.

I'm now out of breath and my feet hurt. I wriggle my toes inside the boots and cross my arms as a cool wind whips around me. I'm wearing a thin cotton T-shirt and a pair of denim shorts, which seemed enough when I screamed out of the house but now feel like tissue paper against my cooling skin. The air seems to have changed as I've been walking. I go to grab my phone and check the time, then realize I left it on the kitchen counter.

I tut and curl in on myself. For all I know, I could have been gone thirty minutes or three hours.

Time is relentless.

One day rolls by after another. There's no letup. No mercy. No chance for you to just pause and figure out what the hell you're supposed to do!

The wind whips my hair across my face and I tuck it behind my ears, wishing I'd brought a tie or something. I usually always have one around my wrist, but of course not today. It's probably sitting on my nightstand. I was too flustered after bumping into Tane in nothing but shorts and a bra to remember the little details, like putting in earrings and sliding on the ring my parents gave me for my sixteenth birthday.

I rub the bare spot on my middle finger, suddenly aching for the thin gold band with the little ruby studs. Why'd I take it off to sleep? I should just leave it on, always.

And why had I accidentally left my clean T-shirt in the bedroom this morning?

It was so freaking humiliating bumping into Tane like that. He was so embarrassed. He couldn't even look at me. It just topped off my morning and was another reminder why I need to get the hell out of here.

I can't have Tane seeing me naked, or half naked. Whatever!

It's embarrassing enough as it is, but with Tane, it's just that much worse.

Because you like him.

"Shut up!" I yell to myself.

I can't like him. That's ridiculous!

I conjure thoughts of Dylan, hoping they'll save me. I wish he was here. I wish I'd gone with him like he wanted me to.

But then I don't, because I can't just abandon my siblings.

He's texted me several times, checking in about twice a week. It's always the same.

Dylan: Thinking of you. How's it going?

Me: I'm okay.

It's shallow bullshit. I'm not okay, but I can't admit that to him. He's not my boyfriend anymore. I want him to enjoy his trip, not be burdened by me and my shit.

He needs to be free.

I wish I was free.

I can't tell him that one moment I feel like I'm floating in space with nothing to hold onto, and the next minute I'm drowning in a sea so thick and stormy I'll probably never breathe fresh air again. I can't tell him that my brother is one snap away from a violent meltdown and my sister is mute.

With a groan, I cover my face with my hands and lurch off the tree stump.

I need to keep moving forward.

Forward and away.

Willow and Oscar don't need me right now.

They've got Beck, Stace and Tane.

The thought crosses my mind again. What if I left them here? What if I chased my plan, headed back to Wellington alone, and then Alaina, Zoey and I could live it up the way we'd spent all of last year dreaming about?

But…

Watching my step down the hill, I think about all the things I'm doing around the house.

I've basically become the master chef, the housekeeper and the laundry maid. If I go, who will fill that space? Will my brother and sister starve and end up going to school in dirty uniforms?

Mum would be appalled.

Dad would be disappointed in me.

"But they're not here!" I yell.

My voice gets swept away on the thick breeze. The clouds above me are a dark gray now, promising rain at any moment.

Beck will be happy.

He wants rain.

I should head back.

Disappointment sears me. Reality is inevitable, and as much as I'd like this wind to whisk me out of it, it won't.

Life, like time, is relentless, and I can't escape it.

With a sad huff, I make it to the bottom of the hill and veer left, figuring I'll cut through the paddock instead of weaving my way back around to the road. When I reach the creek, I notice it's a bit wider here, but I can make that distance, no worries. There's a big patch of muddy land on the other side, and with gumboots on, I'm not worried about getting my feet wet.

Backing up a little, I get in a short run-up and hoist my body over the water, landing with two solid feet that are quickly sucked down into a thick, sludgy mud.

I scream with surprise and let out a horrified gasp as

the land I thought was hard and solid is turning out to be more like quicksand. I sink fast, and mud oozes into the top of Stacey's pink gumboots.

"Gross!" I screech as my socks are soaked through and my feet are rapidly drowned in cold gloop.

Lifting my leg, I try to escape the bog…

But there's a problem.

I *can't* lift my legs.

Either of them.

Whatever the hell I've just jumped into is holding me tight, the mud turning into some kind of concrete that has submerged Stacey's gumboots completely.

"What the f—?" I roar, probably sounding more like a screaming two-year-old than a lion.

This cannot be happening to me.

As if my day wasn't shitty enough. Now this?

So much for freaking dry land and needing rain.

With a loud huff, I cross my arms, my nails digging into my bare skin as I scan the darkening sky and try to figure out what the hell I'm supposed to do.

And then it happens; the hairs on my arms rise as an electric current buzzes in the air.

Looking up at the sky, I let out a disgusted scoff. "Are you kidding me?" I shout.

But the noise is drowned out by a crack of lightning that makes me flinch, and not far behind is a rolling thunder that has every fiber in my body jittering with panic.

33

TANE

Cam left as soon as the lunch dishes were done. I told him he didn't have to stay and clean up, but he said it was the least he could do.

After waving him off, I ran down to the field where Copper and Jax were grazing. Tugging them both inside, I got Jax settled in her stable and peered out the window.

Rain was coming. I could sense it in the air, but maybe I'd have time for a really quick ride with Copper beforehand.

I didn't get out on her yesterday, and I can tell she's begging for a decent canter and a little attention.

"Oh, all right, then." I grin, saddling her up as fast as I can before jumping on her back and heading out of the barn.

I get her into a quick run, and we race down to the road and do the short fifteen-minute circuit. The rain is going to start any moment now, and I'm glad we made it back in time.

Beck's waiting for me when I reach the barn.

"Hey." I'm about to get down from Copper, but he stops me.

"Harper's not back yet."

"What?" I grip the reins, Copper jittering beneath me as she feels my tension. "She left ages ago."

"I know. I'm getting worried." Beck looks up to the sky. "Those clouds are going to open up soon."

"Have you called her?"

"I was going to, but she left her phone in the house." He worries his lip. "I feel like she wouldn't stay away this long unless something was wrong. Am I overreacting?"

"No." I tug Copper's reins and she dances in a circle beneath me. I scan the horizon, hoping to see Harper walking back to the house, but of course I have no such luck. "None of us saw which way she left either."

"I've already checked the south side." Beck clips his helmet on. "So now I'll go east. You head up north. She may have gone to visit her parents or something."

"Yeah, good call."

"I haven't mentioned anything to the others. I don't want to worry them." Beck chucks me a hand radio. "Let me know if you find her before I do."

"Sure." I nod and kick Copper into action, heading down the road leading north of the house.

Dammit. I should have followed her when she first left, but she seemed like she needed some space, so we all gave it to her.

Worry nibbles at me, but I try to calm it with logic. She won't get lost on the farm.

But she may have tripped and twisted her ankle or something. That's not cool.

I give Copper a light kick, knowing I'll feel better once I find City Girl.

The wind swirls around me, and I feel a shift in the air. Glancing over my shoulder, I spot a lightning flash in the distance, and not far behind it is a rumble of thunder that feels a million times louder out here.

"Shit," I mutter, nudging Copper again. "Come on, girl. Let's find her quickly, ay?"

Copper picks up her pace but skitters sideways when the sky lights up again. I should have left her in the barn and taken the bike, but I was already on her and didn't want the delay.

"It's okay, girl." I rub her side, cringing when the first fat drop of rain hits my arm.

It doesn't take long for another one to follow, and soon the rain is pouring down like God unzipped the clouds directly above us.

Spurring Copper to the back of the property, I stand up in the stirrups and yell, "Harper! You out here?"

Even if she did reply, I probably couldn't hear her, so I keep trotting forward, anxiously checking every paddock I pass. I'm getting close to two hills that border our northern property line. On one is the small gravesite where too many ashes have been laid to rest. On the other is the old tree stump. It used to be a beautiful evergreen until about five years ago when a strike of lightning ripped the thing in half. Beck decided it was too dangerous to leave, so he hacked it down with a little help from our neighbors.

I pull Copper to a stop at the end of the road, wondering if I should turn left toward the gravesite or right up to the stump.

"Which way'd you go, Harp?" I murmur.

Probably left. It makes sense that she might want to see her parents.

But then I can also imagine her wanting to avoid them too, not quite ready to accept that they're really gone.

Hell, she probably walked south and Beck's found her already.

Swiping the rain off my face, I radio in for a checkup. "You got her yet?"

"Nah, and this rain's gettin' real heavy. You probably don't want Copper out in this storm."

"I know," I shout back to him. "I'll just give it a few more minutes; then I'll bring her back and swap her out for the bike."

"Hopefully we'll find her by then."

Beck ends the conversation and I nudge Copper forward, figuring I'll at least reach the creek. It won't take long to be running high and strong with rain like this. It's just what we need, a decent deluge. Heck, we could probably use a few days of it.

Checking left, I don't spot her and am just turning around when I think I hear a shout.

"Harper?" I yell and use my heel to spur Copper to the right.

We trot down the edge of the creek and my chest deflates with relief when I spot Harper, knee deep in mud and cursing at the sky like she's trying to take on Zeus.

I pull out my radio. "Beck, I've got her."

"Right, mate. Thanks." I can't be sure, but I think his voice is shaking.

Another crack of lightning illuminates the sky, and I hunch my shoulders, the radio going crackly. "I'll … over to … the cows in … milking."

"Cool. I'll see you as soon as I can," I reply, then clip the radio back onto my waistband before closing the distance.

Harper still hasn't seen me. She's too busy ranting and flipping the bird at the sky.

"I hate you! Stupid rain!" She slashes the drops off her face. "Damn you, thunder and lightning!"

"You all right?" I shout to get her attention.

She gasps and whips around to face me, nearly losing her balance. Flapping her arms in a circle, she finds her center, then slicks back the wet hair clumped against her cheek. "No! I am not all right! I had a plan! And it wasn't this! I'm supposed to be in Wellington right now. With my friends, going to parties and spending the day at the beach, not standing in a pile of swampy mud getting rained on!" Her chest heaves, water dripping off her chin as she pulls a wet clump of hair off her neck. "I hate this place! It stinks. And there's poo everywhere. Probably in these gumboots right now! So much poo!" She kind of sobs, then sucks in a breath and shouts, "And don't even get me started on silage!"

I think she's crying now. It's a little hard to tell with rain streaming down her face, but she is definitely the picture of unhappiness.

Aw, man, I wish I could make it better for her.

All I can do is get her out of this rain. Shifting in my saddle, I calmly ask, "You finished, City Girl?"

"What!"

I dismount Copper and steady her with a pat to the neck before watching my step and trudging over to Harper. "With your rant. Are you done, or do you need to get some more off your chest?"

Her shoulders slump forward and her head droops. "I'm done."

It's then that I notice just how deep she's buried in the mud. No wonder she didn't run home. She's stuck.

"Would you like some help getting out?"

"Yes. Please." She grits out the words.

I smile at her before looking down to assess the situation. It should be a simple tug to freedom. Holding out my hands, I'm relieved when she takes them without argument.

"Just lift your foot." I pull her arms, but she yelps and starts falling forward.

"I can't!"

I quickly step up to steady her, nearly getting sucked into the thick mud myself.

Pulling my foot away, I plant them on firmer ground, straddling the bog she's stuck in.

I can only imagine how ridiculous we must look—drenched and groping each other's arms like we're on the verge of a mud-wrestling match.

"Okay." I grip her arms to steady her. "I'm gunna crouch down and free your feet, all right?"

She nods and rests her hands on my back as I go low and wiggle her feet free. My hamstrings get a good strain in this awkward position, but I ignore the pain and keep tugging. I'm beating this frickin' mud no matter how hard it makes me work.

It's a bit of a mission; her feet are stuck pretty good.

I think we can say goodbye to these gumboots for now.

With a grunt, I finally wriggle her first foot free and she tries to perch it on the ground beside her, but it ends up sinking.

"Ugh!" she cries.

I work a little faster, freeing her second foot and simply standing when I'm done. I bring her with me, and she flops over my shoulder, her wet clothes sticking to mine.

"Whoa! What are you doing?" She slaps my back.

"Come on, City. Let's get you back to the house."

"Put me down!"

"I will in a minute." I grin, kind of liking the feel of her sweet body pressed against mine.

I walk as smoothly as I can, so as not to bump her, and am soon standing next to Copper.

My girl continues to prove her 'best horse in the world' status by remaining where I left her.

"Good girl," I croon.

She whinnies as if to say, *hurry the hell up, man*.

I snicker and lower Harper to the ground, quietly instructing her on the best way to mount the horse.

"I can just walk." Her argument is soft and tiny.

"All that way in socks? I don't think so." Putting my hands under her arms, I heft her up, holding her steady while she swings her leg over the saddle.

She grips the reins and shivers as a blast of wind whips across us.

Lightning cracks again, followed more swiftly by thunder.

Copper skitters. Harper gasps.

"It's okay." I soothe them both, stroking Copper's flanks and giving Harper's knee a gentle pat. "I need you to move your foot." She slips her foot out of the stirrup and I smoothly mount the horse, nestling in behind her.

Copper's not used to this much weight, but after a few little jiggles, she gets herself steady.

Reaching around Harper, I gently take the reins off her and steer Copper back to the barn.

It's hard not to feel every sensation as we ride back— Harper's wet hair sticking to my shirt, rain pelting our exposed skin, the faint charge of electricity buzzing in the air. It's only made stronger by the fact that Harper's slender body is nestled within my arms. I know I shouldn't, but I like having her there.

I wish these could be different times.

I wish Beck had never lost touch with her family and she was here on a regular summer visit to the farm.

I wish we were two people who liked each other, using any excuse we could to hang out.

I wish a lot of things.

But I can't turn back time.

And I can't make Harper love this place.

All I can do is take care of her until she leaves.

34

HARPER

Cold rain hits my skin, but all I can feel is the heat of Tane. His strong, sure body is right behind me, his arms wrapped around me as he guides us back to the barn.

Blinking at the raindrops taunting my lashes, I sniff and wrestle between the urge to get back as fast as possible and the yearning for this ride to be the slowest one I've ever taken.

How can someone feel this good?

He makes me want to lean back or curl against him. He's like a protective raincoat that I want to shelter within.

Another flash lights the sky, and Copper skitters to the right. I gasp but am soothed by Tane's gentle "Whoa. It's okay. It's okay."

He's speaking to his horse, but he may as well be speaking to me.

Copper and I seem to be in the same boat. As thunder rolls across the gray sky, we both flinch. My nerves are wound tight, calmed only by the solid chest behind me.

Swiping water off my face, I blink against the driving rain.

"Here." Tane perches his worn hat on my head.

"Thank you," I barely whisper, tugging it down to my eyebrows. Rain runs over me, relentless tears that make me want to join in, but I can't.

I can't cry.

It'll break me, and I'm not in a position to be broken right now.

I need to be strong. I can't fail my family.

Swallowing becomes impossible as Tane gently guides us back. In spite of the weather, he never breaks into a trot or a gallop. We amble back to the shed, Tane's soft murmurs like a calming shield to counter the storm's temper.

My insides are chaos by the time we reach shelter.

The rain suddenly cuts off when Copper walks into the barn. Shaking her ears, she whinnies and Tane's weight shifts as he gets out of the saddle. I gasp and grip Copper's mane, hoping I'm not hurting her. As soon as

Tane's gone, I feel off balance. There's nothing strong and steady protecting my back. I'm untethered again. Lost.

Tane smiles up at me, reaching out his arms to help me down.

I rest my hands on his shoulders and grip his sodden shirt while he half pulls, half catches me off the horse.

"Oof." I land against his solid chest. His arms hold me to him until I can find my feet.

My socks sink into the hay beneath me.

Copper grunts and shakes her head again.

Tane's still holding me, and all I can do is stare at him. With a slow, fluid move, he grips the bill of his cap and tugs it off. I'm exposed and open, drinking in his tender gaze.

What's he thinking?

No, I don't want to know.

Why can't I stop looking at him?

I don't want to know that either.

The pads of his fingers are feather soft when they touch my wet skin. His thumb rests on the point of my chin, his fingers delicately exploring the shape of my left cheekbone.

I can't breathe.

The kindness in his brown eyes is mesmerizing, and I act without thinking.

Rising to my tiptoes, I plant my lips against his. I don't even know if he sees it coming, but his fingers lightly grip the back of my neck, so I'm pretty sure he doesn't mind.

His lips are soft yet full, confident yet undemanding.

I tip my head, sinking into the kiss likes it's a slow dance I've been waiting my entire life for. His fingers shift from my neck, threading into my wet locks of hair. I scoop my arms under his, clutching the back of his shirt, drawing him even closer to me.

And then he welcomes me in, shifting his mouth so I can truly taste him. His tongue is warm and comforting, brushing against mine and sending spikes of unbelievable pleasure from my mouth to my toes.

It's impossible not to moan, to give away just how much this moment is transporting me. As I softly whimper against his mouth, he grips my waist, his long fingers splaying over my back.

I move my arm, cupping his head as if I can somehow fuse our mouths even closer together. I want to draw him in, be drawn in by him, so there's no air, no space, between us.

So there's only this kiss. This feeling.

This—

What am I doing?

The thought hits me like a bolt of lightning. A crack of thunder booms above the barn as if to back up what my brain is so desperately trying to tell me.

Copper whinnies and shuffles to the side.

My senses come back online, alerting me to the barn, the smell of wet hay, the sensation of wet fabric sticking together.

I'm kissing Tane.

My eyes pop open, waking me from this dream, and I lurch away from his mouth with a gasp. Shoving his shoulders, I step back and bump straight into Copper.

Tane reaches out to steady me, but I bat his hand away.

The move hurts him. I can tell by the flash of confusion that flickers across his face.

But I can't explain myself.

I was just making out with Tane like it was the most natural thing in the world.

But it can't be.

I… He's a dream I can't have.

A dream I don't even want!

His gaze is asking me what's wrong, his wrinkled brow begging for an explanation, but I can't give him one.

I couldn't talk right now if my life depended on it.

All I can do is cover my mouth with trembling fingers and bolt from the barn.

"Harper!"

I ignore Tane's cry and sprint toward the house, my muddy wet socks slapping against the stairs when I reach them. The rain continues to stream over me, and another flash lights up the sky.

I slump onto the back steps, slipping off my socks and throwing them into the dirt. They land, two muddy, drenched worms getting pelted by the rain, like the water can somehow beat the dirt free.

My arms go limp at my sides.

I let the rain pelt me too. Let it soak right into my bones.

Tears try to burn me from the inside out. But I won't let them fall.

The sky will have to cry for me today.

For this poor, confused girl who just wants to call her mom and figure out what the hell she's supposed to do.

35

TANE

Maybe I should have chased Harper. I'm not sure.

My body is still on fire after that kiss.

Holy shit, that kiss.

Mate, I have never felt anything like that before.

I've kissed a few girls, I know what I'm doing, but none of them have ever owned me so easily. Harper's tongue, her heat, her warmth, her delicate moan. Her fingers grasping my shirt and then cupping the back of my head, her lithe body pressed against mine like it was born to be there.

My body responds to even the memory of it.

I scratch my wet hair and blow out a breath, trying to calm my vibrating muscles down. Having her jerk away like that was a cold shower. Or maybe a bucket of icy water.

A hard snicker pops between my lips. I need to focus on that part.

The cold part. The *realistic* part.

I probably shouldn't have touched her face to start with, but she just looked so vulnerable. I wanted to make her feel better, to take that pained, lost look out of her eyes.

Then she just launched herself at me, and I was held hostage. Happily so.

Closing my eyes, I rest my forehead against Copper's neck.

"Did you see it, Cop? Were you watching?"

She whinnies.

"She wanted me, right?"

Silence.

I step back with a frown. Why else would she have kissed me?

But then she just took off.

Maybe I could have been any guy. Maybe she just needed a kiss.

The thought settles inside of me. It leaves a paper cut

against my heart, but logic is telling me that's all it was. A heated, desperate moment. She's hurting. Going through some tough shit. I can't expect more.

I guess all I can do is enjoy what I had and hope like hell that I can get over it, and not spend my days and nights pining for another taste of the delectable Harper Hughes.

36

STACEY

Jonas tastes good. That's my primary thought as I dip my tongue into his mouth.

It's a gorgeous, sunny day, a total contrast to the storm from yesterday. It blew through overnight, and I woke up to twittering birds outside my window and sunshine bathing the landscape.

There's something about the sun and heat that always makes me feel better. It got me out of bed, helped me push thoughts of Bianca aside.

Getting a text from Jonas a couple of hours ago was the icing on the cake.

The stupid garage is now painted, so Beck let me borrow his car so I could meet Jonas at a secluded spot about twenty minutes from the farmhouse.

It's actually part of a hiking trail that leads up to a lookout, but after about ten minutes of walking, Jonas grinned and pulled me off the path and through a clump of trees until we popped into this grassy circle of sunlight.

"Wow." I grinned. "Good find!" I glanced up at the trees hiding us, then down to the ferns and undergrowth bordering the private spot.

Jonas seemed kind of triumphant as he unearthed a blanket from his bag and spread it out for us. "Leon and I found this last year. It's the perfect spot for a little covert rendezvous." He wiggled his eyebrows at me, and my insides jittered. His innuendo was barely masked, but I decided to take a seat and see where it led me.

It led to me lying down with Jonas draped against my body, his hands exploring the terrains of my legs, butt and back while his tongue and lips covered everything from my nose to my collarbone.

It isn't a bad way to spend the afternoon.

We've already finished our specialty Cokes and nibbled through a bag of chips and two chocolate bars. Making out with Jonas's chocolatey taste is so not a bad thing.

He moans against me, ripping his lips from my mouth and nipping the edge of my jawline before gently sucking on my neck. His hands, obviously bored with outside exploration, are now wriggling beneath my shirt, and as good as that will feel…

"Whoa, Jonas, time-out," I pant, catching my breath as I nudge his hand back into the safe zone.

He groans a soft complaint against my neck, using his tongue to send a delightful shiver down to my belly while he squeezes my butt.

"Stop." I giggle. "My body is already on fire."

"So just roll with it," he murmurs against my skin.

Oh man, that is so tempting, and I'm not opposed to sex at some point, it's just that I've never actually gone all the way. I've gotten kind of close a few times, but I've always put the brakes on before things go too far. I will never forget that squirmy conversation where Mum sat Bianca and me down to go through the basics and then encouraged us to hold out for the right guy.

"Sex is meant to be super special. Don't sell yourself short for a quick rush. It's called making love for a reason."

I don't know why her words are lingering inside of me now. I kind of wish they wouldn't. Jonas is the hottest guy I've ever dated. I've never physically wanted someone more, which means my "let's think a minute" brakes are lacking in strength. If we step this up a notch, I could easily cave on a whim.

Do I want that?

My body screams YES!

A rush like that would be the ultimate distraction.

But my brain reminds me that I'm only on my second date with the guy.

"Come on," he whispers against my ear. "It'll be fun."

"I'm sure it will," I counter, finding the willpower to push him off me before resting my weight on my elbows. "But it's only our second date. Isn't that kind of fast?"

He flops onto his back with another pained groan, then squints against the sun and smiles at me. "Fair enough." He runs his knuckles down my bare thigh, the whisper touch stoking the fire I'm trying so hard to control. "If you weren't so gorgeous, this would be a lot easier."

I grin and roll onto my side, resting my head on my hand and gazing down at him. "Come on, you like me for more than my body, don't you?"

"Of course!" His eyes bulge and he runs his hand down my arm. "I had so much fun hanging out with you and my friends the other night. I can't stop thinking about you. That's why I had to see you today. That's why I wanted you all to myself."

I bite my lips, warmed by his compliment.

He wrinkles his nose at me, reaching up to peck my mouth before flopping back onto the blanket. "I'm looking forward to a repeat with my friends, though too. I'll try to set something up next week."

"Okay." I nod, already excited over future plans.

"School's going to be so great with you there."

I grin, still floating over the fact that this guy likes me so much. How'd I get so lucky?

"How do you think your sister will fit in?"

The happy butterflies flitting through my chest suddenly seize up and start to disintegrate, the simple question burning their wings to ash.

I swallow and shrug, looking over Jonas's head and focusing on the crown ferns, tracing the vibrant green leaves with my eyes.

"Stace?"

"Don't know." I shrug again and reach for a stick near the edge of the blanket. I start picking at the rough edge. "I mean, she might not even be coming back. It's kind of up in the air right now."

"Wait, so she's going to stay in Australia with your horrible grandmother?" Jonas gives me a confused frown. "What do your parents say about that?"

Irritation buzzes through me. From butterflies to chainsaws. Awesome!

I manage to work the bark lose near the top of the stick and start peeling it back. "Why do you even care?"

"What do you mean?"

"Well, now you're suddenly so interested in my sister. Are you hoping for a two-for-one kind of deal?"

"What? No." He frowns and leans away from me like I've just sprouted horns. "I just want to know you."

"Well, maybe I don't want to share everything." I throw the stick away, sitting up with a huff.

Jonas gapes at my crossed legs and slowly rises, resting his weight on his hands. "What is your problem? Why are you getting so pissy?"

"I'm not pissy. I just don't want to talk about my sister!"

"You really hate her that much?"

"Of course I don't hate her! I love her. She's all I've got left! And now she's gone because she can't stand the sight of me!" My voice cracks, breaking apart as a nugget of truth comes flying out.

I bite my lips together, wishing I had the power to grab at my confession and swallow it back down.

My cheeks flame red; I can feel the prickling heat spreading over my skin. I want the hot, *sensuous* heat back. I'm tempted to grab Jonas by the collar and haul him on top of me. Screw waiting. I'll take sex now. Anything to stop this hideous conversation.

I reach for Jonas, but he leans away, gently capturing my wrist and placing it back in my lap.

"What are you talking about?" His eyes narrow. "Did you do something to piss her off?"

"I don't want to talk about this." I force a smile and try to throw in a little, sexy eyebrow raise. I'm about to say, "So how about that sex?" when he gives me a stern look.

"Stacey. Are you… are you lying to me or something? What did you do?"

His eyes scorch me, and I sit back on my butt, wishing I could somehow break contact with that curious gaze of his.

"I won't care," he whispers. "Whatever it is, I'm sure it's not that bad."

"I don't want to talk about it," I grit out.

"Come on." He gives me a light nudge on the shoulder.

No! My brain rebels. I can't say it. I won't. No one will understand, not even Jonas.

Spinning around, I snatch my sandals and tug them on.

"Where are you going?"

"Home." The word tastes like ash in my mouth.

Home? I don't have a home!

"Don't go," he whines, like I'm being annoying.

I shoot him a fierce look. "All you seem to want to do right now is talk, and I'm not in the mood, so I may as well leave!"

My sparking words fire his own anger and he practically growls, "A second ago, you weren't in the mood for sex either, so what *do* you want?"

"I want my old life back!" I scream, tears punching onto my lashes like my shout has somehow powered them out me. "I want my parents to be around! I want my sister back!"

Tears splash onto my cheeks and I slash them away, pissed off that I can't just stay mad and irate. I'm hating myself for spilling more of the ugly truths out into the open.

I don't want this to be my reality! I want the lie! The daydream!

"Your parents?" Jonas whispers, even more confused than he was before. "Where... Where are they?"

I swallow and pinch my nose. I can't say the word dead. My tongue can't even form it.

"Stacey," Jonas clips as he yanks on his shoes and then stands. "Why are you lying to me?"

I jump to my feet, pulling my shoulders back and spitting, "Because I don't like the truth."

The corners of his eyes twitch before narrowing to thin, hard slits. "Yeah, well, I do."

I scoff and shake my head. "You can't tell me you've never lied."

"You're right. Everybody lies!" He flicks his arms wide, then points at me. "But I *never* lie to my friends. The people I'm closest to *know* me, just like I know them." His face distorts with a look of disgust. "I'm not hanging out with a girl who's just going to make up bullshit when she's in the mood and then goes psycho when I try to call her on it." He grabs the blanket with a huff, rolling it around his arm before pushing past me with a muttered "Text me when you're sane."

"Whatever!" I scream at his back. "I don't need you! I don't need anybody!"

His feet crunch through the undergrowth, his footsteps quickly fading into the distance. I slump onto my butt, wrapping my arms around my knees. The sun does nothing to warm me or bolster my mood. All I can feel are the cold tentacles of reality, binding me in the clutches of a truth I don't want to accept.

37

HARPER

I screwed up, and I need to make it right.

That kiss is going to eat me alive in more ways than one. I force my brain to focus on the slightly hurt look Tane gave me when I pushed him away. That's what I need to mend. My physical response and soaring emotions over being that close to him...well, those are things I just have to forget.

I'm a practical girl.

I can do it.

Clearing my throat, I walk into the barn, pausing in the large doorway, struck still by the gentle beams of light angling into the cavernous space. It's like a painting—beautiful, peaceful.

And not what you want.

The thought makes me frown, unsettling my treacherous heart. Why can't I just listen to this logic and feel good about it? I'm a city girl who belongs in Wellington, dammit. I won't be wooed by gentle light or the smooth, steady sound of someone brushing down a horse.

I won't be wooed by a country boy.

I have a plan. I need to stick to it.

Crossing my arms, I shuffle across the hay, fighting to keep my chin up and my stance strong.

"Hey." I punch out the word and then try to soften my greeting by resting my shoulder against the stable wall. Going for casual. Unaffected.

My heart thrums wildly in my chest as I force a closed-mouth smile.

Tane stops brushing and looks over his shoulder, his face warming with a genuine grin.

Of course it has to make my insides curl with desire.

It's not fair that he's so gorgeous.

"Howdy, little lady."

I snicker at his fake accent. And he's adorable too. This feels like a losing battle. My heart is shaking my resolve. My instincts are telling me to close the space, feel those lips, disappear again.

But my brain won't let me. I can't. I'm a mess right now, and kissing won't solve my problems.

"You right?" Tane's deep voice is soft and easy, his patient gaze so alluring.

I swallow and bob my head. "Can we talk?"

"Sure." He holds out his brush. "Come on over."

"Uh." I hesitate, then inch toward him.

"Nice gumboots, City." He winks at me, cutting the tension with those three easy words.

I glance down and wriggle my toes inside the boots. "Yeah, well, I still have to replace Stacey's."

"Does she know they're gone yet?"

"I don't think so, but I'm going to head into town first thing tomorrow. At least if she finds out before then, I can promise her replacements before I leave."

His easy smile falters, but then he takes my hand, laying the brush inside of it. "Here." He pulls me a little closer to Jax and shows me what to do. "Brush with the grain. That's it. She loves this spot right here."

I move to it, running the brush across the animal in short strokes. "Like this?"

"Yeah. You got it."

He bobs beneath Jax's neck, and I wait until his head

pops into view before saying, "I'm sorry about yesterday. The whole kissing you thing."

He keeps his eyes on his own brush, his lips twitching with either a frown or a grin. I'm not sure. I wish I knew.

"It's okay," he finally murmurs, smiling. "I didn't mind it."

I can't help a blushing grin and look down so he can't see me properly. "I just... I shouldn't have done it. I mean, I'm leaving on Sunday, and even though we'll hopefully come back for visits, it's just not... I shouldn't be kissing you when there's no future in it."

He stops and studies me, his brown gaze making me feel transparent...unhinged. "There's nothing wrong with a toe-tingling kiss every now and again."

A flash of desire shoots through me and I swallow, resuming my brushing with fervor.

"I'll never regret it, even if I don't get another one." His easy smile and wink only make me like him more.

Why do these gooey feelings come so easily around him? I barely know this guy!

I focus back on the brushing, relieved by the silence that descends between us. It's a peaceful, calm kind of feeling. The sounds of our brush strokes, the pale light bathing Jax's coat...those things stir something in me that I'm not sure I've ever felt before. Almost like this need to be still. To soak in the light for a moment.

I don't get it. Unless I'm sleeping, I like to keep busy, but now I just want to stand in this ray of light?

What is wrong with me?

Wiping my forehead with the back of my hand, I move down Jax's body, wondering how long I'm supposed to brush her for.

"Hey, you want to go for a ride?"

Tane's question jolts me.

"Uh...what?"

"I can saddle up both horses for us. Jax is lazy as, so she'll just plod along after Copper. You don't have anything to worry about. We'll take it slow."

I can't stop a grimace.

Tane just laughs, then looks extra cute when his eyebrows kind of wrinkle. "Come on, please? It'll probably be the last chance before you leave."

How am I supposed to deny that face? "Yeah, no, of course. Yeah. Um...okay."

"Yes." He elongates the *s*, then starts saddling up Jax, explaining everything as he goes, like he's forgetting this is my one and only time.

"Hold these." He passes me Jax's reins, and I nervously wait beside her while he saddles up Copper.

Glancing up at Jax, I give her an edgy smile, then lightly pat her nose. She grunts in approval, so I keep my hand there, then scratch between her ears. She seems to like that too, her ears flicking.

"Okay. Let's get you up." Tane comes back around to me and helps me mount in one easy movement. I let out a surprised gasp and he chuckles while adjusting the stirrups to make sure it's comfortable for me.

"That about right?"

"Thanks," I murmur, wriggling my gumboot and clutching the reins.

"Just relax. All you gotta do is hold on, 'kay?"

I nod.

"Let's go." Tane mounts Copper, then gives her a light nudge with his foot. She ambles forward, Jax following automatically.

We're soon walking in tandem, Tane pointing out different things on the farm. It's a good day for it. The intense rain has brought a fresh vibrancy to the land. The grass seems greener somehow, and the air has a clean crispness to it.

That won't last long. The early afternoon heat is kicking

in already, but a light breeze is countering it. I let it ruffle my hair, enjoying the soothing sensation.

Tane leads us up past that stupid boggy creek. I glance at the spot Stacey's gumboots are now buried and think about how Tane came to find me. He rescued me. Once I'd gotten done screaming at the sky, I would have had to try and figure a way out of my predicament. Tane saved me that trouble, and I need to thank him for that. But it seems weird to just suddenly blurt it out.

When he looks my way, I beam him a grateful smile. He grins back as if he can read my mind, and I figure that will be enough for now. I'll work on a proper thank-you before I leave.

Walking up the hill, Tane leads us up the switchback trail, past the old tree stump and to a spot that looks out across the neighboring farm. Paddock upon paddock. Different shades of green. The canvas is interrupted with cows and bordered by straight rows of poplar trees. It's idyllic, made only more tranquil by the farm-house in the distance.

"It looks like a painting," I murmur.

"The sun sets right over there." Tane points. "I some-times ride out here to watch it. It's my favorite spot on the farm. And when the sky is light with pinks and purples and golds, yeah, it's totally a painting."

I breathe in the fresh air, my heart swelling as my imag-ination colors the sky just the way Tane described it.

"You can see everything from up here." Tane turns in his saddle, pointing out different things. I glance over my shoulder and see the farmhouse and freshly painted garage in the distance. It's an interesting perspective, seeing how the barn and milking shed are situated. My eyes scan back around, grazing over another hill to our left.

"My parents are buried over there." Sadness roils through me. "I didn't understand why they wrote that in their will, but maybe from this spot, I can."

"Did your dad ever talk about Beck? I mean, after the fallout?"

I cringe as flashes from that awful picnic burn my brain. "The fallout. That's a good way to describe it."

"I still only vaguely remember what happened. We were playing. I remember feeling happy, which was so unlike me." The edge of his mouth rises, then falls. "But then there was shouting from my mum, mostly. And then came this thick, oppressive tension. Next thing I knew, we were in the car and Beck was yelling that she shouldn't have spoken that way. But Mum was too drunk to really take it in. I remember sitting in the back, wanting to cry, because I thought it was over. I thought Beck was gunna kick us out and we'd be scraping for scraps again."

My heart twists. Scraping for scraps? What kind of life was Tane living before Beck found him and his mum?

Understanding starts to inch its way into me. "Beck wouldn't have kicked you out."

"I know that now." Tane sighs. It's a deep, heavy one that makes his shoulders droop. "He caught Mum sleeping with his worker only weeks before he was supposed to go to the South Island with your parents. He actually seemed kind of excited about the trip. Excited, but nervous."

My lips part in surprise.

Whoa. Dad definitely didn't know that.

"He never explained why he pulled out last minute. My dad was kind of hurt over it. He was planning on coming to visit so he could have it out with Beck. Finally put a stop to all this distance."

Tane swallows. It's thick enough for me to hear. Copper shifts, obviously sensing his tension. With a few calming strokes, he settles her down and starts talking again. His voice is kind of raspy and rough. "I think he was ashamed. Ashamed that the woman he cut you guys off for went and cheated on him. Like maybe he'd fought for nothing. But he had the farm to think about too. I couldn't have managed on my own, and it was too late to find a relief milker. They're all booked up around Christmas." His expression is tormented as he looks at me. "I'm sorry my mum screwed everything up. So many wasted years. So much hurt and misery.

He should have been on that holiday with your parents."

I appreciate the sentiment, but all I can do is sniff and croak, "If he had been, he'd be dead too."

My quiet statement steals the last of my peace. Anxiety writhes inside of me, desperate to show, to get out. Tears burn my throat, but I swallow and blink as fast as I can to stop them.

Tane's looking at me. I can feel it, but if I catch that kind, brown gaze, I'm going to fold. So I keep my eyes focused on the poplar trees in the distance.

"I'm so grateful Beck's alive, but I'm sorry you lost. I'm so, so sorry."

Shit, don't, Tane. Please stop talking! I'm going to lose it!

Shaking my head, I manage to grit out, "You didn't kill them."

He's still looking at me. I can sense it. He wants me to turn and meet his eyes, but I can't. Gripping the reins, I shift in my saddle. Jax moves beneath me, giving me a start. I yelp and Tane quickly reaches forward, grabbing her reins and quietly soothing her.

"It's okay, girl. It's okay."

Jax lets out a horsey grunt and calms beneath me.

I lean forward and stroke her neck. "He keeps these

horses because of Abby, doesn't he? She always loved them."

"Yeah, maybe." Tane smiles at me. "Financially, they do nothing for him, but... he always likes to have a couple of horses around. He bought me Copper. Beck just kind of knew I needed her." He sits back and gazes into the distance. "He saved my life, that guy. When I got here, I was an angry, lost kid. My dad had—" His voice cuts off and he looks down. "Mum met Beck and it all happened kind of fast, but she needed a home, and Beck was offering one."

I want to ask about his dad but can feel the *don't go there* vibes radiating off him, so instead I softly whisper, "My parents never really gave her a chance. I mean, maybe they would have, but... I don't know... bad communication and stubbornness, I guess. They missed Abby too. You never got to meet her, but she was something special. Beck's one and only. His soul mate. When they were together, they were...the couple you wanted to be like. She and the boys, they were Beck's entire world. His whole happiness. And when they died, he just..." My nose starts to tingle, and I have to swallow before I can keep talking. "I don't know how you get over something like that. Ever."

Tane doesn't say anything, and when I glance at him, I nearly drown in that pained look in his eyes. His forehead wrinkles and he swipes a finger under his nose.

"I'm sorry for what went down with your mum, though. Do you miss her at all?"

His shoulder hitches. "I know I should. She's my flesh and blood. She wants me to move to Upper Hutt. Is pissed off that I sided with Beck. She's angry that he kicked her out. She said I don't understand, but she doesn't see what a bitch she can be. She's selfish. Heartless! But Beck put up with all of her shit. I never understood why. I was too busy being grateful to try and analyze it. I owe him. I owe him everything."

"So, that's why you stay, even though he's not your dad?"

"He's the closest I'll ever get to one." Tane's gaze warns me not to challenge him, and I stay quiet as he looks out over the landscape. "There's something about this place. This land. It heals. It takes the pain away. It gives you something bigger than yourself to focus on." He looks at me again. "This place saved my life."

His face is so beautiful right now. He's quietly asking me to believe him, and I do.

Blinking, I turn to gaze at the view, assessing the land and wondering if my parents always wanted to come back here one day. They wanted to be buried here. It must have been special to them. Maybe they had long-term plans of leaving Wellington and retiring in the country.

But that doesn't fit.

They're city people. We love the city. They never spoke of plans to move back here. We were settled in Wellington. That's our home!

Is it? Will it still feel like home without them?

The question makes me shudder, and I let out a ragged breath.

A soft brush of fingers down my arm makes me turn. "It's gunna be okay, City." Tane's tender voice and expression make my insides quiver. "I know it doesn't feel like it right now, but you're gunna get through this. You're strong." He smiles. "You're stronger than you think."

38

TANE

I can't get my conversation with Harper out of my head. It's taken me until nearly bedtime to figure out what it was that was eating me so bad.

It's my mum.

And Abby.

When Harper talked about Abby being Beck's one and only, it niggled. And then it nibbled, and finally it started to eat big chunks right out of my stomach.

Mum thinks that Beck isn't hurt over what she did to him. Maybe she truly believes that because... well, maybe he never really loved her.

The thought stings big-time. She's my mum, and I know she has her faults, but she and Beck lived together for about eight years. That's a long time to pretend to love someone.

Not really wanting to but knowing sleep will be impossible unless I do, I head down to Beck's room. I actually find him in his office.

He's hunched over his computer screen, paperwork spread around him, his fingers awkwardly tapping the keys. He hates the admin side of farming. Always has. Maybe now's not the best time to talk. He's probably in a bad mood.

I hesitate in the doorway, glancing around the antique-style office with its ugly lampshade and walls of books —everything from *Asterix & Obelix* to *Great Expectations*, plus a row of ancient encyclopedias on the bottom shelf: A to Z. I remember when I first arrived here sometimes sneaking into this room and thumbing through the encyclopedias. I didn't read anything, just looked at the pictures. It was the closest thing I'd ever had to the internet. At school, I hadn't been allowed to use the computers much…on the days I actually *got* to school.

I shake off the dark memories and am about to leave Beck to it when he glances over his shoulder.

"Hey, mate." His eyes warm with a smile and he spins in his chair, obviously relieved by the interruption.

Even so, I hold up my hand. "Sorry, I didn't realize you were working."

"No, come in, please." He points to the chair adjacent to his desk. "I wanted to let you know that I'm interviewing a potential worker tomorrow. His name's

Lincoln. He's from up north and is moving down to be closer to his new girlfriend."

"Oh yeah?" I cross my arms. "Much experience?"

"Yeah, he's been working up in Whangarei for about five years now. Think it might be a good fit, but I'll hire him on a six-week trial basis first. See how things go."

"Sweet." I nod, still lingering in the doorway.

Beck points to the chair again, and when I don't move immediately, his eyebrows bunch with confusion. "You right?"

"Yeah. I, um…" I blow out a breath and scratch the back of my head. It's now or never, I guess. "Can I ask you something?"

"Sure." He points to the chair for the third time, and I shuffle over to it, plunking down as Beck writes himself a note and then swivels his chair to face me.

I look away from his curious gaze and start picking at the fraying hem of my shorts. I don't want to offend him, but I've got to know.

"Did you ever love my mum?"

Beck goes so silent and still that I'm forced to glance up just so I can see what his face is doing. His brown eyes narrow in pain, and then he starts playing with the whiskers of his beard. His chair squeaks when he leans forward and rests his elbows on his knees. "Why are you asking me this?"

I shift in my own seat, tugging at the ends of my shorts and finally confessing. "She's been texting and calling… a lot." I raise my eyebrows. "She really wants me to understand her side. All I can see is two people who have no loyalty and no respect for you. Am I wrong?" Beck tips his head, looking thoughtful and stirring up the unrest within me. "Mum said she wasn't entirely to blame for what she did. That there's things I don't understand, and that you're not perfect."

"Well, that's no secret." Beck releases a dry chuckle. It contradicts the silt washing through my bloodstream, and I frown at him.

"You're perfect to me, Beck. You're the best man I've ever known."

Leaning back with a heavy sigh, he gives me a small smile. "I've made plenty of mistakes, mate, and one of them was probably not loving your mum the way I should have." Scraping a hand through his hair, he lets out another sigh. "Thing is… I met my soul mate when I was twenty-three, and she was my one and only. I never expected to lose her, and when I did…" His expression buckles with a look of such pain that I almost want to cry. "I don't know if I'll ever get over her completely. I don't know how to love another woman the way I loved my Abby." He blinks a few times, then sniffs, his expression clearing back to neutral.

Biting the inside of my cheek, I watch him for a minute before asking, "Why'd you stay with my mum, then? If you didn't love her, why'd you let her move in?"

He studies me for a long beat, his meaningful look enough to make me feel transparent. But then he slowly raises his hand and points at me. "You, mate."

I give him a confused frown. "Me?"

He grins and starts bobbing his head. "You were a skinny, miserable, wild-eyed wreck. You needed me. You needed this place, just the way I did when I was a kid. I was in slightly better shape than you were when the Connells took me in, but not by much. They gave me a home. They adopted me...and it saved my life. "

My mouth drops open without my say-so. I mean, I knew he was adopted, but he's never told me about his life before coming here. Not that I've asked. I don't want to talk about my nightmares from the past, so why would he?

"The first time I saw you, sitting on the floor in the corner while your mum served me coffee...you just reminded me so much of myself. There was this pained rebellion about ya. This tough outer layer that was doing everything it could to protect broken insides."

I swallow and my knee starts to bob.

"I wanted to help you, so I struck up a conversation with your mum, found out everything I could about you two, and when I heard the story, I figured…I've got an empty home. Might as well fill it."

My lips twitch with a grin. I'll never forget the day we moved into the farmhouse. It was the biggest house I'd ever seen. Four bedrooms upstairs, a downstairs wing for the grown-ups. It was insane! I loved all the old knickknacks. It was like stepping into an antiques shop.

"It took you a while, but when you started to open up… the first time I heard you laugh…" Beck grins. "I wasn't willing to let that go, so I… played pretend. Or at least I tried to." His smile fades. "Your mother started to see through it, so she found love with someone else."

"She shouldn't have done it that way." I shook my head, still annoyed with her.

"Yeah, maybe. It took me off guard, pissed me off, but… I didn't love her. I…" Drooping his head, he rests his elbows back on his knees and rasps, "She's not the only one at fault. I was wrong the way I treated her. I never let her in. Couldn't do it. Abby owns my heart forever. I should have just been real with your mum from the start. You guys could have lived here, just as friends, but…I don't know. Maybe I thought I could love her." He shrugs.

I frown at him, wishing I didn't know this. Not wanting to see the cracks in Beck's gleaming veneer. But I guess it makes him more human, in a way.

Pity for my mum stirs. I cross my arms, pushing them

into my stomach to try and squash the feeling. Anger hurts less. It's an easier emotion to deal with, which is why I threw out so much attitude when I first arrived on the farm. It's why I fought and scrapped, rebelled against the kindness. I didn't trust it.

But I do now. Beck won me over, slow and steady. I love him, even if he isn't perfect.

He gives me a sad smile and then once again proves his worth. "You should call her. Go see her for a visit or something. Tell her you understand and forgive her."

I swallow, unsure what I should say.

"Do it." Beck taps my knee. "Life's too short and unpredictable to have regrets."

His expression folds with pain again, and this time, I'm pretty sure he's thinking about his mates—Lance and Richie.

So I nod, because I don't want to let him down. Because doing the right thing will no doubt make me feel better in the end.

"Thanks, Beck," I whisper, rising from my chair.

He nods, and as I walk out of the room, his chair squeaks as he turns to get back on with work.

Slowly climbing the stairs, I flop onto my bed and grab my phone off the nightstand. I don't want to call her now. She might say something to piss me off. I'll wait for a new day, when my emotions aren't as raw and tattered.

Resting the phone against my chest, I gaze up at the ceiling, trying to imagine what it must be like to love a woman so completely that even after she's gone, your heart remains hers.

39

HARPER

I yank a T-shirt out from under my suitcase and start folding it, but I totally muff the job and in the end just dump it in a scrappy pile on top of everything else. My mind is scrambled eggs as I try to single-handedly pack up for our trip back to Wellington.

My siblings are all but useless.

Willow's curled up against her pillows, messaging her friends with a scowl on her face. I want to ask her if she's all right. I want her to tell me what's upsetting her, but she won't. All I'll get is a morose frown, maybe a shrug if I'm lucky.

Storming out of the room, I head for the bathroom to gather up our toiletries. I'll leave the toothbrushes for the morning, but everything else can be packed away. I want to be all good to go so that as soon as Beck and Tane get back from milking, we can say our goodbyes and hit the road. It'll take all freaking day to get back to Wellington, and I want to allow time to stop for lunch and dinner.

"Ugh!" I jerk to a stop in the bathroom door, annoyed by the sight of wet towels clumped on the floor, the reek of the unflushed toilet and the black scunge around the plug hole in the sink.

This place needs a clean and I'm itching to do it, but I'm leaving, and I won't spend my last night here scrubbing away other people's grossness. What's the point? It's not like this is my home.

My throat swells as I snatch my shampoo and conditioner out of the shower. Drying the bottles off with the hand towel, I try not to think. To feel.

I have a plan. I have to stick to it.

We're going home.

What home?

I snap my eyes shut, then force them back open, glaring into the mirror. "*My* home. In Wellington."

The empty house without your parents, you mean.

"Shut up," I grit out, haphazardly throwing the rest of our stuff into the toiletry bag before heading back down the hallway.

As sweet as Tane was yesterday, our conversation on the hill has unsettled me. I can tell he thinks I should stay. When he talked about the land healing him, it was almost appealing.

But I'm a city girl.

I'd be unhappy here. I'd miss my friends.

I need to get back to what I know.

Throwing my toiletry bag on top of my suitcase, I walk to Oscar's room to check that he's packed up like I asked him to.

No such luck. The little slob is sitting on his bed, big headphones covering his ears, and his clothes are spread from one edge of the room to the other.

I let out a little scream, which makes him jerk and look at me like I'm a crazy person.

"What is your problem?" he mutters.

I point at his bag, which is lying open yet completely empty on the floor.

"You haven't even started packing? I asked you to do that straight after dinner! We're leaving first thing tomorrow!" He has the decency to look just a little shame-faced, but that doesn't stop him from staring back at his computer screen to avoid me. "Why are you on your computer again? You've had your allocated screen time for the day. Get off and start helping me!"

"Stop stressing out. It'll take me two seconds to shove everything in a bag tomorrow morning," he grumbles.

Steam starts spurting up my throat, and I lurch across the room and slap his laptop shut.

His eyes bulge at me as he whips off his headphones. His nostrils start to flare, and I shuffle back a step, my heart racing as I will myself to stay strong. This is just a taste of what might await me. I can't fail now.

Nerves scour my insides. Like Stello pads, they go to town, rubbing my guts until I feel raw and bleeding. But I can't let that show. Crossing my arms, I steel myself against the internal massacre.

Oscar pushes his laptop off his knee with a growl. "I hadn't saved! You just lost me my place in the game!" He throws his pillow at me.

I bat it away and it hits the floor with a thump. "Calm down."

"I don't have to calm down! You should have *asked* me to turn it off. Shown a little respect."

"Respect? Why should I respect you when you have no respect for me? I asked you to help me by packing, and you haven't even started! Plus, you're on your computer when you shouldn't be. We've talked about this!"

"You're like the frickin' computer police, Harpy!"

Argh! I hate it when he calls me that. Dad would always put a quick stop to the name-calling, but he's not here right now. Not ever. No one's got my back anymore when it comes to my turd of a little brother.

"Would you guys stop yelling!" Stacey walks out of her room with her iPad in hand. "I'm trying to watch something here."

"Why doesn't she have screen restrictions?" Oscar points at her.

"Because she's not addicted like you."

"Whatever! She's on her phone all the time, texting her stupid friends."

"Excuse me!" Stacey snaps. "My friends are *not* stupid. Who the hell do you think you are?"

I glance at her and quickly mutter, "Don't make him angrier."

"Oh, am I awakening the beast? Is his face about to turn green?"

Oscar growls and stands up too fast, whacking his head on the slanted ceiling above his bed. "Argh!" he shouts way too loudly. His eyes glass over as he rubs his head and points at the door. "Get out of my room!"

"What is going on up here?" Tane appears at the top of the stairs.

He's shirtless, which is so not what I need right now. Even though his sweaty T-shirt is draped over his shoulder, I can still see everything. He's no doubt on his way to the grotty bathroom, and I'll have to spend the next five minutes not imagining him naked under that feeble showerhead.

The thought makes me flush and I squeeze my biceps, rolling my eyes and struggling for composure.

"This isn't your business." My voice trembles, much to my annoyance.

Tane just saunters up to Oscar's door and leans against the frame. "It's in my house, so it kind of is."

"Get out!" Oscar yells again.

"Shut up!" Stacey retaliates, igniting a spark that sets off this powder keg of anger. We're soon all ranting at each other, trying to be heard above the other. Oscar and I are fighting about his computer while Stacey and Oscar are fighting about how horrible the other one is. I'm trying to gain some control while Tane raises his hands and shouts for us all to just calm down.

It's like a red rag to a bull, and soon we're all yelling at him to butt out.

"Oi!" Beck's boom makes us freeze.

I flinch. Stacey gasps. Oscar jerks with fright.

Tane's shoulders droop down with relief, and he turns to look at his "father" standing at the top of the stairs, glaring at each of us.

After a painful beat, he points over his shoulder. "All right, that's it. Get in the truck. All of you."

I share a quizzical look with Willow, who is cowering in our bedroom doorway behind Beck.

The big bear huffs and points at us. "You've got two minutes, now move! Tane, put a shirt on!"

Tane disappears into his room while I share a quick look with Oscar. He grabs his cap and shoves it on before pushing past me to follow Beck outside.

I throw on a light sweater and follow Willow down the stairs. Climbing into the back of the ute without a word, I cling to the edge and wonder where Beck's planning on taking us.

He revs the engine and we lurch off. I fall against Tane and he steadies me, then tries to give me a smile in the fading light.

I can't reciprocate. All I can do is right myself and shift just a little away from him.

The Stello pads are done now. My insides are mush.

Tears burn my throat as Beck drives us out to the back of the farm.

I swallow, not even giving them a chance to form.

I won't cry.

I can't.

40

STACEY

The sky is basically black by the time Beck stops driving. I have no idea where we are in relation to the farmhouse. I have no idea why Beck wanted to bring us out here.

Probably to bury our asses in unmarked graves and be done with it.

I know I'm only kidding, but I wouldn't blame him. The guy's gone from one child to like five overnight.

It should be six.

I shake the thought off and jump down, glancing up at the sky and being struck by the vastness of it. The stars burn brighter out here. There's something kind of awe-inspiring about it. The moon is nowhere to be seen. It must be new, which makes the stars sparkle that much more.

"All right, you lot. Come on." Beck's still barking at us.

I shift away from the ute and approach the circle of logs. The big grizzly bear is getting a fire going. I take a seat next to Tane. Harper is lined up next to Willow and Oscar. As soon as the flames are dancing, Beck finds his own perch opposite us. We make three sides of a triangle now, each length different, each length missing family members that shouldn't be gone.

Beck doesn't say anything, just studies us quietly while cicadas sing a late-night song. It's kind of a peaceful soundtrack, and I focus on the noises of the night so I don't have to think too hard.

It's been a shitty week, and now that Jonas is pissed off with me, I can't see school being any kind of reprieve. There's no joy left, so I've been distracting myself with movies, desperately trying to live in the make-believe as much as I can.

"Your dads ever tell you how we became friends?" Beck breaks the silence, and I glance over at him.

His eyes brush across mine before traveling to Harper. She gives a half kind of nod while I hitch my shoulders.

"You met at primary school." Harper's voice sounds rusty, like she's got a sore throat or something.

"Yeah." Beck nods. "The Connells took me in over the Easter break. I'd just turned five, and I was a skinny little ratbag. I'd never been to any type of school before —no preschool, kindergarten. None of that. The teacher made Lance my buddy that day, and at playtime, he chucked me a rugby ball and said, '*Let's go.*'" Beck's lips twitch with a grin. "So, we ran outside and started playing, and then Richie joined in, and we did that every playtime. Every day we could." He gazes at the flames like he's seeing the memory. Three little boys running around a muddy field, no doubt barefoot, oblivious to the heat or cold. All that mattered was the leather ball and the fun of tackling your mates.

Beck smooths a hand down his beard. "By the end of the year, we were inseparable. None of us had brothers or sisters, so we became each other's family. We were at each other's houses all the time. Mostly here, though." He looks into the distance as if he can see through the darkness. "We explored every inch of this farm. Eeling in the creek. Scaring the shi… scaring the cows. Making the chickens squawk. Building forts." He chuckles. "Mum just kind of got used to us disappearing and turning up when we needed food." His head starts bobbing while his voice gets thick. "We stuck together through thick and thin. Rugby wins and losses, bad weather, failed exams, new girlfriends, parents dying." His voice cracks. "The lot."

I shift on the log but can't take my eyes off him. I'm transfixed by his deep voice and his eerie walk down memory lane.

"They were my best men at my wedding, and when Abby got pregnant with Matt and Charlie, I knew I needed them as uncles for my boys. So, we got together over a beer one night, and we all swore that no matter what came our way, we'd look after our own. If anything ever happened to me and Abby, your parents would look after my boys." His voice wobbles, and he has to swallow before rasping, "And vice versa."

He goes quiet then, pinching his nose and obviously struggling to find his voice. I can't move, and when he sniffs like he's fighting tears, I feel my own build. My eyes start to burn, my nose tingling, and I wonder if I should even bother fighting them.

Beck lets out a shaky breath and scrubs a hand down his face. "We had a forever bond. A forever love. We promised to be mates for life, and I kind of let the team down. When Abby and the boys were taken so suddenly, I just... I couldn't handle being around your happy families. It tore me up. Reminded me of how much I'd lost, so I pushed you all away, and then... well, I let time and distance drive us even further apart."

"And the picnic," Tane mutters.

Beck's head jerks in his direction, and he points across the flames. "Your mum wasn't the only one to blame for that. I should have handled it better. I... She just... I made her feel like an outsider. Like she'd never really fit." He shakes his head. "And I should have told them why I was... with her." He gives Tane a sad smile, and Tane nods his understanding, his face morphing with this grateful kind of pain.

I'm not sure what it means, but I couldn't ask if I wanted to.

All I can think about is Bianca and how I've let the team down.

Guilt ravages me, and this time I don't even try to stop it. I let it claw my back and peck at my brain. It hurts, but I won't deny myself the pain, drawing my knees to my chest and hugging them. My shoes perch on the log and I stare at Beck, ignoring the tears that start slipping down my cheeks.

Beck scrubs a hand down his face again and starts blinking. "I didn't know how to apologize or explain what I was going through. I didn't think they'd understand. You were all so happy. Your happy little family units." His tongue darts out to skim the edge of his mouth. "Then after that picnic... the shouting, the accusations... I thought I'd be excluded for sure, but your parents...they kept me in their wills." His face bunches and tears glass his eyes. "They kept me as your guardian. I didn't expect that, but..." Sucking in a breath, he pulls a note from his pocket. "They wrote to explain."

Clearing his throat, he unfolds the letter with trembling hands and takes a second to compose himself. It doesn't really work; his voice wobbles all over the place as he reads aloud.

"Dear Beck,

Hey, mate.

I know things are kind of disjointed between us right now, but as I sit down to update the wills, I just can't bring myself to take you out of them.

Life's not fair.

It's not fair that the world's greatest dad lost his kids.

If I could have taken that pain for you, mate, I would have in a heartbeat. I wish I had the power to bring them all back. But I have none.

All I've got are my choices.

And here's one of mine...

If Renee or I are taken too soon, I want the world's greatest dad helping out my kids. You are a good man, Beckett Connell. I know my kids would be safe with you, and this is why I keep you in the will. I trust you, even when I don't understand you. I know that at your core, you have a heart of gold.

I won't stop fighting to mend bridges and make things right between us.

We're family, which means we don't always agree, and we don't always understand, but we <u>always</u> love.

It's a forever love.

Mates for life — that's never going to change.

To unbreakable promises,

Lance

PS - Richie here. Everything he just said. Miss you, Becky Boy. Love you forever.

Tears are streaming down Beck's face by the time he's done. They dribble into his beard, and I think my broken heart is now two panting shards inside my chest.

"I didn't make things easy on them, but I'm not going to break my promise or this bond." He wrestles the note back into his pocket and glances around the fire, his voice growing stronger. "I'd do anything to turn back time, but I can't. All I can do is honor my brothers by keeping my promise. I'll be whatever you need me to be: dad, uncle, friend, coach. I'll take any role you want me to. I commit one hundred percent to taking care of you guys. And I want you *all* to stay."

He looks around at each of us. When he gets to me, I slash the tears off my cheeks and try to smile but can't manage it.

"I want to become a family. Mates for life. But that choice isn't mine." He bobs his head and points at the ground. "All of you, right here, right now, need to make a decision. If you want to stay, you're welcome. But you have to commit to making this work: to compromising, to thinking about each other before yourself, to working together so we can help each other through this, just the way your parents wanted us to."

He pauses again, letting his words really sink in.

I let them wrap around me, slither into my heart and mind.

"But I won't force you. If you want me to support you from afar, then I'll make that work too." He rubs his beard and looks down, giving us all space to think.

My heart starts thrumming, one thought cascading through me on repeat.

Tane shifts beside me, shuffling his sneakers in the dirt. "I'm in. I'm with you all the way, Beck."

"Thanks, mate." He gives him an affectionate smile before looking across the flames. "Ozzy, how about you?"

He looks up and nods. "I want to stay."

Harper's lips part in surprise, and she starts rubbing her forehead.

"Willow?" Beck asks.

She shrugs and then nods, like she doesn't care either way.

"No." Harper shakes her head. "No half-ass answers. If you want to stay, you have to say it. I need to hear the words."

I hold my breath, surprised by the strength in Harper's voice. I thought the whole Willow talking thing was a lost battle.

Willow shifts uncomfortably, tucking her hands beneath her legs while biting her lips together.

We wait it out, the silence almost unbearable. Even the cicadas have gone quiet.

Finally, after what feels like an eternity, she softly speaks. "Stay. I wanna stay."

Harper's lips form a wonky line, like she's fighting tears that will not be allowed to fall. With a firm sniff, she sits up straight and swallows, her gaze locked on the flames.

Beck's voice is gentle. "Harp, we know you have plans in Wellington. A whole new chapter beginning. Uni. It's important. We all understand. We—"

"I'm staying," she blurts, then nods like her head is a bouncy ball that's just been smacked against concrete. "For now, at least. I can delay my studies for a year." She puts her arm around Willow's shoulders. "It's the right thing to do."

"Thank you." Beck smiles at her. "We need ya."

She gives him a shaky smile in return, and then all eyes land on me.

"Stace?"

"Well, of course I'm gunna stay." I lift my hands. "But…" I let out a breath and have to swallow before I can find the courage to say what has to be said. "Not without Bianca. She should be here right now. I never should have let her walk away so easily. I never should have hurt her like I did." Tears attack me again, sticking pins into my eyes and making my voice shake. "I need to get her back. Can you guys help me?"

"You bet." The sweet smile on Beck's face makes me feel warm and forgiven. I don't deserve it, but I bask in it for a moment.

He didn't even ask me what I did to make Bianca escape me.

I think I'm beginning to understand Mum and Dad's choice now. Beck is a pretty damn good backup plan.

Slapping his legs, he lets out a dry, gruff kind of laugh. "So, this is it. Mates for life."

"Mates for life," I whisper, then let out a watery laugh and bob my head.

41

HARPER

So it looks like I'm staying.

I don't know how to feel right now. The battle that's been raging ever since arriving here has been won for me. Won by Oscar. Won by Willow and her four little words.

She spoke! She actually spoke!

And said the very words I thought she wouldn't.

She wants to stay.

It's so unexpected I can barely think straight.

All I know is that I can't leave my family. Mum and Dad wouldn't want me to.

So it's over.

I'm staying.

The battle has ended.

But is it really a win?

I can't decide.

Glancing across the fire, I catch Tane's gaze on me. His lips aren't moving, but his eyes are smiling. Their warm glow hits me right in the heart, and it starts to beat wildly.

I wish it wouldn't.

It kind of scares me how easily I could fall for the farm boy.

I still don't know if it's the right thing to do. I feel broken right now. My plan is shattered, my dreams for the future shoved onto a back shelf. Nothing is working out the way I thought it would.

Do I truly open my hand and let go of everything I was holding onto?

I said I'd delay studies for a year, stick around until everyone was settled. Then I can move back home and pick up from there. Zoey and Alaina will only be one year ahead of me. It'll be all right.

One year.

I hold Tane's gaze, my insides jittering with a mixture of nerves and excitement.

A year on the farm. With him.

An unexpected warmth curls through me, and my lips rise at the edges before I can stop them. He smiles back and flashes me the quickest wink, and my stomach pitches with giddy pleasure.

I warn myself against it.

I'm only here for a year. One short year.

I won't let myself get too attached. That would be foolhardy.

I glance at my siblings and remind myself why I'm staying.

It's not for Tane. It's for them.

To get them settled. To make sure they're happy.

I mustn't forget that.

Even as all the good reasons filter through my brain, I find my eyes tracking back to the country boy.

Oh man, this year could potentially be the longest one of my life.

42

STACEY

The sun is diluted by a thin layer of cloud cover. I don't mind so much. It's hot today, and even though I love hot, the cool breeze tickling my skin is delicious.

My insides are buzzing and vibrating as I walk around Hamilton Lake with Jonas. He's not holding my hand or anything. We could be siblings for all people know, ambling along while we wait for our parents or something.

I step to the left to allow a jogging mother and her two kids on scooters to dash past us. Jonas's elbow bumps into mine, and I flash him a nervous smile.

His lips tip with a half grin. "So, are you actually going to say anything, or are we walking around the lake in silence?"

A soft giggle spurts out of my mouth, and I focus on the

pug sniffing in the grass ahead of us. Its owner chats on the phone, letting out a high-pitched cackle, which sends the pukekos dashing for cover.

"Um…" I lick my lips and glance up at Jonas, wishing I'd remembered my shades. It'd be nice to have the dark lenses for cover right now. "Uh, thanks for agreeing to meet with me."

"No worries." He says that, but I'm not sure he really means it. His sideways glance is a little wary.

"Look, I'm sorry for lying and saying some of the stuff I did." I swallow, annoyed at the sudden burn of tears.

Why'd I forget my shades! This is so embarrassing!

"The truth is, I do need you. I mean, I really like you, and I don't want to…to not be friends or to not hang out anymore. That might just break my heart a little bit, you know?"

His smile is slow to form, but one eventually pulls at his lips, and he's soon grinning down at me. "I like you too."

Warmed by his sweet words, I find the courage to start talking. "Okay, so, here's the truth…"

I tell him everything. Well, almost everything.

By the end of my big spiel, he knows that my parents died in a car accident at the end of December, and I'm now living with Beck Connell. He knows of Tane, because he's part of the rugby team and everyone loves the first fifteen, apparently.

The way Jonas spits out those words makes me think he and his friends *don't*, but I figure pointing that out probably isn't a great idea right now.

I also tell him that Bianca and I got into a big fight because I was mean and thoughtless. I nearly choke on those words, but I can't keep denying the truth. I acted like a bitch, and Bianca deserves so much better.

"So, Beck and I are flying to Sydney on Tuesday. I'm hoping to convince her to come home with me."

"Why don't you just call her?"

I shake my head, having thought of that already. "I have to make the big gesture, so she knows how much I mean it."

We stroll past the bright orange fitness area, and I glance at a guy doing pull-ups like it's the easiest thing in the world.

Jonas takes my hand, threading his fingers through mine. "Well, I'm looking forward to meeting her."

I squeeze his hand, warm fuzzies flittering through me like butterflies. "I really want to look after her, you know? She's shy and struggles with meeting new people, making friends."

"She can hang with us. We'll look after her."

I bob my head, unsure what Bianca would think about Jonas and his crew. Leon would no doubt creep her out. Uncertainty rides through me as I bite my lips together and try to talk myself out of the concerns.

It'll be fine.

She can hang with us until she makes her own friends. She just makes connections slower than I do, but that doesn't mean she's not a totally likable person. She'll find her people. I just have to look out for her until she does.

"What if you get to Australia and she says she loves it there and doesn't want to come back with you?"

The thought is like a sharp slap to the face, and I frown at Jonas without meaning to.

"Whoa." He chuckles, raising his free hand in surrender. "Sorry. Wrong thing to say?"

I glance to the ground as we step onto the wooden walkway over the water.

"It's just..." My shoulder hitches. "We're family. We should be together. Now that Mum and Dad are gone, we need to look out for each other."

Jonas swallows. "I'm really sorry about your parents."

I shake my head. "I don't like thinking about it."

"I won't mention it again, and..." He tips his head. "I understand why you lied."

"I'm sorry I did," I whisper. "It's just not news you want to share with the guy you're crushing on."

He smiles and raises our joined hands to his lips, lightly kissing my knuckles. "You can tell me anything. Like I said, I'm always honest with my friends. Family... well, sometimes you've got to tell a little white one to get out of doing something crap, but... my friends, I guess they're kind of like my family. They're the only people who understand me. They're the only ones who matter. I'm loyal to them above all else."

I smile at his words, but when he glances away from me, my lips dip into a thoughtful frown. I'm not sure how much I agree with him.

In Uncle Lance's letter, the one Beck read out around the fire, he talked about forever love. Even when you don't understand each other, you keep loving. You keep fighting to stay together. You forgive. You compromise. Because that's what family is about.

That's why I have to go and fight for my sister.

We'll never think the same. We'll probably always confuse each other.

But she's my sister for life.

I don't say anything as Jonas and I continue our slow walk around the lake. For the first time since Bianca left, I'm actually feeling kind of peaceful, and I don't want to disturb that feeling by disagreeing with Jonas.

I really like him, and he's forgiven me for lying.

I want to start the school year with him by my side. I want him to hold my hand and steal kisses. I want him to take me on dates and make me feel good about life again.

I need him.

And I won't do anything to screw this up again.

43

TANE

Man, I feel good.

I clomp up to the house, stoked with how quickly things seem to be falling into place.

Beck's just introduced me to the new farmhand, Lincoln. He's putting the guy on trial. Linc, as he likes to be called, seems nice enough. Early thirties, wasn't raised on a farm but grew up in the country. He's met himself a Waikato girl and wants to be close to her. Seems kind of loved-up about the whole thing, which makes me laugh. The poor guy is gone for this woman. She must be something special.

He'll move into the cottage where Grant used to live, and it takes the pressure right off me. I can now start school without worrying about Beck being worked off his feet.

He and Stace leave tomorrow on their "Bring Back Bianca" mission. He's asked me to manage the farm for the two days he's gone. I'm kind of nervous, but at least I'll have Linc to help me. Harper's going to get Oscar and Willow sorted for the new school year, and then she'll be heading down to Wellington to organize their house. I heard her invite Willow and Oscar to join her, but they both said no, as if they were afraid or something.

I guess I get it.

If Beck suddenly died, this house wouldn't be the same.

I sit on the back steps and pull my gumboots off before stripping off my overalls and walking into the house.

My phone dings, and I check the message.

Mum: Thanks again for your call last night. It meant a lot. I hope I can see you soon.

Me: Yeah, I'll come down. I promised I would. But you've got to promise that you won't pressure me to stay.

Mum: I won't. I promise. I just want to see ya.

I reply with a smiley face and try to figure out when the

best time to go to Upper Hutt will be. It's a freaking long drive, but now that I'm repairing bridges, I feel like I shouldn't leave it too long. Mum's my family, and even though I don't always understand her, I need to keep loving her anyway.

A two-night visit won't kill me, and it'll mean the world to her.

Scratching the top of my head, I remember about that haircut. The principal at North Ridge High likes his students looking their best. Cam and I are already prefects, and if I'm wanting team captain, I need to set a good example. I'll have to fit that in this week.

I slide the laundry door open and am greeted with the delectable sight of Harper pacing the kitchen. She's in a pair of white shorts, which accentuate her luscious tan, and an oversized T-shirt thing that drops off her shoulder. I bet she has no idea how sexy it is.

The kettle pops and she storms across to it, pouring the bubbling water into her mug. Smells like instant coffee. I grin, wondering if she's coming around to it, or whether it's still an endurance test to drink the stuff.

She spins for the fridge and jumps when she sees me.

"Oh. Hi."

"Hey." I smile, but she just buries her head in the fridge, taking way too long to retrieve the milk.

When she said she was staying, I was so stoked I couldn't hide it.

But she's acting kind of weird and edgy around me now.

I don't know what's going through that brain of hers, but I'd love to find out.

Her kiss still filters into my dreams at night, the way she moves, the unchecked smile that sometimes takes over her face. They linger around me like a sweet-smelling perfume.

Now that she's staying, is there hope for more with her?

Will she let me kiss her again?

Hold her hand?

Be the guy she turns to?

Aw, man, I want that so bad. But I get this feeling that just going for it is the wrong move. I need to take my time, reel her in slowly. She doesn't seem the type to cope well with pressure, so I'm not going to put any on her.

She's got enough on her plate right now.

I just want to help her. I can't make this about me and what I want.

What does *she* need?

That's the only question I should be asking myself right now.

She stirs in the milk with gusto, tapping the spoon on the edge of the mug before chucking it into the sink. It clatters loudly, and she flushes while putting the milk away and then slamming the fridge with a sniff.

"You okay?"

She flinches again, then gives me tight smile. "Yeah, just…" She rubs her forehead. "My brain is going nuts. There's so much to do. I have to get Willow and Oz enrolled at their new schools tomorrow, and then there's uniforms to purchase and stationary to get, not to mention going back to Wellington to pack up all our stuff. I need to decide what to do with the house. Probably rent it out to start with, but I have to organize that too. And Oz and Will don't want to come, which is fair enough, and they should really start school fresh and not completely drained from a trip that will no doubt be harrowing." She barely pauses for a breath, then keeps jabbering. "I have help down in Wellington. I mean, my girls will help me. They've already said they will, and I have great neighbors too, so that's all good. But then I need to get back here with all our stuff. I've never driven a trailer or truck before, and I don't know how I'm supposed to get our car back as well. I need to look into the cost of movers, but I'm guessing it's really pricey and—"

I stop her panicked babble by gently pressing my finger against her lips.

She starts and jolts back from me, her eyebrows starting to dip.

"You need to stop talking and take a breath." I smile. "Breathe."

She sucks in a breath, and I can't help a soft chuckle.

"Now let the breath out."

She huffs it out and I twirl my finger in the air, encouraging her to take another one.

We do this three times before I'm satisfied that she's not going to self-combust on the kitchen floor.

"It's all gunna be good. I can come down and help you. I've got to go visit my mum anyway, and she's living less than an hour out of Wellington. We'll coordinate our trips, and it's all gunna be sweet as."

She gives me a doubtful smile, which makes me laugh.

"Come on." I take her hand and pull her to the table. "Let's start with a list."

Her expression suddenly melts with affection as she takes a seat. "A list? You make lists?"

"Yep. It's the best way to get that hailstorm out of your head."

I rummage in the kitchen drawer for a pen, then grab

some paper. I have no idea why she's smiling at me like I'm a champion, but I'll take it. I'll freaking lavish in it. That look on her face is nothing but beautiful.

"Right." I take a seat beside her and poise my pen over the paper. "It's time to make a plan."

She rests her chin on her hand, her eyes gleaming at me. Her grin holds some kind of secret I don't understand, but I'm looking forward to finding out. It feels good to help her, feels even better that she's going to stay, and I can keep doing things to make her go from panicked babble to smiling at me.

"Mind if I write?"

"Sure." I slide the paper over to her and grab her mug of coffee, taking a quick sip before starting to pepper her with logistics and questions.

She writes furiously, and the next hour disappears as we share an instant coffee and figure out what the next two weeks of our life is going to look like.

Our life.

Yeah, I kind of love the sound of that.

Keep reading to find out what's going to happen next on the Connell farm.

Will Bianca agree to come home?
Will Harper finally stop fighting her feelings for Tane?

What challenges will this makeshift family face as they start at North Ridge High?

Find out in Broken Girl vs. Fix-It Boy

BROKEN GIRL VS FIX-IT BOY

She's closed her heart to protect her family. Can he open it back up to let love bloom?

"I didn't think it was going to be possible for this series to get

even better, and yet I have fallen even harder for all these teenagers…" – Amazon reviewer

TANE:

Harper wants me. I can feel it every time she looks my way.

Her lips tell me I'm the guy for her. Our attraction is irresistible. Magnetic.

But she's fighting it.

She's pushing me away at every turn. All I want to do is help her heal.

Why does she have to be so stubborn?

Why does she want to do this all on her own when I'm here to make things better?

I can't quit on her.

I'm not going to let her keep hurting herself this way.

I don't care what it takes. I'm winning Harper's heart, because *my* heart won't let me do anything else.

Broken Girl vs Fix-It Boy is the second book in the poignant Forever Love YA contemporary romance series. If you like tear-jerking moments, triumphant journeys, and characters with depth, then you'll adore Jordan Ford's emotional love story.

Buy *Broken Girl vs Fix-It Boy* to see young passions heal painful wounds today!

PREVIEW

BROKEN GIRL VS FIX-IT BOY

BIANCA

"Stacey? What are you doing here?" I gape at my sister, trying to figure out why my stomach is jumping with glee.

I don't want to see her!

That's what I've been telling myself every day since I left.

But it's a lie.

She's there, and all I want to do is run around the table and hug her.

I've missed her so much. I've never felt as lonely as I have here in Oma's sterile, pristine colonial. I thought I'd thrive in this neat-as-a-pin environment, but it's felt like a prison. Who knew how relaxing a little chaos could be?

"I'm here to take you home." Stacey's voice shudders, and her blue eyes are starting to glass with tears.

But she hurt me.

She doesn't respect me.

She never sees me.

We can't live in the same room together. I can't move back to Hamilton. I ran to save myself.

"I don't know what you think you're playing at, Beckett Connell, but you can't just show up here and kidnap my granddaughter!" Oma spits a little fire at the man Dad wanted me to live with.

"It's her decision," Beck calmly argues.

We can't see them right now. They're in the drawing room. I glance at the door and wonder what I'm supposed to do.

It's my decision.

So what decision do I make?

"I saw a pineapple at the airport this morning." Stacey gives me a hopeful grin, and before I can stop them, my lips turn up at the corners.

HARPER

Tane's eyes are a darker shade of brown in this light. It's hard not to study them as he looks across the table at me.

He's been nothing but amazing since showing up at my door in Wellington. I seriously couldn't have done this without him.

And now we're nearly back in Hamilton. Only a few more hours left and we'll be living under the same roof for an entire year.

My stomach quivers.

"You're nervous again," he teases, nudging my ankle with his foot.

I try to hide my blush by looking down and stirring the froth on my latte. I notice that Tane ordered one too. I'll bring him around to real coffee, and now that we have a decent coffee machine in the trailer Tane's towing, I don't have to have that instant crap ever again.

"What are you worrying about?" he gently presses me.

I don't know what it is about his sweet-tempered ways, but they seem to tug words out of me.

Sitting back with a sigh, I lick the back of my teaspoon and confess, "This year. It's like this big giant looming over me. I don't know how to face it. I don't know how to live on a farm or how to be a mum."

His lips twitch. "No one's asking you to be a mum. And this is only a giant if you choose to look at it that way. Step a little closer and just take one day at a time. Today, all we have to do is drive home and unload the cars and trailer. Tonight, you can figure out what tomorrow holds. Just stop projecting so far into the future. You'll do your head in."

"You make it sound so easy." I tuck an escaped hair back into my side braid.

"That's why I'm good for you." He winks.

"Good for me?" I can't fight my smile, and try to hide it by tapping my fingers on the tabletop and focusing on the varnished surface.

Shuffling in his chair, Tane rests his arm in front of mine and draws a gentle line down each of my fingers. "I could be good for you," he whispers. "If you'll let me."

Desire whips through me like a tornado, but I curl my fingers and gently slide my hand away.

The move injures him, but he does a pretty decent job of trying to hide it. His smile is still kind and sweet.

I try to soften my retreat with the best explanation I can. "I'm broken right now, Tane. You don't want me. I'm not good for anybody."

His lips smile, then dip a couple of times before he softly disagrees with me. "You'd be good for me, City. Real good."

TANE

Getting the tribe to school on time was a mission. I'm going to have to put a rocket under Stacey's bed to get her ready in the morning. Holy crap!

Harper was amazing, as usual, sorting everyone out. We only got back yesterday, and I was shattered from the long drive, but I can't miss the first day of school, so I dragged my butt here, along with two reluctant girls and one who couldn't shut up about Jonas.

Manu told me a couple of things about the guy. He's not perfect, but he ain't trouble either. Still, I'm gunna keep my eye on him. Stacey's been through enough. She doesn't need any extra heartache.

"Tane!" Cam raises his hand at me, and I lope across to him, doing our little shake ritual before raising my chin at Logan and Sione.

Manu cruises past with his half-cocked smile, and I turn my back to the boys so I can have a more private chat with Cam.

"Bad morning?" He snickers.

I raise my eyebrows at him. "Let's just hope they get better."

Cam's grin grows a little wider but starts to fade when

he gazes over my head. I glance behind me to spot my redhead "cousin" walking past with Stacey and Willow.

"Who's that?" he whispers.

"Oh, that's Bian…ca." I catch the way Cam's eyes track the cherry blossom, the way his lips part in wonder. I lightly smack him in the chest. "What are you doing? What is that look on your face?"

"Nothing." He blinks and tries to hide the fact that he was full-on drooling. "What?" He shrugs, but his gaze swings back to where she was standing just moments ago. She's moved on already, and his eyebrows wrinkle.

I narrow my gaze, crossing my arms and clearing my throat so he'll look at me.

Oh yeah, I see you, Cameron Jones. I see the way you're checking out my family.

Cam clears his throat, tucking his hair behind his ear. "So she arrived safely, then?"

I don't let up with my glare until his cheeks start to flame red, and then I can't help my bemused smirk.

Cam glances at me and shoves my shoulder. "Shut up. She's gorgeous!"

Looks like Jonas isn't the only guy I'm gunna have to watch this year.

I start to laugh in spite of myself. Of all the guys in the school, Cam is the least of my worries. If anything,

Bianca is one lucky lady. Not many girls catch Cam's attention. The fact that she made him blush, well... that says it all.

He's gunna have his work cut out for him, though. If Willow's the quietest person I've ever met, Bianca would rate pretty damn high on the shy scale.